LOVE WINS

BY

LORRAINE BEARD

ISBN: 978-1-3999-5107-4

Book cover designed by Sandie Worrell.

1

The coldness of the room penetrated Eddie's greatcoat, and the sound of his father's snores filled his ears, as he stood looking down at his girls sleeping curled together on the narrow bed, candlelight illuminating their pale faces. How had it come to this? This was the last place he wanted them to be. Lizzie was no longer here to keep them safe, and he only had thirty-six hours left of his leave to come up with a plan to get them away from here and to safety.

He'd insisted the girls were evacuated once he'd heard Lizzie was dead, but his father, who had never taken any interest in his granddaughters, had gone against his wishes and refused to let them go. Anger burned within him. His father didn't want to take care of his girls. He wanted them to take care of him. No one knew better than Eddie how demanding Gareth Davies was. He'd always protected Lizzie and their daughters from all that, but because of the war, he wasn't able to protect them any longer.

Lizzie had known about his father's cruelty, well some of it anyway. Lovely, sweet, gentle Lizzie, who came from a family so very different from his own. Lizzie had been shocked by his father's behaviour. She'd never been physically strong, and Eddie had done all he could to keep her safe. He'd failed his wife. If he'd been here, she wouldn't have been out in the cold, queuing for essential food, so she would never have become so unwell. No doubt the fear of the air-raids and spending night after night in a damp shelter were also to blame. It hurt so badly that he wasn't able to save Lizzie, but he still had a chance with his girls.

"Mam?" Lily's voice came weakly from the bed. "I want Mam."

A lump formed in Eddie's throat, preventing him from speaking.

Barely awake herself, Eliza turned and pulled her younger sister into her arms. "Shh, Lily. Don't cry. I'm here."

Eddie's feet seemed frozen to the spot, but somehow he moved towards them. He kept his voice low, as he said, "Eliza, Lily, it's me. I'm here too."

"Dad!" Instantly recognising her father's voice, Eliza sprang from the bed.

Eddie placed the candle on the chest of drawers and caught her as she flew into his arms.

"You came home!" Eliza cried, clinging to his neck. "I prayed you would, and you did. Oh Dad, you've come to take us away from here!"

If only it were that simple. His daughter's complete trust in him to do what was needed caused his throat to tighten again. He looked to where Lily seemed to be still sleeping, before he managed to say, "It's so good to see you, Eliza."

Sitting on the edge of the bed, he lifted his eldest daughter onto his lap. Eliza was twelve years old now, and although she wasn't as delicately built as her mother and sister, she was far too thin.

She clung to him as she had when she'd been much younger. "I miss Mam," Eliza sniffed. "I didn't know what to do, but you came back. Lily isn't well again. She's scared of the bombs, and of…" She stopped and lifted her head slightly, nodding in the direction from where the snores still came.

"Tell me everything, Eliza. I'll do what I can."

"Can't we just get our house back? It hasn't been bombed yet."

"If I could, I would. But listen, I can't stay. I have to go back to the army."

Silent sobs shook Eliza's slim body. "What will we do?" Turning her face up to look directly into her father's eyes, she pleaded, "Don't go again. Please, Dad, I don't know what to do. Can't you make us get evacuated? Just don't tell him where we are."

Eddie hugged her closer and stroked her dark brown hair. He could try insisting they were evacuated, but there was nothing to stop his father from bringing them back. For some reason, he seemed determined to have them here, but his reasoning was a mystery to Eddie.

When Eliza shivered, he looked about the room for another blanket in which to wrap her, but could see none. Of course, there wouldn't be. He hadn't had more than a thin covering over him when he was a boy. This small room looked exactly as it had when he'd lived here. Only the essentials and nothing of warmth and comfort. It had been a little more pleasant until his mother died when he was twelve, the age Eliza was now. Then he'd been left alone with his father. He'd always been able to run upstairs to the Lewis's though, until Ruthie had told him they couldn't be friends anymore, and that he wasn't to go up there. He'd never understood why. Someone had obviously hurt her. He knew that now, but he hadn't at first. Why hadn't she let him help her? They'd always been there for one another before. He even used to think they'd end up marrying one day. However, she'd made it clear she didn't want anything more to do with him, so that was that. Then he'd met Lizzie. Lizzie was the best thing to have happened to him, and she'd given him Eliza and Lily. He'd loved them all with everything he had.

"Please Dad," Eliza spoke in a shaky whisper. "Don't make us stay here."

"I don't want you to stay here, you or Lily. I just don't honestly know what to do for the best," He spoke truthfully to her. Eliza had always been a sensible child.

"You could send us away in secret." She was looking at him intently again as she spoke quickly and quietly. "We could change our names and pretend to be someone else, so he can't find us and bring us back."

Her determination and logical thinking reminded him of Ruthie. Why was he thinking of her again? He hadn't seen her in twelve years, at least, not to speak to anyway. He had to focus on his girls. Please Lord, he prayed silently. Show me what to do.

Eddie spoke gently to Eliza. "If it were that simple, I'd do it. But the authorities aren't going to let me change your names to hide you from him. If there were any of your mam's family left, I'd send you to them, but your uncle is away in the air-force. I don't have any more family. I'll come up with something," he tried to reassure her.

"I'll run away then!" Eliza stated. "When Lily is better, I'll run away to the country and keep her safe."

"Eliza, you can't do that. How would I ever know where to find you? Besides, you'd have nowhere to live, and no money."

"There must be somewhere!" Desperation filled her voice. "There must be some family you've forgotten about." She buried her face in his coat, sobbing uncontrollably.

Eddie held her as she cried. She was right. There was someone who he hadn't asked, but could he? Would she even speak to him? What would it do to them all if the truth came out?

"What's that noise? Stop it right now!" a voice bellowed from the other room.

Eddie felt Eliza's arms tighten around him. She was clearly afraid of her grandfather.

"Make me some tea, girl!" His voice came again.

Eliza went to pull away from her father, but he held her a moment longer, whispering, "I'll go. You and Lily stay here."

Eliza slid from his lap and scrambled back into bed next to her sister, while Eddie got to his feet. Before going to see his father, he took off his coat and laid it over his girls. That should help a little, he thought, as he picked up the candle and made for the door.

"What have I told you about using candles, girl!" Gareth barked as Eddie opened the door into the main room. "They are for my use only."

"I lit it, Dad." Eddie took a step towards him, holding it up to illuminate where his father lay on the bed in the corner, the smell of alcohol emanating from him. "Why are you denying my girls the use of a candle?" he added.

"Eddie!" Gareth Davies tried to rise to a sitting position, obviously surprised to see his son.

"Why were you wanting Eliza to bring you tea at this time of night? The girls should be sleeping."

"Rubbish! It won't hurt them. It wouldn't hurt the youngest to do a bit either. She won't last much longer than her mam if she doesn't toughen up a bit."

Eddie found it hard to keep his anger in check. In two strides, he was at his father's bedside. Leaning over him as much as he dared, he almost growled at him, "Don't you ever speak about Lizzie or my girls like that again. They are not your slaves. Now, I'll make you that tea, and then you and I need to talk."

Eddie straightened up and moved to the stove, turning on the gas. As he slid the kettle into place, he wondered what good anything he could say to this man would do. Lord, soften his heart, he prayed.

Five minutes later, he handed a mug of steaming tea to the older man, who was now sitting up in bed. Taking a seat on one of the old wooden chairs at the table, Eddie took a sip of his tea before he said, "I'm sending the girls to the country, where it's safe from the bombs." He somehow restrained from adding, and you.

"I need them here, and they should be with family."

Eddie knew his father didn't care at all about Eliza and Lily being with family. He tried again. "I'd feel happier if they were away from Cardiff. There are going to be more raids, I'm sure of that."

"If the whole of Cardiff thought like that, they might as well all leave and invite the Germans to take over Wales. Moving half the schools into the country won't do anyone any good. They won't know what it is to live in hard times. No, I say they stay."

Eddie realised he wouldn't get anywhere with his father. He'd always been the same. Once his mind was made up, there was no changing it. "Why do you really want them here?" He hoped he hadn't beaten Eliza and Lily in the way he'd experienced as a boy. Surely even his dad wouldn't beat girls, would he? Eddie remembered seeing bruises on his mother's arms and neck from her husband's rough treatment, but would he beat Eliza and Lily? That was one of the things he'd been concerned about since hearing they were living under his roof. "You're not raising your hand to them, are you?" His hands tightened on the mug as he waited for his father's reply.

"Seems to me they could have done with that over the years."

Eddie jumped to his feet, glaring down at Gareth, whilst struggling to hold back his anger. "If I find out you've laid a hand on either of them, you'll regret you ever thought about it." Eddie knew he needed to control his temper. Lizzie had been a Christian when he'd met her, and he'd soon realised that being angry was not pleasing to the Lord. He'd worked hard to stay calm over the years. Not having to see his father much had helped, but now the anger was returning. He didn't want to end up like the older man. Help me, Lord, he prayed. I don't have much time and I don't know how to keep my girls safe.

The eerie wail of the air-raid siren began to moan, rapidly raising in pitch to alert everyone of its urgency. Eddie slammed his mug on the table. "Come on!" he said, looking at his father, who hadn't moved. "Which shelter do you use?"

Gareth laughed. "We don't. We stay here. Reckon the little one makes as much noise as the bombs."

Eddie was not listening. He ran into the bedroom, where Eliza and Lily were scrambling under the bed.

"Come on!" He reached to pull them back out. "We're going to the shelter."

"He says we're not to go there…" Eliza stopped half under the bed.

"I'm your dad, and I say you do. I'll take you. Get your shoes and coats on."

It took some time for the girls to get organised. Lily seemed hardly able to stand, so after pulling on his coat, Eddie swung her up into his arms, wrapping the garment about them both. Eliza picked up the blanket along with a small bag. Flinging the strap over her head, she hurried alongside him.

By the time they reached the blacked-out street, the bombs were already falling. Eddie felt Eliza holding tightly to his arm as they ran towards the nearest shelter.

The squeal of falling bombs drew nearer, mixing with the drone of planes and the anti-aircraft guns firing into the sky. Eddie knew the sound came from the direction of the docks, but this street was only a stone's throw from there. He had to get Eliza and Lily away from here. "You'll be safe in the shelter," he tried to reassure them. Eliza's question about finding more family came back to him. He only had one option left. What did he have to lose by trying?

They were almost to the shelter when a deafening boom filled the night, lifting Eddie right off his feet and pulling Eliza away from him. He tried to reach out to grab her, but she wasn't there. He was aware of flying through the air before he landed hard on his side. Pain burned in his shoulder and for a moment he forgot where he was. Then the memory of running to the shelter with his girls came back to him. Where were Eliza and Lily?

2

As Eddie made to move, he realised that miraculously Lily was still in his arms, but it was too dark to see if she was hurt. The sky was now brighter than it had been, as the houses on the opposite side of the street were burning.

"Lily, are you alright?" He got to his knees and looked down at his youngest child, pushing her pale blonde hair back from her face. Thank you, Lord. I didn't land on her, he prayed.

Her eyes fluttered open, and she began to cry, causing her to cough.

At least she's alive, Eddie thought as he got awkwardly to his feet. "Eliza," he called over the roar of fire and bombs. "Eliza, where are you?"

"Dad! I'm here! Where's Lily?"

Eddie heard Eliza's voice and hurried in that direction. He tripped over several objects before he finally reached her. Why wasn't anyone else here to help?

"My foot!" Eliza cried. "It's stuck."

Another explosion shook the night as Eddie dropped to his knees beside his eldest child. Lily slid from her father's arms and moved forward to hug her sister, while Eddie set about moving several chunks of masonry and releasing her foot.

"Did it hit Granddad's house?" Eliza asked.

It was the first time he'd known her to call his father that. Eddie pushed down the hope that it had hit his father's house. Despite all he'd done, no one deserved to die that way. "No. It hit the other side of the street. Eliza, you're not going to be able to walk on that foot. I'll carry you."

"I'll walk." Eliza tried to stand, but cried out in pain and fell back to the ground.

"We'll get you on my shoulders. That way, I can still carry Lily," he told her, as he moved into a different position and helped her up. Pain shot up his neck and down his arm, but he did his best not to show it. He had to get the girls to safety.

Eddie struggled to his feet, then bent to lift Lily back into his arms.

"I'll walk, Dad," she said shakily, but knowing she was too weak, Eddie held her closer.

Bombs still fell nearby as Eddie hurried along the streets, flames casting an eerie glow all around them.

"Dad, the shelter is that way," Eliza called to him over the noise.

"This is our chance, Eliza. I'm going to try to find you somewhere safe."

Eddie walked along as quickly as he was able, his two daughters clinging tightly to him. What if she no longer lived there? What if her house had been bombed? What if she, too, was dead? Eddie tried to ignore the icy stab of fear inside him. This was truly his last chance. Had he given Eliza false hope? Please Lord, he prayed silently, let her be there, and let her be willing to help. He tried reasoning with himself that the place where she was living was further from the docks, so was less likely to have been bombed, but there was no guarantee.

Several times, Eddie had to find different routes to take, as fires burned brightly in some streets, while others were completely impassable due to collapsed buildings.

Leaning close to her father's ear, Eliza asked, "Where are we going?"

"Somewhere where I think you will be safe." He was thankful Eliza didn't ask any further questions, which was most unusual for her. Maybe he should have taken them to get medical care first. After all, he didn't know how badly hurt they were, but a plan was forming in his mind, and this was his chance to carry it out. Had the Lord given him this opportunity?

Eventually, they reached an area where the bombs seemed further away. Eddie paused to regain his bearings before turning onto another street.

As they neared their destination, Eddie wondered at the wisdom of this idea. What if she was down in a shelter? Anyone with any sense would be right now. It was too cold to keep the girls out here any longer than necessary.

He knew the address by heart. He'd never been inside the house where she lived in the downstairs half, but he had passed it several times, just to make sure she was alright. He'd never seen her up close, but had caught a glimpse of her on one or two occasions. The curtains and doorstep always looked neat and tidy, and he told himself that was enough to know she was alright. He'd been concerned when she'd disappeared, but after asking around a bit, he'd managed to find her.

The all-clear siren sounded in the deserted street as Eddie lifted his hand to knock on the door. He wondered whether he should take Eliza and Lily to be seen to, then come back, but decided against it. You never knew who you'd see, and right now he didn't want to be seen around here. Both girls were crying. He knew Eliza was in a lot of pain with her foot, and Lily just seemed weak and exhausted.

Eddie was surprised when the door opened and there she stood. "Hello Ruthie," his voice shook a little. "May we come in?"

"Eddie?" Ruthie stared at him. "I heard a child crying, else I wouldn't have answered the door. What's happened? Come in." She pulled the door wide open and stood aside.

Eddie walked into the dark room and stopped for fear of walking into something.

Ruthie closed the door, then went to light a lamp. "Power's off again," she explained. "Good thing I kept Mam's old lamps."

The room was soon lit, and Eddie noticed how neat and tidy it was. He wouldn't have expected anything different from Ruthie, as her mother had been the same. When they were growing up, after his mam had died, Eddie was ashamed of the state of the downstairs half of the house where he and his father lived. Ruthie had offered to come in and help him and his dad keep house. Eddie always felt better in there, knowing Ruthie had tidied and cleaned it for them. He did what he could himself, but his dad would beat him if he caught him doing "women's work", as he called it.

"These are my girls, Eliza and Lily," Eddie explained. "We got caught in the raid."

"Bring them over here," Ruthie said, leading him towards a couch which stood against one wall.

Eddie laid the shivering Lily down, then wondered how to get Eliza, who was also shivering, from his shoulders. Now he'd reached his destination, his own pain had increased in intensity. It seemed Ruthie knew what he needed, as she lifted Eliza down with ease. Ruthie had always been strong and capable, and she'd always known what he needed without him even saying anything.

After she'd settled Eliza on the couch, Ruthie hurried from the room, returning almost instantly with several blankets. The next few minutes were a blur to Eddie, as he and Ruthie worked side by side, wrapping the girls up as warmly as possible, then inspecting Eliza's foot. Ruthie told him she'd done some first aid training and that she didn't think it was broken. She got some bandages and expertly wrapped it. She then checked both girls over for cuts and bruises, of which they both had several, although Lily seemed to have got off more lightly, probably because she'd been in her father's arms.

After cleaning the cuts, Ruthie suggested putting the girls to bed in her own room. "You don't want to be taking them out in the cold again."

Eddie agreed gratefully, and they carried them to Ruthie's bed, where she saw they had enough blankets to keep them warm.

"What about you?" Ruthie asked. "Sounds like you might have landed hard, too. Is there anything you'd like me to check over?"

"I'll be fine," Eddie told her. He had to say what he'd come for, before he changed his mind.

No sooner had they got back to the kitchen, the air-raid siren sounded again.

"It's further across town," Ruthie explained. "We'll be alright here."

"I was surprised you weren't in the shelter when we got here," Eddie said.

As she moved to put the kettle on, Ruthie stated, "I just stay here."

Eddie noticed the sadness, or whatever it was, in her reply. He had hoped she would have found some sort of happiness by now, but that was more difficult to come by than ever during a war.

Neither of them spoke until Ruthie brought two mugs of steaming tea to the table and sat down opposite Eddie. Looking directly at him, she asked, "Why were you so far over this side of town?" As an afterthought, she added, "And how did you know where to find me?"

"I've always known where you were. I couldn't just let you disappear," Eddie told her.

"But why were you over here tonight? Why bring the girls out in the raid?"

Ruthie had always been good at getting to the point. At least, she had been until she suddenly stopped wanting to be his friend. He'd missed her directness over the years. Of course he'd loved Lizzie, but she and Ruthie were completely opposite from one another. Ruthie was practical and knew how to handle almost any situation, while Lizzie needed his love and protection.

"I'm home on leave. I was taking the girls to the shelter when the bomb exploded."

"What about Lizzie?" Ruthie questioned.

"She's gone. I came back as soon as I could. Ruthie," Eddie cleared his throat before he went on, "Ruthie, I need your help. Lizzie is gone, and I need you to take my girls." Eddie shuffled his feet nervously under the table.

"Can't they go to the country with other evacuees?" Ruthie's surprise was evident.

"They are with my father. He won't let them go."

Ruthie stood quickly to her feet, visibly shocked and seeming to find it difficult to get her breath. "Your father? No! I mean, I can't. What about Lizzie's family?"

"They should be with family, yes. There's no one left on Lizzie's side, that's why I'm asking you. You were like family to me when we were growing up. I trust you with them, Ruthie."

"Eddie," Ruthie sat down again and rested her elbows on the table, her hands covering her face. "We were close, yes, but I told you we couldn't be friends anymore." The words sounded silly and meaningless even to her own ears.

"I knew something must have happened to make you say that. I never thought you really meant it."

Ruthie screwed her eyes up tightly, trying to stop the tears from escaping. She hadn't allowed herself to cry in years, and she wasn't about to start again now, with Eddie Davies, of all people, sitting across the table from her. Telling Eddie they couldn't be friends any longer had been the hardest thing she'd ever done. Well, almost. There was only one thing more difficult than that, and Eddie had helped her out there. She couldn't allow herself to think about the last time she'd spoken to him.

"Please, Ruthie?" Eddie became more insistent. "I have to get them away from him. I found them with only a thin blanket over them in a freezing cold house. He won't allow them to use candles and expects them to be his slaves. You know how he treated me. I haven't had the chance to find out yet, but it wouldn't surprise me if he hadn't beaten them. You know what he's like when he's had a drink."

"Oh yes, I know what he's like." Ruthie's voice was flat.

"So, will you take them? He'll do all he can to find them, just so he can use them as his slaves, so I was thinking it would be best if you could take them to the country."

"What?" Ruthie's voice came out on a squeak.

"Please, Ruthie, you're the only one I can trust with them. I'd stay if I could, but I have to get back to the army."

"The country? I don't know anyone in the country. I don't even know how to get there."

"I've got time. I'll take you all there tomorrow."

"Tomorrow? Eddie, have you gone mad? You come here in the middle of the night and want me to take your girls to the country tomorrow!"

"Yes. I know it's a lot to ask, but I've got some money I can give you. I'll see that my army money gets sent to you as well."

"Eddie! I don't understand. Why not just take the girls? I'm sure you could find a nice family to take them in. They do that all the time now with evacuees."

"He'll get them back. If there's any record of where they are, he'll find them. And if anything happens to me, I need to know they're safe."

"But why me?"

A sudden thought struck Eddie. What if Ruthie had married? A quick glance at her hand told him that wasn't so. Before he could put it off any longer, he spoke the words he never thought he'd speak. "Eliza is your child."

3

"She can't be. You took her to the orphanage. Lizzie had her own baby," Ruthie exclaimed in barely more than a whisper.

"I'm sorry, Ruthie, I shouldn't have come out with it like that." Eddie got to his feet and moved quickly around the table, resting his large hand on her thin arm. "I told myself I'd never tell you. I've never told anyone else."

Ruthie allowed herself to lean against him for a moment before pulling away and staring up at him. "I trusted you," she stated.

"I'm sorry." Eddie moved his chair around from the other side of the table and sat next to her. "I meant to do as you'd asked, but Lizzie and our little girl were so bad. I'd come to you to see if your mam would come and help them, remember? But she'd already died of the flu. I couldn't believe it when I found you with a baby in your arms. I really was going to do as you asked and take her to the orphanage, but I'd left Lizzie alone so long already, and I thought I'd check on her and our baby first, but our little girl was dead. Lizzie was barely alive herself, but she knew something was wrong with the baby. I didn't want her to give up, so I put your daughter in her arms." Now Eddie was speaking the words he'd kept inside for so long, he found it difficult to stop.

"How do I know you're not just saying that to make me take your girls away?" Ruthie wiped a tear from the corner of her eye. She'd spent the last twelve years wondering what had happened to her daughter. Eddie was the only one she trusted to take the child whose existence she'd hidden to the orphanage, but he hadn't kept his word.

"It's true Ruthie. If you saw Eliza, I mean really looked at her, you'd see she looks like you. Her ways are like yours too. She's confident and capable, she's always looked after her mam and Lily. Everyone says she looks like me, but I know different. I know she's like you."

"And Lizzie just accepted my baby in place of her own?" Ruthie questioned in disbelief.

"She never knew. It was weeks before she was well enough to see her properly. I told her babies change a lot when they are first born. Like I said, everyone was convinced she looked like me. She was so small too, the same as our baby, but she soon grew stronger."

"She was very early," Ruthie told him. "I didn't know if she'd live either. I often wondered if she had survived and where she was. But Eddie, what if someone found out? If people knew I'd had a baby, things would have been even harder than…"

"No one ever knew, and no one ever needs to know. What do you mean, Ruthie, even harder? What's been happening?"

Ruthie began to cry uncontrollably, her head resting on her arms on the table.

Eddie wasn't sure how to help her. How had things got this difficult between them? Deciding there was nothing to lose, he put an arm around her shaking shoulders. "I'm sorry Ruthie. Whatever it is, maybe I can help?"

"No one can." She sniffed, raising her head slightly.

"Please tell me what's been happening. I know you said we couldn't be friends, but we were best friends once, right from when we were small."

"I've been so alone," Ruthie explained. "After Mam died of the flu, there was no one."

"You must've had friends? I mean, you always did before."

Ruthie shook her head. "I couldn't. None of them were real friends, not like you and I were. We used to tell each other everything, and I knew I'd never be able to do that with anyone again. I just had to be on my own."

Eddie wanted to tell her that the Lord had always been with her, but now wasn't the right time. Neither his nor Ruthie's families went to church. It was only Lizzie who had talked to him about the Lord. Lizzie helped him see all the ways Jesus had been alongside him through all the hard times.

Lizzie had been so kind and gentle. Eddie first met her as he walked home one evening. He'd heard a cry and had gone to see what was happening. Finding two drunken men trying to pull a young girl into an alleyway, he'd gone over and seen them off, before taking the girl to a café where they'd shared a cup of tea. He'd bought it for her, but she'd insisted he share it.

Lizzie told him she'd recently moved to Cardiff from the country, after her parents had been killed in a fire at their farm. She was now living with her grandmother. Her brother was working elsewhere, and Lizzie had been to get a few things her nan needed from the shop. She wasn't at all used to city life. Eddie had walked to the shop with her, then walked her back to her nan's house. He'd called by several times after that, so Lizzie wouldn't be afraid of going to the shop on her own, and she'd soon learnt to depend on him. The most sensible thing to do was to marry her.

Before they'd been married three months, Lizzie's nan died, leaving the young couple alone in the house.

They'd spent many happy years there together, until war broke out, forcing him to leave Lizzie and the girls for the army.

He was brought back to the present as Ruthie sighed heavily. "I suppose she would look like you," she said firmly.

"Hang on a minute!" Eddie pushed his chair back in surprise. "I don't know who it was you were seeing, but you know I never touched you like that."

Ruthie twisted her fingers together while her eyes seemed fixed on a spot on the floor. "You never worked it out, did you?" Her voice was low. "The reason I stopped coming round to your house, the reason I couldn't look at you or be around you."

"You'd found someone else." Eddie tried to keep the hurt from his voice.

"No Eddie, there wasn't anyone else. I had no choice in it. You want to know why Eliza looks like you? It's because you share a father. Eliza is your half-Sister."

"No!" Eddie leaned back in shock. "You mean…? Ruthie, I never knew. I would've protected you." He shook his head in disbelief. "Makes me want to kill him!" Eddie felt anger rising in him. It burned through his whole body. All he'd learnt over the years about controlling his temper threatened to leave him. Why did he not know? How could he have been so blind?

"Has he hurt them?" Ruthie lifted her gaze, fear and sadness in her eyes.

Eddie shook his head. "I don't honestly know. Oh Ruthie, I'm so sorry. I don't know how I never knew."

"I didn't want you to know. I was so ashamed."

"But it wasn't your fault. If I'd known, I would've helped you."

"It was too late by then. I didn't think he'd actually go through with it, but one day he did. That's when I pushed you away. I just couldn't face you. After that, I tried to keep away from him, but one evening he caught me again, out the back of the house."

"I would've taken you away."

"Then you wouldn't have met Lizzie. It had to be that way."

"Did anyone else know?" Eddie enquired.

"Not for ages. Mam only knew about the baby just before she died, but she never knew who the father was. I kept wearing a big coat whenever I went out. I didn't think I could hide it much longer, then she came early. It all happened at once. Mam got the flu, and I was looking after her. Then I knew the baby was on its way. I was so frightened, but I had to keep quiet and not let anyone know. Mam died just before the baby was born, and I didn't know what to do!" Ruthie lowered her head to her arms again. It was some minutes before she could go on.

"I knew I had to get someone to see to Mam's burying, but I didn't know what to do with the baby. I thought I'd be able to take it straight to the orphanage when it came. I'd found the place several weeks before and planned on going in the night and leaving the baby on the doorstep, but I was feeling bad myself. I knew I'd caught the flu off Mam, and I didn't know if I'd make it there and back. When you came looking for Mam, I knew I'd have to tell you about the baby and ask you to take her to the orphanage. I really thought you had."

Eddie was silent for some time before he said, "I would've done it, but it just didn't feel right. She was your child, and I was afraid she might end up with the wrong people. When our baby died, and yours was so small and helpless, I knew that if anyone could give her all the love she deserved, it would be Lizzie. Lizzie had enough love to go round everyone. I knew she'd never make it if she knew our daughter was gone. I needed to give her hope, and your little girl was the chance to give her that."

"All these years I've wondered what happened to her. I wondered what her name was. I wondered if she'd been found in time, but I told myself you would have made sure she was."

"Her name is Elizabeth Ruth," Eddie explained. "Lizzie was too weak to think of anything, so I named her, after both her mothers."

"Lizzie didn't mind you naming her?"

"No. We'd already talked about Elizabeth if it was a girl. Lizzie said we should shorten it to Eliza. She knew you were my closest friend growing up, and how I used to run upstairs to your place when things got bad, so she was happy I'd given her your name as a middle name. Lizzie always said she wished she could meet you and thank you for being there all those years. You and Lizzie would've got on well. But I was too afraid to let the two of you meet once we had Eliza. I thought you'd see her and realise what I'd done."

"I didn't recognise her tonight. How could I not know my own daughter?" Ruthie began to cry again.

"You weren't expecting anything. You were concerned with helping the girls."

"I still wish you'd let me look at your shoulder. I can see you've done something to it," Ruthie suddenly changed the subject.

The all-clear sounded, interrupting their conversation. It also seemed to bring Eddie's mind back to his original question.

"Ruthie, I know all this has come out of the blue, but will you take Eliza and Lily to the country? There's no way

I'd let them go back to him now, not knowing what he did to you. Please, Ruthie, will you take them? I know it's a lot to ask. I don't even know what you'd be giving up here. I believe the Lord led me to you tonight."

"What will everyone…? I mean, people will wonder where they've gone." Ruthie answered his question with one of her own.

"Everyone can see the other side of the street was bombed. For all I know, the whole thing might've gone by now. I'll say we were going to the shelter, and they were blown away from me. I know it's wrong to lie, but I have to keep them safe. I just hope it's not too late."

Ruthie had never known so many emotions in such a short time. Tonight, she'd bandaged the foot of her own child. Lifting her from Eddie's shoulders, she'd held her daughter in her arms for the first time in twelve years. She knew nothing of looking after children, but she was being asked to do just that. Could she measure up to Eddie and Lizzie's standards? What if the girls didn't like her? Could she bear being so close to her own child and not say anything? Lizzie had been such a good mother, and she would never want to take that away from Eliza, who would soon be a young woman.

Ruthie had also just shared the secret she'd kept for years, having told herself that she would take it to her grave. Now Eddie knew what his father had done, and he'd believed her. Why hadn't she trusted him all those years ago? Would things have turned out differently if she'd confided in him when it first happened? She likely wouldn't have spent all these years shut away from the world and everyone else. She went to work in the factory, but only spoke to the other women when necessary, not wanting to risk getting close to anyone.

These rooms in the downstairs of the house had been hers since the day she left her home above where Eddie grew up, three weeks after Eliza was born. For the first two weeks, Ruthie had been so unwell with the flu, she wondered if she would be joining her mother. There were times when she wished for that to happen. She'd thought there was nothing left to live for, but she'd survived. She knew she couldn't stay in that house, so had moved across Cardiff to this one. Since then, these rooms had been her place of safety. Could she leave that and go to the country? A thought struck her. Lizzie had loved and cared for her child. She could do the same for Lizzie's daughter, as well as getting to know her own. She never thought she would have that chance. She'd be near Eliza, and no one would ever have to know the truth and think badly of either of them. "Yes." She turned to look directly at Eddie. "I'll take them. I'll do whatever I can for them."

4

Eddie stood looking at his daughters where they slept side by side on the bed. Had it only been a few hours since he last looked down on them sleeping like this? Here they were wrapped in warm blankets and resting peacefully. Now they were safe, at least, much safer than they had been in his father's home.

In the dim lamplight coming from the main room, Eddie turned away from the bed and allowed his eyes to scan his surroundings. The small room held little of value. In fact, it was quite bare. How had Ruthie ended up living like this, he wondered. Suddenly feeling uncomfortable standing in her bedroom, Eddie hurried back into the other room, closing the door silently behind him.

Unsure of what to do, Ruthie stood from where she'd been sitting at the table. "Are they alright?" she asked.

"Yes, they're sleeping," Eddie replied. "I need to go and get things sorted, then I'll come back for you and the girls. Can you be ready to leave later today?"

"I'll be ready." Ruthie didn't tell him that there wasn't much to pack, and there was certainly no one she needed to say goodbye to.

"Can you keep it to yourself that you're leaving?"

"Yes. I'm paid up with my rent, but word will soon get around when I'm not at work."

"I'm sorry to ask you to leave like this, but I don't want him trying to find them." Eddie moved from foot to foot.

Ruthie didn't need to ask to whom he was referring. She had no desire to have Eddie's father come after them, so leaving without saying a word wouldn't be difficult.

"Like I said, I'm going to sort out a few things, then I'll be back."

"You will be careful, won't you, Eddie?" Ruthie had no idea why she spoke the words aloud.

"I'll be back before you know it," he assured her.

"What should I tell the girls when they wake up?"

"Tell them I won't be long. Tell them I'm going to make sure they never have to live with him again."

"But who should I say I am?"

"Say you're their auntie."

When Ruthie looked at him quizzically, Eddie continued, "I'll think about it while I'm gone. Just say I'll answer all their questions when I see them."

Eddie moved towards the door, and Ruthie went with him. Before opening it, he turned and pulled her into his arms. "I've missed you. Thanks for doing this for me. I'm sorry I never knew what was going on." He allowed himself to hold her a moment more than was necessary, before stepping out into the street, closing the door quickly and quietly behind him.

Out in the wintery night once more, the icy wind blew into Eddie's face, bringing the smell of smoke with it. He wanted to hit something! He wanted to throw something! No, he wanted to kill his father. How dare he hurt Ruthie like that! How dare he destroy her life! Eddie began to run. He needed to get this sorted out. He hadn't felt anger like this in years!

His feet pounded the streets as he made his way back across the city. Fires seemed to burn in all directions, especially down by the docks, but Eddie gave them little thought. He passed people searching in piles of rubble, and whereas in normal circumstances he would have stopped to help, he just kept on his way.

Many roads were now impassable, but eventually Eddie found his way to the street where he'd grown up. Only when he turned the corner did he stop. The left-hand side was a pile of smoking rubble, with small fires burning here and there. Some of the houses on the side where he'd lived had also been destroyed, but his father's house stood intact.

The rage that had driven him to run across the city now left him, and a strange stillness took its place. He wanted to have it out with his father, but his feet were fixed to the spot. Suddenly, he heard Lizzie's voice gently saying, "They are safe. The Lord kept them safe and led you to the right place. Don't mess it up now."

Don't mess it up? He almost questioned aloud, so clear had Lizzie's voice been. Eddie stood, unable to move amid the chaos. His breathing and heart rate slowed, and he seemed more able to think again. Please, Lord, he prayed silently, keep me calm, and give me the right words.

Eddie walked slowly towards his father's home. Opening the door, he was immediately hit by the smell of alcohol coming from the man sprawled on the bed in the corner. He took a candle and went into the room where his girls had slept just a few short hours ago. He gathered up their few belongings, placing them on the bedsheet and tying them into a bundle. Lizzie's hairbrush caught his attention when he saw it resting on the chest of drawers. He held it for almost a minute, before adding that too.

Once he had everything, he picked up the bundle and walked noiselessly back through the house. He placed it outside on the doorstep, then closed the door softly.

In the main room once more, he stood over his father, saying harshly, "Wake up!"

When there was no response, he crossed to the far corner to grab the broom. He held it at arm's length and poked his father with the bristly end. "Wake up!" he demanded.

With a loud snort, Gareth Davies sat straight upright, looking for something to hurl at his son. Spotting an empty bottle in his father's easy reach, Eddie knocked it onto the floor with the broom, the shattering glass causing the older man to stare at him in shock.

"What's all the fuss?" the old man demanded.

"The bomb exploded as we were on our way to the shelter," Eddie stated. He didn't want to lie outright, but he needed to put his father off the idea of looking for the girls. "The other side of the street is almost completely flattened, some of this side too."

"So, you were caught in that, then? Thought you might have been." A smile crept onto the older man's face. "Safe as houses in here I was! Told you they didn't need the shelter. Suppose you've tucked them up in bed and told them they don't have to do any work."

Eddie took in a breath and let it out again, before he said quietly, "They won't be coming back here."

Gareth's eyebrows shot up in surprise. "You mean…?" He left the sentence unfinished.

"Seems you'll have to do your own work from now on," Eddie responded coldly.

The old man actually began to chuckle. "You come in here all high and mighty, insisting they go to the shelter, and get them killed. Seems your old dad had the right idea after all!"

Eddie clenched his fists. Only the knowledge that his daughters were safe with Ruthie kept him from hitting his father. He cared nothing for the girls, and Eddie could not understand his attitude.

Not trusting himself to speak, Eddie turned and left the room, banging the front door behind him. He gathered up the bundle and marched down the street. He hadn't needed to lie, his father just presumed that Eliza and Lily had been killed.

Eddie felt bad for not helping those searching the rubble and putting out the fires, but he had to come up with a plan. He needed to think. Without realising where he was going, he found himself in the graveyard. The sky was bright with the glow of fires and the moon had also reappeared. As there was no stone, it took some time for him to find Lizzie's grave. There hadn't been time or money for a proper marker, but there was a simple wooden cross with her name on it. He dropped the bundle, sinking to his knees on the fresh mound of earth.

"I'm sorry, Lizzie," he said quietly. "I'm sorry I left you and the girls alone. I let you down, but I'm going to make up for it now as best I can. I'll make sure the girls are safe. Oh Lizzie, now you know what I did. Eliza is still our daughter though, just as much as Lily. You were her mam. I'm sorry I wasn't honest with you, but I didn't think you'd make it when the baby died. You'd been so happy about our little girl. I didn't want you to know she was gone. I thought you would give up too. I got a lot wrong, Lizzie, but I'm going to try to make it right. Ruthie will look after our girls, I know she will. I'll take them far away from here, somewhere where it's safer from bombs."

As Eddie talked softly to his dead wife, a plan formulated in his mind. There was a man in his unit who constantly spoke about the place he'd come from. There had been some confusion about himself and this man, as the man's name was Eddie Davis. He himself was Eddie Davies, and they had often both responded when their names were called during their training together. They had discovered that, although Eddie Davis was from England, not Wales, he didn't live very far away. He lived in a place called the Forest of Dean, and "A right nice place it was and all!" according to him. Lots of trees and wide-open spaces. People were sending their children there out of the city, so that's where Eddie would take Ruthie and his girls. He'd find someone to take them in. All he needed now was to borrow a car.

***

"Eliza, where are we?"

"Eliza opened her eyes at the sound of her sister's frightened voice. The bed was soft, and they were warm! It had been so long since they were warm that she didn't want to wake up, in case it was all a dream. The pain in her ankle brought the memory of the previous night back to her. Had that really all happened? Did their dad really come home? Yes, she was sure he had. Then the siren had gone off, and he'd insisted they went to the shelter. The bomb exploded, and she'd flown through the air. Dad and Lily found her, and Dad had got her leg out from where it was trapped. It was definitely all real because her ankle hurt bad.

Her Dad got her onto his shoulders, and had carried Lily in his arms. He'd walked for ages, but she didn't know where to, because she'd kept her eyes closed some of the time. Then she remembered they'd come to a house, where a kind lady had seen to her ankle. She didn't recognise her, but her dad seemed to know her. That was it! The lady said they could sleep in her bed.

"Eliza, I need a wee."

Eliza sat up and looked about her. She didn't know what the time was, but most likely having heard Lily's voice, the kind lady appeared in the doorway.

"Good morning," she said, with what seemed like a forced smile. "I hope you both slept well."

"Yes, thank you," Eliza said. "I'm sorry, but Lily needs to…"

"That's out the back. Come with me, Lily, I'll show you. I'll come back and help you, Eliza. You might not want to be putting much weight on that foot today."

Lily slid out of bed and stood on shaky legs looking at Eliza. Knowing that she would indeed need help herself, Eliza nodded at Lily, saying, "Go on, you'll be alright. I'll get my foot going and be up in a minute."

Ruthie held out her hand to Lily, who took it shyly, but when she made to take a step forward, her legs shook so much that Ruthie slipped her arms around her. "I'll tell you what," she said, "I keep a pot under the bed for emergencies, and I reckon this might be one." Reaching down, she slid out a chamber pot and helped a now shivering Lily to lift her clothes and sit down, turning away while the little girl used it.

Eliza didn't know who this lady was, but she seemed kind. She now came around the bed and asked her how her ankle was.

"It hurts a bit," Eliza replied.

Ruthie guessed correctly that it hurt a lot, but Eliza wasn't about to complain.

"Where's Dad?" Eliza asked, as she wondered how she was going to get out of bed. Would she also be allowed to use the pot? She didn't like the idea of using it, but didn't think she could make it out the back with her ankle hurting like it was.

"He's gone to see to a few things," Ruthie told her. "He said you won't have to go back to where you were living."

"We don't?" Lily's voice came from the far side of the bed.

"That's what he said. My name's Ruthie, by the way. I don't expect your dad will be too long." Ruthie stopped herself from saying anything more. This was such a strange situation. Here she was, face to face with her baby. She wasn't a baby anymore though, she was a twelve-year-old girl, quite grown up too. Eddie was right. Eliza did look like her. Her dark hair curled in the same way, whereas, although Eddie's hair was a similar colour, it was straighter.

Lily stood up, and Ruthie suggested she take her into the other room where it was warmer.

When Lily looked inquiringly at Eliza, she nodded. She somehow felt that this lady was someone they could trust.

Eliza watched as Ruthie easily lifted her sister into her arms, and carried her from the room, soon returning to ask if she needed any help. Eliza slid to the edge of the bed and tried to stand. Her ankle wasn't strong enough to take her weight, but she was sure she could hold on to the bed to get to the pot.

Ruthie recognised in Eliza the determination she'd had at her own age, as she said, "I'll be alright thank you."

Ruthie left the room, saying over her shoulder, "Call me if you need me."

Eliza used the pot, then wondered how to empty it. She stood looking at it for some time, before, holding onto the bed for support, she almost hopped across the room. She pulled the door open, and Ruthie was instantly there to help her. "I'm sorry," tears threatened to spring from Eliza's eyes. "I can't carry the pot to empty it."

"Don't you worry about that." Ruthie put her arm around the girl's thin shoulders and guided her to a chair. If Eliza knew she was her mother, she wouldn't feel any embarrassment about not being able to empty the pot. She mustn't think that way. Eliza could never know who she really was.

Ruthie let go of her daughter and hurried back to the bedroom. Standing by the bed, she wondered what she'd done. Had she really agreed to take Eddie's girls to the country? She could change her mind. Yes, he couldn't force her to go, but she dismissed that idea as quickly as it had come. Now she knew where her child was, she wasn't going to take any chances with her safety. She hadn't been able to keep herself safe, so why did she think she could keep Eliza safe? She was wiser now, she reasoned. Her mother hadn't talked to her about what men could be like. Maybe she wouldn't talk to Eliza about it, but she would keep an eye on her. Going to the country was the safest thing to do.

5

A misty haze hung over Cardiff as Eddie knocked on Ruthie's door for the second time in a matter of hours. Ruthie was quick to open it and hurried him inside. He was relieved to see Eliza and Lily on the old warn couch, Lily lying on Eliza's lap and Eliza with her foot resting on a chair. Ruthie had covered them with blankets to keep out the winter chill.

Both girls immediately turned questioning gazes on him as he entered the room and placed the bundle on the floor.

"Where did you go, Dad?" Eliza asked, as he bent to kiss them.

"I went for some of your things. I knew Ruthie would look after you both. Did you sleep well?"

"It was nice and warm!" Lily exclaimed. "Eliza's foot is really hurting her."

"It's okay," Eliza said quickly.

"We'll find someone to have a proper look at it when we get where we're going," Eddie told them.

"Where are we going?" Eliza questioned as she watched Ruthie close another box after packing it full of her belongings.

Eddie glanced at Ruthie, who nodded in agreement. He knelt beside his girls to give his explanation. "You won't be going back to your grandfather's place."

"Good!" Lily exclaimed. "He was mean!"

"Where will we go?" Eliza asked seriously. "He said he would find us and bring us back if we tried going somewhere else."

"That's why we've got to be clever about it. Ruthie is going to go with you."

"Why can't you take us, Dad?" Lily asked.

"Because I'm in the army," Eddie explained.

"But if we can hide from him, can't you hide from the army?" Eliza wondered thoughtfully.

"Afraid not. The army is better at tracking people down than your… him." Eddie had no desire to refer to his father as their grandfather.

"But what if he finds us?" Lily asked fearfully.

"You have to trust me, and Ruthie. We'll make sure he doesn't find you."

"Where are we going?" Eliza repeated her earlier question. "I don't think I can walk far."

"Don't worry Eliza, you won't be walking, you'll be going further than that. Now, I need a word with Ruthie, then we'll come back and tell you what's going to happen."

"But if we go too far to walk, how will me and Eliza go to Mam's grave?"

Lily's question was almost Eddie's undoing. He swallowed three times before he managed to say, "I'm sorry girls, but you won't be able to go there for a time. You can remember your mam in your heart though, like I remember you all when I'm away. You know she's with Jesus now. She's not hurting anymore, and she would want you to be safe." Eddie quickly stood up and asked Ruthie, "Can I have a word?"

"You'll have to come in here a minute," she said awkwardly, indicating the bedroom.

Eddie followed her into the room and closed the door. Leaning against the wall, he began in little above a whisper, "I don't know how to thank you, Ruthie."

"I was thinking," Ruthie spoke in the same low whisper. "Lizzie looked after my daughter, so the least I can do is the best I can for hers. And Eddie, I should thank you. Thank you for keeping my baby safe and loving her." Before Eddie had a chance to reply, Ruthie changed the subject, asking, "Where can we go? And how will we keep him from finding us?"

"I was having a think about that. I still think we should say you are their aunt. I was going to say you were my sister, but given what I've just learnt about my dad, I don't think that's such a good idea. Maybe Lizzie's sister?"

"But I'm nothing like Lizzie. She was so small and delicate and…" She couldn't go on. She'd envied the dainty girl and everything about her when Lizzie first got together with Eddie, but after a while, those feelings faded. Eddie had deserved better than her. She was glad he had Lizzie.

"Half-sister then if you like," Eddie suggested.

"Probably best. I know nothing about Lizzie, and the girls are bright."

"Okay, so you are Lizzie's half-sister. That should work. If the girls believe that too, they are less likely to say anything wrong."

"Eddie, I'm afraid I won't be good enough."

"You? Never. Ruthie Lewis, you are the strongest person I know."

"Maybe at one time." Ruthie's voice was hardly audible.

"How long do you need?" Eddie asked. "I spoke to someone about borrowing a car, but I didn't bring it now as I didn't want to draw attention."

"Can you give me an hour?"

"That's fine." He was relieved she wouldn't need much longer. The sooner they got away, the better.

"I should be in the factory, but after last night, no one will come looking for a day or two. Most people will be at work by the time you come back, so there's less chance of seeing anyone."

"That's good. Someone I was with in training came from the Forest of Dean. It's not so far away, and it's right out in the country. He'll never find you there. I can take you there today and find somewhere for you to stay, then I can return the car and be ready to get back to the army."

"I've heard of the Forest of Dean. I see you got some of the girls' things. I presume that's what's in the bundle. How did you get them past him? You sure he didn't follow you here?"

"He couldn't stand. Besides, I put the bundle outside before I woke him. I told him about the explosion as we were going to the shelter, and he presumed the worst. I didn't want to lie, but I didn't have to in the end. I just let him think what he wanted."

Eddie opened the door and moved to stand once more by his daughters. "I'm going to get a car, then I'm taking the two of you, and Ruthie, to the country. He won't find you there. Ruthie is your aunt. She's your mam's half-sister, so she'll look after you well."

"Mam never said she had a sister!" Eliza exclaimed in disbelief.

"We didn't grow up together," Ruthie explained quickly, "so I expect it was a bit difficult for her."

"Now girls," Eddie began, "Ruthie needs to finish getting things ready, so don't bother her with questions. Mind you give her a hand too."

Eddie promised to return soon and left the house, leaving the three of them wondering what would happen next.

When Ruthie got out the remains of the bread, announcing she would slice it and make sandwiches to take, Eliza offered to do it for her. With a bit of help from her newly acquired aunt, she settled herself at the table and set about her work. There was a lot to think about. She'd never heard her mam mention a sister of any kind, but what did it matter if this Auntie Ruthie was going to take them to the country where it was safe?

Ruthie moved quickly and efficiently around the rooms, gathering up what she wanted and disregarding the rest. Whoever found it could keep it if they wanted it. People would know she'd gone away somewhere, but no one would look for her. No one would miss her. She supposed that was her own fault really. She hadn't wanted to get close to anyone. She'd just sort of existed. Had she wasted her life? Most likely, yes. It didn't seem fair that so many people were being killed and families were missing those they loved, while she, who mattered to nobody, was still here. Now she would matter. Now Eddie needed her to do something, and she'd do her best. She finally had the chance to be with her child. She hadn't dared give her a name when she'd held the tiny baby in her arms, but she was Eliza. Elizabeth Ruth. What was Lily's full name? she'd have to find out. Eddie kept mentioning God. It seemed he was a Christian now. Ruthie had never thought much about God. If he did exist, he hadn't cared much about her. She didn't have time to think about that. She wondered what kind of work she would find in the country. What did people do there? She hoped she wouldn't have to milk cows. She'd never met a cow in her entire life!

Time flew by and Eddie soon returned. In just a few minutes, he carried her belongings and the bundle he'd got from his father's home into the car. He then came back and lifted Eliza easily into his strong arms. At her protest, he said quietly, "We need to be gone as soon as we can."

At this, Eliza ceased to protest, but Ruthie instantly recognised the same independence in her daughter as she'd had at her age.

Lily made no resistance as Eddie lifted her up and cuddled her tightly. Eliza and Lily were obviously very close, but Lily didn't seem to have the energy to be independent. She hoped a bit of country air would do the little girl good. She reminded Ruthie of a porcelain doll she'd once seen, with her pale skin and light blonde hair. It looked like a gentle breeze would blow her over. She'd need to take special care of her. It was clear Eddie was concerned about her health.

Ruthie followed Eddie outside and shut the door, not bothering to lock it. She glanced back at her home for the last twelve years, but felt no real loss at leaving it. It hadn't been a home, just a place to sleep and exist.

She slid into the car next to Eddie and glanced over at the girls huddled in the back seat, blankets wrapped about them. "We'll be alright," she told the two fear-filled faces staring back at her. "We'll find somewhere nice in the country, and there'll be lots of things to tell your dad about when you write to him."

"Will we still be able to write letters to you, Dad?" Eliza asked.

"Of course. You write to me, and I'll write back to you."

"Will we go to school?" Lily questioned. "Eliza couldn't go when I wasn't well because she didn't want to leave me on my own. Eliza likes school."

"Eliza can go to school, and you, when you're well enough," Eddie told them.

"The country air might help you get better," Ruthie said hopefully.

"Lizzie always wanted to go back to the country," Eddie told Ruthie over the noise of the car engine. "I should've taken her, but I didn't know anything other than working on the docks. I should've done it before I was called up, then she might still be here and…"

"You always did your best, Eddie Davies! That I know," Ruthie stated confidently.

"I don't know. You're probably right about Lily. The country air will most likely do her good."

"There are so many fires still!" Eliza exclaimed. "Did our whole street get blown up?"

"Not all of it, so I got a few of your things from the house."

"Will there be bombs in the country?" Lily asked sleepily. "I don't like bombs."

Ruthie didn't imagine anyone liking bombs. "I don't expect there will be many. They're usually after the docks and the factories here."

After several diversions, Eddie drove the car out of Cardiff. By this time, both girls were sleeping.

Keeping her voice as low as she could, Ruthie asked, "I know Eliza's name is Elizabeth Ruth, but what about Lily?"

Eddie smiled. "Liliana Grace," he told her. "Lizzie heard of Liliana somewhere in a book and decided it suited the angelic little girl who arrived after so many miscarriages. We didn't want fun made of her, so we shortened it to Lily."

"She's a Liliana Grace if ever I saw one," Ruthie agreed. "I really will do my best for them both."

"I know you will, that's why I came to you last night." Eddie made a turn onto another road before he went on, "You know there's always a chance I might not make it? I mean, I'll try my best to get back, but you know how it is in a war."

"Don't say it, Eddie." Ruthie turned away to stare out of the window.

"I don't want to, but we must be prepared. Lizzie is gone, so I have to be sure. I'll do my best to survive this war, but if I don't, will you keep the girls?"

Ruthie found it difficult to hold back her tears. "Of course I will. I'll do whatever I can to make sure they never come into contact with someone like him again. You have to make it home though, Eddie, you just have to."

"I'll keep praying I will. Can you and the girls do the same?"

"I've never prayed before," Ruthie admitted.

"The girls pray. Lizzie taught us all how to talk to the Lord, then to listen as well. Sometimes I'm all too good at the talking, but not so good at the listening. Lizzie was good at listening."

"Do you honestly think it works? Prayer, I mean."

"I know it does."

"But if it does, why did Lizzie die, and Eliza and Lily end up where they were?"

"God doesn't always give us what we want. I don't understand it myself. Lizzie could've explained it better. I know it's a lot to ask, but could you see the girls go to chapel as well? I'm not saying you have to go with them, although I wouldn't be without the Lord in my life now. You know how I used to be? Having Jesus in my life made me different."

"I can see that. The old Eddie would've got really mad when I told you what happened."

"I was angry. I haven't felt anger like that in years, but He calmed me down. I can't explain how knowing Him has made my life better. I wish Lizzie could've talked to you. Eliza and Lily have a strong faith, at least I hope they still do. I don't know what losing their mother will have done to them."

6

Dad! I'm going to be sick!" Lily's urgent cry came from the back seat.

Eddie quickly pulled over to the side of the road and jumped out. As he ran around the car, Ruthie was already ahead of him, as Lily had been sitting behind her. She had the door open in no time and had lifted the little girl from the car. Eddie watched as Ruthie placed Lily on her feet and held her as she emptied the contents of her stomach onto the grass.

When Lily had finished, she cried, "I didn't mean to!"

"It's alright, we know you didn't," Ruthie spoke gently to her. "It was most likely because you're not used to being in the car and you fell asleep."

"Perhaps you'd better sit up in the front with us," Eddie suggested. "It won't be long now, I don't think. Are you feeling better?" He took out his handkerchief and wiped Lily's face.

"I think so," she sobbed.

They returned to the car with Lily on Ruthie's lap. "You tell us if you feel sick again," Eddie told her. "It's easy enough to stop."

As they started off once more, Eliza buried her face in the blanket and tried not to cry. It should have been her who helped Lily, not Auntie Ruthie or whoever she was. Did she think she was going to be like their mam? Well, she wasn't. She'd looked after herself and Lily since her mam was gone. She'd done it before really, as her mam was often not well. She didn't need anyone else. She was glad they were going away from Cardiff. At least they didn't have to live with that horrible man who called himself a grandfather anymore, but her dad should have just brought her and Lily, not this Auntie Ruthie. They didn't need her.

Eliza decided there and then that, once her dad was back in the army, she'd tell Auntie Ruthie she could go back to Cardiff if she wanted, because she and Lily would be just fine. Evacuees were going to the country all the time! They didn't have someone else with them.

Eliza tried to move into a more comfortable position. Why did she have to hurt her ankle? If she hadn't done that, she would have got Lily out. She would have helped her to the pot this morning, too. It just wasn't fair!

A short while later, they had to stop once more for Lily to be sick. Again, Ruthie got out with her, and her dad joined them. Eliza pretended she was asleep and hid her head under the blanket. Lily would probably end up liking her, she thought to herself, but she wasn't going to like her. Why had her mam never said she had a half-sister? She must be really bad if Mam didn't talk about her, she decided.

Soon Eddie announced he thought they were there. He pointed out sheep grazing beside the road and Eliza sat up to see. There they were, heads down, eating grass, with their backsides sticking out into the road.

"They look funny!" Lily giggled. "Oh look! There's a tiny one there!"

"Oh yes!" Ruthie agreed. "What a tiny lamb."

"I thought it was a baby sheep," Lily sounded confused.

"It is," Ruthie explained. "A baby sheep is called a lamb."

"Like baby dogs are called puppies and baby cats kittens," Eliza joined in, not to be outdone.

"And baby pigs are piglets and baby cows calves," Eddie continued.

"Will we see pigs and cows?" Lily asked.

"I don't know, maybe." Eddie stopped at a junction, trying to decide which way to go. After a quick prayer for guidance, he turned left. A little way down the road, he spotted a chapel. Of course, that would be a good place to ask about somewhere to stay, but it wasn't Sunday. What if there was no one there? He decided he'd might as well find out, so pulled over and stopped the car.

"Are we going to live here?" Lily questioned.

"I'm going to ask about a place for you to stay. I won't be long. Why don't you all get out and stretch your legs."

Eddie disappeared up the path which led to the chapel, and Ruthie opened her door and got out, lifting Lily with her. "Would you like a hand, Eliza?" she asked kindly.

"No," Eliza shook her head. "I'm staying here." Her mother's voice in her head caused her to add, "thank you."

Ruthie pulled her coat around herself and Lily. "It seems colder out here," she observed. "Perhaps we'd better stay in the car, not that it's much warmer."

"I like it here." Lily smiled as Ruthie got back into the car, wrapping a blanket more securely around the shivering child.

"It does seem a nice place, very quiet," Ruthie agreed, but her thoughts were on Eliza. Was it her imagination, or did Eliza resent her being here? No, she was imagining things. They were all tired, that was likely it.

It didn't seem long before Eddie reappeared, closing the gate behind him. "No luck?" Ruthie asked as he got into the driver's seat.

"As it happens, there was someone there. She was playing the organ. There's a farm not too far from here where they might have room. They had some evacuees there, and some land girls, but they've all gone home. The farmer and his wife come to this chapel."

"That does sound promising. I think I might enjoy working on the land. It'll be much better than being stuck in a noisy factory."

"How about we eat that food you brought, then go on up and see?" Eddie suggested. "Shame it isn't warmer out, this would be the ideal place to sit on the grass and have a picnic."

Ruthie took out the food and offered it around.

"Lily might be sick again if she eats," Eliza said protectively.

"I won't," Lily said adamantly. "It was because of the car, Auntie Ruthie said that."

"Well, if we can't go to that farm, we might be in the car longer again," Eliza said with a sigh.

"I'm sure Lily will be fine," Eddie reassured her.

They all ate as much as they wanted, then Eddie set off up the road. As they turned left, Lily exclaimed, "Look! There's a school!"

"I imagine that's where the two of you will go if you stay here." Eddie smiled at her.

After passing a cluster of houses, they turned right onto a farm track. It wasn't long before Eddie stopped the car in the yard, where they were greeted by a madly barking collie dog.

His barking, along with the noise of the car, soon brought a woman from the house. She looked to be in her forties and smiled as she hurried towards them. "Quiet Ben!" she told the dog firmly, while still smiling, and the dog instantly ceased to bark.

Both Eddie and Ruthie got out, leaving the girls inside.

"Hello," the woman greeted them. "Can I help you?"

Ruthie noticed instantly how different her way of speaking was.

"Are you Mrs. Turley?" Eddie enquired.

"That's me. And who be you?"

"My name's Eddie Davies. I just stopped down at the chapel and was sent up here. You see, I'm home on leave and when I got back to Cardiff, the raids had got worse. My wife died while I was away and I'd feel better about going back if her sister and my two girls were out in the country, away from the bombs."

"And you've brought them all the way here yourself? You must be concerned. Come on in and I'll make us some tea, then I'll find Mr. Turley."

Turning back to the car, Ruthie wondered which of the girls she should help. It would be easier supporting Eliza as she hopped along, but she didn't seem to want anything from her. Instead, Ruthie gathered a sleepy Lily into her arms, pulled the blanket around her, and followed Eddie, who was assisting Eliza.

The warm farmhouse kitchen was a complete contrast to the cold January air outside. Mrs. Turley fussed around pulling chairs closer to the stove, then making the tea.

"How did you hurt your foot?" she asked Eliza.

"A bomb went off when we were on our way to the shelter," Eliza explained. "It blew me away from Dad and Lily, then some things landed on my foot."

"I'd like her to have it seen by a doctor," Eddie said. "Is there one around here?"

"Yes, we still have a doctor. He's too old to go to the war, so we're thankful for that. After you've warmed up a bit, I'll tell you where to find him. I'll go and get Mr. Turley now, and we can see what we can do."

Ruthie looked about the kitchen. It looked so large compared to the tiny rooms she'd lived in all her life. She noticed an open Bible resting at the other end of the table. That would please Eddie, she thought.

Eliza was enjoying the warmth of the stove. She'd been warm last night in Auntie Ruthie's bed, but here it was even warm without having to be under lots of blankets. This will be better for Lily, she supposed.

Mrs. Turley soon returned with her husband. He too was smiling as they entered the kitchen, where he came to warm his hands by the stove.

"It's getting colder!" he announced. "Wind's getting up too."

"They don't want to be talking about the weather!" His wife smiled. "As I told you, they're looking for somewhere to stay."

"For Ruthie and the girls," Eddie put in.

Looking at Ruthie, Mr. Turley asked, "Have you ever worked on a farm before?"

"No," Ruthie shook her head. "But I think I'd like it. I'm not afraid of hard work."

"And how about you girls? You reckon you won't mind living in the country?"

"We won't mind," Eliza spoke quickly. "Lily is really scared of the bombs."

"I'm not surprised! Reckon I would be too!" exclaimed Mrs. Turley. "We haven't had any around here, though."

"Really?" Lily lifted her head to look at her.

"Not one. You sometimes hear the planes going over, but there's been no bombs."

"I reckon it will work out all round to have you here," Mr. Turley stated.

"I'll see that Ruthie has enough money to pay you," Eddie explained.

So it was settled. Over tea, they learnt that Bill and Ada Turley had two sons, John and Joe, who were both away in the war. They'd had several evacuees here, but they'd all returned home. They hadn't done much better with land girls either.

"Didn't know what to do with a bit of dirt!" Mrs. Turley laughed.

Eddie brought in the belongings from the car, and helped Ruthie and Mr. Turley to carry them upstairs, where Ruthie and the girls were to share one room, with a large bed standing in the centre. Once that task was complete, and he'd been fed to Mrs. Turley's satisfaction, Eddie knew the time had come for him to leave. Ruthie left them alone as he said goodbye to Eliza and Lily, telling them to do as Ruthie said. He promised to write, and come home just as soon as he could.

Ruthie went out to the car with him, while the girls stayed in the warm kitchen. "What if I get it wrong, Eddie?" she said in some panic. "I don't know anything about looking after the girls."

"Your mam did, so just think back to what she would have done. You'll be fine Ruthie, I know you will. Mrs. Turley will be a good help too, I'd imagine. I'll call in and ask the doctor to come and see Eliza on my way by. Don't let her give you any trouble mind, she's an independent one, I know."

Ruthie fought back tears as Eddie got into the car and drove away down the farm track. Whatever had she done? Here she was in the middle of nowhere, living in a house with complete strangers. She'd known Eliza and Lily for less than twenty-four hours, now here she was, having agreed to take care of them for Eddie.

What was she thinking? Eliza was her own child. She'd never thought she'd see her little girl again, let alone sleep in the same bed as her. When Eliza had become sulky earlier, she'd reminded her of Eddie's father. The face she'd pulled had told Ruthie she wasn't happy. But no. Eliza was nothing like him. She was more like Eddie, but more than that, she was so much like herself. Eddie was right when he'd said Eliza was independent. She'd have to tread carefully with her. It would be less complicated with Lily. All she seemed to need was to feel safe.

How long had it been since she herself had felt safe? Too long, she realised. Many years too long.

7

Ruthie lay still on the edge of the bed, listening to the sound of the rain as it drummed on the farmhouse roof. Lily lay sleeping peacefully beside her, but she was sure Eliza was still awake. Eliza looked as pleased as she herself had been when Lily insisted on sleeping in the middle. Lily seemed to feel secure with her, but it was clear her own child didn't trust her. Had she found it that difficult to trust when she was Eliza's age? No, she hadn't been that way. She was a little older than Eliza when her father died, but she had still been able to trust people. That only changed when… The thought caused her to sit upright in the bed. Had Eliza experienced the same treatment at the hands of Gareth Davies? After all, she'd shared a house with the man who had changed the path of Ruthie's own life.

Sensing the older girl's eyes on her in the darkness, Ruthie lay back down. She didn't want Eliza asking her questions, not that she was likely to speak to her any more than was necessary.

Seeing her daughter had brought back so many memories. She'd both loved and hated the child she carried. No, hate was too strong a word, but as soon as she'd known she was having Gareth Davies' baby, she couldn't imagine being a mother to it. She'd known girls who'd had babies without being married, and she knew what they were called. Some of them fought to keep their babies, but they'd been conceived out of love. Her child was conceived out of fear. She wished now she'd told her mother what was happening. She would have known what to do. However, by the time the baby was on its way, and she couldn't hide it any longer, her mam was too unwell to be of any help.

Ruthie had known all along that she would give her baby up. What other choice did she have? She didn't want a constant reminder of her terrifying experience. However, not having the baby around hadn't lessened the memories. Now, that baby had grown into a twelve-year-old girl, and she was lying on the opposite side of the bed.

The slight movement of the mattress told her that Eliza was as restless as she was. She wanted to reach out to her, but she didn't know how. In a low whisper, Ruthie asked, "Are you alright, Eliza? Is your ankle hurting?"

Ruthie wondered if she would get a response, but after some seconds, Eliza said, "It's not so bad now." She hesitated before continuing, "It's just so quiet here apart from the rain."

"It is, isn't it? It seems strange to me, too." Ruthie was relieved that Eliza had spoken to her. "It would be quieter still without the rain, I suppose."

While visiting the toilet in the shed behind the house before going to bed, Ruthie nearly screamed when a nearby owl chose that moment to hoot. Eliza and Lily had been told to use the pot in the house, what with Lily being unwell and the doctor advising Eliza to stay off her ankle for a day or two. He'd cleaned the wound, but was happy with the treatment Eliza had received. Ruthie found herself going alone to the outhouse. Her heart pounded in her ears as she went into the unknown darkness. Her imagination ran wild, until she told herself that there was no one nearby to harm her. On her return to the house, she'd broke into a run when one of the cows in the barn let out a loud "Moo!" Life on a farm would take some getting used to, she realised.

The wind was blowing wildly when Ruthie awoke some hours later. The room felt cold, and for a moment, she wondered where she was. The sound of Lily coughing reminded her of all that had transpired over the last two days.

Above the noise of the wind and rain, Ruthie thought she heard some noise from elsewhere in the house. She slipped noiselessly out of bed and found her clothes in the darkness. As she tried to dress quietly, Lily's voice came from the bed.

"Auntie Ruthie, where are you going?"

"I'm not sure what time it is, so I'm going downstairs to see."

"Is it time to get up?" Lily's voice still sounded weak.

It was still dark, but then it didn't get light early at this time of the year. Without the noise of other people going about their business in the street, it was difficult to know the time. "I'd stay there a while longer if I were you. See if you can get a bit more sleep. I'm going to see what I can do to help Mr. and Mrs. Turley."

Ruthie finished dressing and made for the door, stubbing her toe on the leg of the bed as she went. She bit her lip, rather than exclaiming aloud, before she continued on her way and finally made it out onto the landing.

Down in the kitchen, she found Mrs. Turley preparing the breakfast. "Good morning, Ruthie. I hope you slept well."

"Yes thank you, Mrs. Turley. I left the girls sleeping, is that alright?"

"That's fine. They need the rest, I'd say."

"What can I do to help? Should I go out and help Mr. Turley?" Ruthie had noticed the man's big coat was missing from the hook just inside the door.

"I'll go out there this morning if you can finish the breakfast for me? Probably best if you make a start in the daylight with the animals. It's blowing a gale out there!"

"I can do the breakfast, yes. I'm happy to do whatever you need."

Ruthie soon found her way around the kitchen. She used to enjoy cooking with her mam but hadn't given it much thought since she'd been living alone. It felt good to be cooking for more than just herself again.

She had a good breakfast ready by the time the Turleys came in from the barn. The girls had also made their way into the kitchen and helped as much as they were able.

The five of them sat around the table together. Before they began, Mr. Turley asked a blessing on the meal and on the day ahead. He had done the same the previous evening and, although Eliza and Lily seemed used to this kind of thing, it was all new to Ruthie.

There was general conversation while they ate, then as soon as they'd all finished, Mr. Turley reached for his Bible. "I hope you don't mind, but we're halfway through the gospel of John," he told them.

"I like John!" Eliza replied. "It was one of Mam's favourite books too."

Ruthie listened as Mr. Turley read aloud. She'd not taken much notice when the Bible was read to them in school, but found herself wishing she had. Those who read the Bible and talked about Jesus seemed somehow different.

Once he'd finished reading, Mr. Turley rose quickly, saying, "I'll be going back out then."

"What would you like me to do?" Ruthie asked.

"Come with me," Mr. Turley said. "I'll show you around a bit and see what you make of the farm."

Ruthie felt a little nervous about this new kind of work she was to do, but she knew this kind farmer would be a good teacher. She would do her best with whatever task he gave her, even if it involved cows.

Mrs. Turley sent Lily back to bed, then moved a chair nearer to the sink so Eliza could sit to dry the breakfast things.

Eliza liked Mrs. Turley. She was always happy and friendly. The fact that she and Mr. Turley were Christians also put her at ease. They would be safe here, if only Lily would get well again soon.

Mrs. Turley sang to herself as she filled the sink and began washing the dishes. As she handed the first plate to Eliza, she asked, "Is there something bothering you? I know living in the country will be different, but I'm sure you'll get used to it."

Her kindness brought tears to Eliza's eyes, but she didn't want to cry. "I think I'll like living here. It's very quiet, but I'll get used to that."

"I can't help feeling that something is on your mind," the older woman said kindly.

Eliza wondered how someone who didn't even know her could know that. She began, "I miss Mam. I know she's with Jesus now and it's better for her, but…" Eliza hesitated, then blurted out, "I don't know why Dad brought Auntie Ruthie here. He could have just brought me and Lily, like other evacuees."

Mrs. Turley took her hands from the water and looked straight at Eliza. "It was very good of your dad to bring you all the way here. Most evacuees come by train, you know. I'm sure he had his reasons for bringing your auntie as well."

"I suppose so, but we didn't know her until the other night. I mean, Dad said she's Mam's half-sister, but we've never heard of her before. What if she isn't?"

"Oh Eliza!" Mrs. Turley's smile widened. "I don't think there's any doubt about that. I'm guessing she looks very much like your mother. I mean, if I didn't know any different, I would think she was your mam. The two of you look so much alike."

Eliza was confused as she answered, "No, Mam didn't look like her. Lily looks just like Mam."

"Well, there you go then. Lily looks like your mam, and you look like your auntie. You don't need to worry about that, Eliza. I'm sure there must be some reason you haven't seen her before."

Eliza didn't reply, but sat wondering how it could all be. Perhaps Mrs. Turley was right. Why did everything seem in a muddle at the moment? Her mam would say she should be grateful. Yes, she should. She and Lily didn't have to live in fear of what would happen anymore. Not of the bombs, and not of their grandfather. It didn't seem like Mr. Turley liked to drink, so that was certainly a good thing. She hadn't known people could drink like that, or what it would do to them until they were forced to live in the pokey rooms with that man. No wonder their dad hadn't made them visit him. She wondered how many more people there were in the family they didn't know about. She knew her mam had a brother, but he was in the war. She'd seen him a few times, and he seemed nice enough. Maybe Auntie Ruthie would be alright after all, but something still bothered her. If she was nice, why hadn't they seen her? She only lived in Cardiff, so why were they sent to their grandfather if Auntie Ruthie lived so near? Their mam had cried when she knew she didn't have long left and said they might have to live with their grandfather for a while, but their dad would make sure they were alright. She said she wished there was another way, but they were to keep praying about it and God would make a way.

Well, God had made a way. He'd brought their dad back safely, and he'd brought them here, but she still didn't understand about Auntie Ruthie.

At dinner time, Eliza took the opportunity to have a good look at Auntie Ruthie, realising they were similar in many ways. Afterwards, when she and Lily sat together, Eliza reading to her younger sister, she looked up from the book and asked, "Lily, do you think Auntie Ruthie looks like Mam?"

"No!" Lily laughed. "She looks like you. She talks like you sometimes, too. I like her. She will look after us now."

"I looked after us!" Eliza said indignantly.

"Yes, but Auntie Ruthie can look after both of us. You won't have to stay home from school because of me."

"I didn't mind. Anyway, you'll soon be better, and you'll come to school too."

"Will everyone talk funny, like Mr. and Mrs. Turley?" Lily smiled.

"I expect so. Not unless there are evacuees."

"Will they talk like us?"

Eliza thought before she said, "I think it depends where they lived before."

"Why do you talk different because you live somewhere?" Lily questioned in some confusion.

Eliza sighed. "I don't know, Lily, it's just the way it is, I suppose. Remember the Italian café Mam and Dad took us to? The Italian people came from another country, so spoke another language before they came here. They have a different way of saying the same words."

“Which country did people here come from?” Lily enquired.

“We are in England now, not Wales, so I suppose that’s why they talk different.”

“Mr. Turley was saying about cows yuttin’ and I didn’t know what he meant. He said they yut grass in the summer. He meant eating!” Lily began to giggle and soon Eliza joined her.

“Mam would have liked it here,” Eliza said. “She would have liked Mr. and Mrs. Turley, too.”

“Auntie Ruthie said we can pick wildflowers in spring and put them somewhere to remember Mam if we want to, because we can’t go to the cemetery.”

Eliza was immediately defensive. “Mam’s not in the cemetery, she’s with Jesus.”

“But…” Lily’s voice shook a little. “you said we were going to take flowers to where she was buried in the spring. I told Auntie Ruthie we would be sad because we couldn’t.”

“We don’t need to,” Eliza said sharply, before picking up the book and continuing to read, the moment of laughter the two sisters had enjoyed now forgotten.

Lily usually enjoyed hearing Eliza reading, but today she wasn’t really listening. Why didn’t Eliza like Auntie Ruthie? She was glad she was there. Eliza never got mad with her before, but now she was mad with her and Auntie Ruthie. Lily’s mind drifted to the promise Mrs. Turley had made earlier that day. She’d said that once she was stronger, Lily could help her in the kitchen. Mrs. Turley made good food, even though there were rations. She said she had a special recipe for a cake, and Lily couldn’t wait to help her make it. Mrs. Turley said her boys, John and Joe, liked that cake, and Lily knew she would like it too.

She was glad they didn't have to go back to Cardiff. Mam had grown up in the country, and now she would be even more like her. She could see why her mam liked it so much. She'd told them a lot of stories about living on a farm. Now she and Eliza had the chance to do many of the same things.

8

Life at the farm soon settled into a pattern. Ruthie found that, although farm work was physically tiring, it was far better than the work she'd done before. Even the cows weren't quite as frightening as she thought they would be.

On Sunday mornings and evenings, they made the mile-long walk to the chapel where Eddie had asked for help when they'd first arrived in the village. Ruthie found she enjoyed the services in the simple building. The sound of many voices raised in song was somehow comforting, and the words the preacher spoke made a lot of sense. Eliza and Lily also seemed to enjoy the services, along with Sunday school in the afternoon. Mr. Turley read even more of the Bible on Sunday mornings, carefully explaining what he was reading. The best part of the day came after chapel in the evening, when Mrs. Turley sat at the old piano and played hymns for them to sing along to. Ruthie found the words of those hymns really speaking to her. They told of how Jesus loved them, that he was a friend to them, of all God had created, and so much more. When Ruthie had admitted to Mrs. Turley that she didn't really know much about Jesus, she'd suggested they take a part of each day to talk and pray together. Ruthie had been concerned that she wouldn't be doing enough work on the farm, but both Mr. and Mrs. Turley assured her that getting right with God was more important.

Most of the people in the village seemed friendly, although some didn't seem too keen to have yet more outsiders move in. The girls had started at the local school, which had apparently doubled in size since the beginning of the war. They came home with many tales of what various members of their classes had got up to.

Eliza's ankle had healed well, and she would have run to school each morning if Lily could have kept up with her. Eliza had made two good friends, Florence, a local girl, and Stella, an evacuee from London. The three girls spent as much time together as they could, joining forces to either help on the Turley farm, or on the farm where Stella was staying with Florence and her family.

Lily had missed the first week at school, but now she too had a friend, Elsie, another evacuee from London. Elsie wasn't as fortunate as Stella, as the family she was with seemed to see her more as an inconvenience, which was difficult to imagine, as a sweeter child you couldn't find.

"Elsie was late for school again today," Lily told them one evening as they ate together around the large, well-worn kitchen table. "She dropped an egg when she brought them in, because her hands were so cold, so she had to clean the whole of the kitchen floor."

"That doesn't sound right to me," Mrs. Turley said. "I'm sure it must have been an accident."

"It was. Her hands are all cut because they're always so cold. She didn't want to show me them, but I saw," Lily informed them.

"I think I might pop over there tomorrow," Mr. Turley announced. "I haven't seen Dan for a while and it sounds like 'im and me should have a talk about evacuees and what they should be expected to do."

"Stella says she doesn't want to go back to London. She wants to stay with Florence's family forever!" Eliza stated.

"Yes, they are a good family," Mr. Turley confirmed, "but not everyone is as good as they are."

Ruthie noticed the expression on Eliza and Lily's faces, and knew they were thinking of life with their grandfather. She wondered about the extent of his cruelty to them and wanted to ask them about it, but Eliza still seemed wary of her.

"Auntie Ruthie, can we write to Dad tonight?" Lily asked.

"I told you I'd do it for you, Lily!" Eliza exclaimed irritably. "We don't need anyone else to help."

Ruthie didn't know who to respond to first, or quite how she should respond. She just sat open-mouthed.

It was Mr. Turley who said calmly but firmly, "Eliza, Lily was right to ask permission from your Auntie. After all, she's paying for the letters to be sent."

Eliza lowered her head and stared down at her lap, but said nothing.

"What do you need to do, Eliza?" Mr. Turley questioned.

"Sorry," Eliza's voice was quiet.

Ruthie thought it sounded as though Eliza was trying to fight back tears. "Of course you may both write to your dad tonight. I know he'll enjoy another letter." What would Eliza's letter contain, she wondered. What would it take for Eliza to like her?

Ruthie helped Mrs. Turley to clear away after the meal, while Eliza and Lily sat at the table to write to their father. Ruthie knew she should include a letter to Eddie as well, but what could she say?

It seemed Mrs. Turley knew Ruthie had things on her mind, as she didn't talk incessantly as she usually did. Once the clearing away was done, Ruthie went out to help Mr. Turley finish the night-time rounds. The air was still, and something felt different.

"We'll have snow before morning," Bill announced, as Ruthie joined him in the barn.

"Do you think?" she asked in some surprise.

"Yes, I'm almost certain of it. The animals that need shelter are all inside though, so there's nothing to worry about. I'll take a shovel to the house in case we need to dig ourselves out."

"Will there be that much?" Ruthie was shocked.

"Might be, you never know."

Ruthie enjoyed working alongside the farmer. She hadn't been sure how she'd feel about working with a man, but she didn't feel afraid of Bill Turley at all.

Of a sudden, with what seemed like some urgency, Ben bounded towards them and nudged Bill's leg.

"What is it, Ben?" he enquired, leaning down to pat the dog on the head.

Ben looked up at him then walked away, turning back to check his master was following.

Ruthie was surprised when Mr. Turley followed the dog to the far end of the barn. Why would you follow where a dog was leading, she wondered.

When Bill suddenly exclaimed, "Oh!" Ruthie jumped so much, she heard her heart in her ears. She still wasn't used to life out here in the country, and if something surprised Bill Turley, it must be bad.

"Come and see who Ben found, Ruthie!" he called.

What could it be? Ruthie worried, cautiously walking towards him. As she drew level with Mr. Turley and looked to where his lantern was shining, she saw a small figure huddled in the straw. Recognising the child's worn-out coat, Ruthie dropped to her knees, exclaiming, "Elsie! What are you doing out here? You must be frozen!" Looking up at Mr. Turley, she explained, "This is Lily's friend, Elsie."

Ruthie lifted the little girl into her arms and stood up. "She's freezing!"

"Let's get her in the house in the warm," Mr. Turley said. "I would take her myself, but I think she's afraid of me. It's a good thing Ben found her."

Ruthie caught sight of Elsie's face, which she'd tried to keep hidden, and knew instantly why the little girl had run away. "You're safe here, Elsie," she told her. "No one will hurt you here."

"I didn't mean to…" Elsie's voice was barely audible. "I didn't mean to spill the water."

Bill Turley had now also seen the child's face. "And they beat you for spilling water?"

Ruthie detected anger in his tone, although he was trying his hardest to stay calm.

"I dropped an egg this morning too!" Elsie burst into tears.

Mr. Turley took off his coat and wrapped it around the slight figure. "I don't know what's been going on there," he said, "but you won't be going back. You'll stay here with us tonight. I know Lily will be very happy about that. Then tomorrow, we'll see what can be done."

Back in the warm kitchen, three pairs of eyes turned to look at them. "Elsie!" Lily cried, jumping up from the table and running towards them, flinging her arms around both Ruthie and the child she was holding.

"Ben found Elsie out in our barn," Mr. Turley explained. "She'll be staying here tonight."

"Come by the fire and get warm!" Mrs. Turley took Elsie from Ruthie's arms and sat in the chair by the stove. "Eliza, you know where we keep the spare blankets, run and get me a couple, please. This child is frozen!"

Eliza ran from the room, while Lily hovered near her friend. "Will Elsie be alright?" she asked.

"She'll be fine," Mrs. Turley reassured her.

"But the bad farmer hit her! Elsie said I mustn't tell that he hits her sometimes, but he shouldn't, should he? I said that Mr. Turley doesn't hit us!"

"No one should hit anyone," Mr. Turley stated.

Ruthie and Ada Turley worked together to treat the various wounds Elsie had received, while Lily talked gently to her friend. "Can Elsie stay here with us?" Lily asked.

"She'll stay here tonight, then tomorrow I'll go and see the authorities," Mr. Turley told her. "Whatever happens, she's not going back to that farm, that's for sure."

"I want to go home!" Elsie cried. "I want my mum!"

"But there are bombs in London!" Lily exclaimed.

"I want my mum!" Elsie wailed.

Ada rocked her gently and soon Elsie cried herself to sleep.

"Can Elsie sleep in our bed tonight?" Lily asked. "I'll look after her."

"I don't know if you'll get any sleep with four in a bed," Mrs. Turley said thoughtfully.

"I think we'll manage one night," Ruthie smiled. "It's time you were in bed too, Lily."

Ruthie carried the sleeping Elsie up the stairs, with Lily close beside her. Elsie looked as though she could do with a good bath, but they'd worry about that tomorrow. Soon the two girls were lying side by side, Lily holding her friend's hand protectively.

As Ruthie was about to leave the room, Lily asked, "Auntie Ruthie, why are some men bad?"

Ruthie sat on the bed and took Lily's other hand. How would her mother answer that, she wondered. "I don't really know," she said honestly.

"Is it because they don't know Jesus? Because when you know Jesus, you want to be good."

"That's likely it, Lily. I would say the people who Elsie was staying with don't know Jesus." Ruthie was glad Lily had found her own explanation.

"Do you know any bad people?"

Ruthie closed her eyes, but instantly opened them again when the image of Gareth Davies looming over her came into her mind. "Yes Lily, I did know a bad man once." Taking the opportunity Lily had given her, she asked, "Do you know any?"

"My Grandfather was bad. He hit Eliza and me, but mostly Eliza, because she tried to stop him hitting me. Elsie didn't have anyone to stop that man hitting her. I told her to tell our teacher, but she wouldn't. She said that if she did, she'd get shut in the cellar."

"It sounds like you have been a very good friend to Elsie."

"She's my best friend!" Lily said with a yawn.

"Shall I ask Eliza to come and hear your prayers?" Ruthie asked, remembering the usual night time routine the girls shared.

"You can hear them." Lily yawned again. "And Jesus hears them and that's the most important." Closing her eyes tightly, she began, "Dear Jesus. Thank you for my friend, Elsie. Thank you that Ben found her in the barn and that she can stay here tonight. Help her not be frightened and make the bad farmer and his wife be sorry for hurting her. Thank you for Eliza and Auntie Ruthie and Mr. and Mrs. Turley. Keep my dad safe in the war and make him come home soon. Amen."

Ruthie echoed Lily's amen, then saying goodnight, she left the room.

She was surprised to find Eliza sitting on the top of the stairs, her elbows resting on her knees.

"Are you alright, Eliza?" Ruthie asked, coming to stand beside her.

"Why are some people so cruel?" Eliza got straight to the point.

Ruthie hesitated only a moment before sitting down on the top step beside her daughter. "I wish I knew the answer to that," she said honestly. Taking a deep breath, she asked, "Are you thinking about your grandfather? Lily said he used to hit both of you, but you did your best to make sure he didn't hit her."

"Yes," Eliza nodded. "Sometimes I couldn't stop him though. Sometimes he hurt Lily. Mam and Dad said we shouldn't hate anyone, but I do hate him!" She began to cry.

Risking being pushed away, Ruthie put her arms around Eliza and held her close. This was the first time she had allowed her near her, and Ruthie didn't want to get it wrong. "I'm sorry he hurt Lily, and I'm sorry he hurt you, Eliza. No one should be treated like that." Tears came to Ruthie's own eyes now as she realised she was comforting her own little girl for the first time in her life. Now she was holding her like this, she never wanted to let her go. Eliza could never know that the man she hated was, in fact, her own father. If he had known she was his child, would it have made any difference? No, of course it wouldn't have. She remembered the beatings Eddie had endured. Gareth Davies didn't care who he hurt. Maybe it was wrong to hate, just as Eliza said, but how did you not hate a man like him?

"I'm glad we don't have to live with him anymore," Eliza stated.

"I'm glad you don't either," Ruthie replied.

"Why did we have to? I mean, why couldn't we have come straight to you when Mam died?"

Ruthie wondered how to answer this question and spoke as honestly as she felt she could. "I didn't know your mam was dead. I didn't know you were living with him. As soon as I found out, I knew you couldn't go back there."

"But if you're Mam's half-sister, why didn't we know you before?"

Ruthie hesitated, thinking about how to respond.

Eliza went on, "Did you and Mam have a row?"

"No, nothing like that. I can't imagine your mam having a row with anyone," Ruthie replied truthfully.

"Lily is like Mam. She doesn't like it when people fall out. So why didn't we see you?"

"I'm afraid I can't answer that, Eliza. Sometimes things just happen, and we don't see those we love. Sometimes it's out of our control."

Eliza was obviously dissatisfied with that answer, as she gently pulled away from Ruthie and got to her feet.

Ruthie stayed where she was, wondering if tonight had been her only chance to hold her daughter in her arms. If so, she wanted to remember the moment forever.

9

Something woke Ruthie. What was it? She listened hard, but couldn't hear a sound. That was it! She couldn't hear a thing. She was wondering if perhaps there was something wrong with her ears when she heard a child crying next to her. Immediately she remembered that tonight, there were four of them squashed into the bed. The crying child was Elsie. Ruthie spoke gently to reassure her, but once she was quiet again, Ruthie's attention was drawn back to the strange silence.

She crept out of bed and tiptoed to the window, where she pulled back the blackout blind and looked out onto the yard below. The moon shone brightly, illuminating a world of white! Mr. Turley's snow had come after all!

Ruthie almost felt like a child again. There was something about snow that invited you to go out and run in it. This snow was clean and white, and with the animals, apart from the sheep, in the barns, it would stay that way.

As she crept back into bed, Ruthie tried to recall the last time she'd felt so carefree. Try as she might, she couldn't remember. She only knew that it was before she'd started helping Eddie and his father out with the washing and cleaning.

As Ruthie lay there, the clock chimed four. Mr. Turley would be going outside soon enough, so she decided she'd might as well get up herself. Bill didn't expect her to help first thing, but she usually did.

How excited the girls would be when they saw the snow, she thought, as she dressed quickly in the cold room. She tucked the blankets more tightly around them as they slept, then crept out onto the landing.

The morning work passed quickly, and Ruthie and Bill returned to the house where the three girls were eager for their breakfast, so they could go out in the snow.

The bruising on Elsie's face was even worse now, and Mr. Turley told her he'd be getting the doctor to have a look at her, as well as making sure the authorities knew no child was to be placed at that farm again.

Breakfast was eaten hurriedly, and Ruthie thought that even the time of Bible reading was shorter than usual.

"You girls better go out and see if that snow's any good before school!" Mr. Turley announced. "I reckon you'd better take Ruthie with you as well. I've seen the way she's been looking at it all morning!"

Dressed in warm coats, hats, scarves, and gloves, Ruthie and the girls went out into the yard. Snowballs were thrown and snowmen hastily built. Even Mr. Turley joined in the fun.

All too soon, Mrs. Turley called them in for "something hot inside them" before the girls were to leave for school.

They were banging the snow off their boots, when Elsie let out a cry and pointed to the other side of the yard, where a tall thick set man was striding towards them.

"It's him!" Elsie shrieked, as she threw herself into Ruthie's arms.

Ruthie held her tightly as she hurried into the house, ushering Eliza and Lily ahead of her. Turning to close the door, she saw Bill and Ada Turley standing on the step, a united front against the man who had hurt Elsie.

"It's alright," Ruthie said, as she sat in the rocking chair and lifted Lily onto her lap beside Elsie. "Mr. and

Mrs. Turley will sort things out. You won't have to go with him, Elsie."

"But he said he'd make me go back if I ran away. I want my mum!" Elsie cried loudly.

"Mr. Turley won't let him take you!" Lily said confidently. "He stopped the bull going in the wrong field the other day, and the bull is bigger than that mean farmer!"

Eliza knelt down in front of Ruthie and rested her hand on Elsie's shoulder. "You are safe, Elsie," she told her. "Shall we pray to Jesus about it?"

"What will he do?" Elsie asked.

"We can ask for you to be kept safe," Eliza told her.

"Me and Eliza prayed to Jesus when we had to live with our mean grandfather, and now we're here and it's nice," Lily stated.

"Did Jesus bring you here?" Elsie's eyes widened.

"No!" Lily smiled. "Our dad came back from the war and brought us here. He brought Auntie Ruthie too, and she's the best auntie."

"Thank you, Lily." Ruthie hugged her. "I think Eliza has the right idea to pray for Elsie."

Eliza began, "Lord Jesus, thank you for bringing Elsie here where she could be safe. Please make it so that Elsie has somewhere nice to live, like we do now. Help Elsie to know that you are always with her and that she can talk to you any time. Help the mean farmer and his wife too and show them how to be kind. Amen."

Lily spoke next. "Thank you, Jesus, for my best friend, Elsie. I'm glad she's here with me and Eliza and Auntie Ruthie and Mr. and Mrs. Turley. I wish she could stay with us. Help Mr. Turley get rid of that man, like he did with the bull! Amen."

Ruthie had never prayed aloud before, so she surprised herself as she began, "Thank you, Lord, for this place of safety for the girls." Her mind suddenly went blank, and she didn't know how to continue. Who did she think she was anyway, trying to pray? She was wondering if she should add an amen after such a short prayer, when Elsie spoke through her tears.

"Don't make me go back there, Jesus! I want my Mum!"

The kitchen door opened and Ada entered, a swirl of snow accompanying her. "Don't you worry," she announced, "Mr. Turley saw him off. He's gone to speak to the authorities now."

"Did he stop him coming in like he did the bull?" Lily asked.

"I suppose he did, yes!" Mrs. Turley laughed.

"We're going to be late for school!" Eliza exclaimed, jumping to her feet.

"I don't want to go to school!" Panic filled Elsie's voice. "He might come and get me!"

"You won't be going today, Elsie, Love. We'll take you to the doctor and I expect the authorities will want to see you once Mr. Turley has spoken to them," Ada reassured her.

"Can I stay and look after Elsie?"

"Thank you, Lily, but she will be alright here with Ruthie and me. Your job is to tell your teacher that Elsie won't be in school today because she isn't well. You don't need to tell anyone any more than that. Can you do that for us?"

"Oh yes, I'll do that. Will Elsie still be here when I get home?"

"I don't know," said Mrs. Turley honestly.

Lily hugged her friend goodbye and reluctantly left for school with Eliza.

It was decided that Ruthie would take Elsie to the doctor. He was disgusted by what he saw, but said her cuts and bruises would heal in time.

When they arrived back at the farm, Mr. Turley had just returned from speaking to the authorities. "Someone will be out to see Elsie this afternoon," He told them. "They're going to have a few words with Dan and his wife."

They need to have more than a few words, Ruthie thought.

At first, the lady who came to see Elsie didn't seem very friendly, but she promised she wouldn't be going back to the farm. She also said that they'd make sure no other evacuees were sent there. As for where Elsie would go next, she didn't know. She seemed relieved when the Turleys said the child could stay with them for as long as was needed.

When Elsie said she wanted to go home to London to be with her mum, the lady admitted they were having trouble finding her, what with all the raids on the city.

Elsie seemed convinced that they'd soon find her, and she'd come and take her home, but Ruthie was less sure that would happen. She didn't think it was wise for Elsie to be told they couldn't locate her mother. Hadn't she been through enough?

After her day at school, Lily was pleased to find her friend still at the farm. The two younger girls helped Mrs. Turley prepare the meal, while Eliza asked if she could go to play in the snow with Florence and Stella.

"Course you can!" Mrs. Turley told her. "Just mind you're back before it be dark."

Eliza smiled to herself as she skipped through the snow across the yard, waving to Auntie Ruthie and Mr. Turley, who were mending a fence. She raced along the road and soon caught up with her friends. "Florence, why are you taking a tray?" she asked.

"It'll make a right good sledge!" Florence informed her.

"We gonna go down that 'ill on a bloomin' tray?" Stella asked in disbelief.

"'An't you been down an 'ill on a tray before?" Florence asked in surprise.

"Didn't 'ave 'ills like that where I lived in London!" Stella snorted.

"Nor Cardiff," Eliza added. "We'd slide about in the streets, but it didn't last long. It got dirty very quickly."

Soon the three girls were laughing and squealing as they took turns sliding down the hill on their tray. Time soon passed, and the darkening sky told them it was time to head home.

As they walked along, Stella swinging the now dented tray at her side, Florence asked, "You found out why you 'adn't seen that auntie of yours before you came here yet?"

"No," Eliza sighed. "I tried asking her last night, but she didn't really answer. She said her and Mam didn't have a row, but that's all. I still think she's hiding something."

"Ask 'er again!" Stella said matter-of-factly.

"Mam would have said I shouldn't ask again," Eliza shook her head. "She's nice to me and Lily and everything. I just don't think she's Mam's half-sister."

"I got it!" Stella stopped suddenly, dropping the tray to the ground with a crash.

"What?" Florence and Eliza both turned to stare at her.

"My mum's got everyone written in the Bible, you know, all the family and that and who was born when. Turns out me sister was already on the way when me mum and me dad got married. She found it in the Bible because she said babies take nine months to come and there was only six between when they got married and when she was born."

"'Ow's that going to help Eliza?" Florence asked, bending to pick up the tray.

"Well, if 'er auntie's got a Bible, it might say in it she's got a sister."

"Auntie Ruthie has got a Bible, and I've got Mam's too," Eliza said thoughtfully.

"You could 'ave a look," Florence encouraged.

"I don't know that I should look in Auntie Ruthie's Bible without her permission, it's hers."

"I thought the Bible was God's!" Stella exclaimed, as they began walking once more.

Eliza contemplated the idea all the way home, but came to the conclusion that it wouldn't be the right thing to do.

There was much conversation around the table that evening as they ate together. Elsie was so relieved she didn't have to go back to the cruel farmer and his wife, she talked more than ever before, mostly about her mum, who she believed was going to come for her any day now.

"Mum sent me a card on my birthday!" she told them excitedly.

"When was your birthday?" Lily asked.

"The first of December. I was seven," Elsie informed them.

"Oh! The same day as Eliza's!" Ruthie said enthusiastically. At the confused expressions on Eliza and Lily's faces, she continued, "Obviously Eliza is older, but…" A sudden realisation hit her. Eddie had said his daughter was born two days before her baby. What had she done?

"Eliza's birthday is the end of November," Lily told her.

"Of course it is! I reckon the snow's made my brain go funny!" Ruthie tried to laugh off her mistake, and quickly rose from the table on the pretence of getting herself some water.

Mrs. Turley tried talking about several other things. Her husband and the younger girls joined in the conversation, but both Ruthie and Eliza were silent for the rest of the meal.

10

Ruthie sat in the dark kitchen, her elbows resting on the table. Everyone else had long since gone up for the night, but she couldn't make herself climb the stairs and get into bed alongside the girls. She'd failed Eddie, and she'd failed his daughters. Why had she mentioned Eliza's birthday? Eliza hadn't said a word since then, and Ruthie could see they were back to square one, or less than that, if that was possible.

Lily had seen it as a simple mistake, but Eliza was reading some significance into it. The older girl wouldn't give up on it now, she knew that. Eliza was so much like her, she knew how her daughter would be thinking.

The girls were safe and happy here, so maybe the best thing for it was to leave them and go back to Cardiff alone. Eddie would understand. After all, he wouldn't want anyone to find out the truth.

Ruthie didn't want to leave, but it was for the best. She'd begun to feel alive again and hated the idea of giving that up, but Eliza and Lily must come first. It didn't matter what she wanted, after all, she'd given up the right to happiness when she'd asked Eddie to take her baby to the orphanage.

Mr. Turley would tell her how to get to the train station, and she'd be gone… But where to? She couldn't just reappear in Cardiff after over a month and expect to pick up where she'd left off. There was nothing there for her anyway. She could go wherever she liked. But where? She'd grown to love Eliza and Lily and would miss them terribly. She'd even been looking forward to the day when

Eddie would return. She had no right to look forward to anything. She'd go to France and care for those wounded in the war. Yes, that's what she'd do. No one would know her, and she wouldn't let herself get close to anyone. She'd managed alright like that in Cardiff for the last twelve or more years, so why not do it again?

***

Eliza lay wide awake, listening to the two younger girls sleeping. Auntie Ruthie, or whoever she was, still hadn't come to bed. Now Eliza knew for certain something was wrong. Why did Auntie Ruthie think her birthday was in December? It might have just been a mistake, but her expression when Lily pointed it out was one of fear and guilt.

Eliza thought back to her conversation earlier that day with Florence and Stella. She'd known it wasn't right to look in Auntie Ruthie's Bible as Stella had suggested, but now she thought she might just have to. Her mam would surely have written a half-sister in her Bible too. Eliza had never read that part of the Bible before, but now she would. She couldn't sleep anyway, so might as well do it now.

Eliza slid quietly out of bed, shivering as her feet hit the floor. She wasn't sure if it was from cold or fear, but decided it was most likely both.

She crossed to the chest of drawers and felt for the candles on top. With shaking hands, she struck a match and lit one. Please, Lord, don't let Lily and Elsie wake up, she prayed silently.

Eliza dripped a bit of wax onto a dish and stood the candle in it. Once she was sure it was secure, she went to fetch her mam's Bible. She read from it every day, and just holding it made her feel closer to God and her mam.

She easily found the part where her mother had written in hers and Lily's names, along with their dates of birth. Elizabeth Ruth Davies, the twenty-ninth of November nineteen-twenty-eight. Liliana Grace Davies, the tenth of July nineteen-thirty-four.

Above their names were those of their parents, Elizabeth Jane Evans and Edward John Davies, as well as their dates of birth. There was also the name and date of birth of Mam's brother, David John Evans, and those of her mam's and dad's parents and grandparents. There was no mention of Auntie Ruthie at all.

Eliza closed the Bible and took it back to its usual place. She stood for some minutes, contemplating her next move. She knew it was wrong to go through Auntie Ruthie's things, but she just couldn't help herself.

She'd seen Auntie Ruthie's Bible a few times, and easily located it. With shaking hands, Eliza carried the book into the light and opened it. It was very much like Mam's, but whereas her mam's was well read, Auntie Ruthie's didn't seem to have been opened much. What if there are no names and birthdays in it, she wondered, turning the pages as quietly as possible.

Then she found it. The page didn't seem as full as the one in her mam's Bible, but at least there were names.

Leaning over to read the unfamiliar writing, Eliza found the name Ruth Ann Lewis, along with her date of birth. Above that were the names of her parents, neither of whom were anything like her mam's.

Eliza was about to give up and close the Bible when her eye caught something in a different handwriting. Below Ruthie's name it read, baby girl, the first of December nineteen-twenty-eight.

Eliza straightened up and stared at the words. What did this mean? That was when Auntie Ruthie had thought her birthday was. Did she have a daughter the same age as Eliza, and that's why she got muddled? Did she look kind of strange because her baby had died or something? No, there was nothing about the baby dying. Looking closely at the page again, Eliza saw that Ruthie's mother had died on the same day the baby was born. None of this was making any sense. What was she thinking? Auntie Ruthie wasn't married! She shouldn't have had a baby.

Eliza replaced Ruthie's Bible and blew out the candle. She intended to get back into bed, but hesitated. Why was Auntie Ruthie not telling the truth?

Before she had time to change her mind, Eliza crossed the room and opened the door as quietly as she could. Noiselessly, she crept down the stairs, intentionally avoiding the ones which squeaked.

In the kitchen, she met an unexpected sight. A candle burned low in a jar, illuminating Auntie Ruthie. She sat at the table with her head in her hands, tears streaking her face.

"Auntie Ruthie?"

Ruthie hadn't been aware of anyone entering the room, and jumped when Eliza spoke.

"What's wrong, Eliza? Can't you sleep? Is something wrong with Lily? Or is it Elsie?"

"Auntie Ruthie, who are you really? I looked in Mam's Bible and in yours and there's no mention of you being half-sisters in either," Eliza blurted out.

Ruthie let out a long sigh. How was she going to answer this? She should have left earlier, but the snow had put her off. Yet again, she'd got it wrong.

"Your Bible says you had a baby girl, but you're not married. Did you muddle me up with her? Is that why you thought my birthday was the first of December?"

Tears rolled freely down Ruthie's cheeks, and she gasped for breath. What was she going to do?

Eliza stepped cautiously closer, unsure of what to do herself. "Mam said some women who have babies without being married are bad, but she said that some couldn't help it because they had no choice. She said we weren't to be unkind to anyone."

When Ruthie was still unable to speak, Eliza went on, "Please tell me? What happened to the baby?"

"Oh Eliza! I don't know what to say."

"Tell me the truth. Mam and Dad said we are always to tell the truth, because that's best."

"Sit down, Eliza, and I'll tell you."

Now more confused than ever, Eliza pulled out a chair and sat down. Ruthie reached for her hand and she allowed her to take it.

Through her tears, Ruthie began, "There are different types of bad people, some beat people, and some men do other things which they shouldn't. There was a man who used to drink a lot, and one day he… How do I say this? Eliza, do you know how babies are made?"

Eliza nodded, her cheeks reddening. "Mam told me before she died. She said I had to tell Lily, but not until she's a lot older."

Ruthie continued, "I didn't want him to, but he was bigger than me, and much stronger. I had no choice. I kept out of his way after that, but I soon found out I was having a baby."

"It wasn't your fault," Eliza said, her voice shaking slightly. Her parents always told her not to ask nosy questions. What had she done? She'd made Auntie Ruthie tell her about something she hadn't wanted to.

"No, it wasn't my fault. The thing was, though, I wasn't married, and I had no way of looking after a baby," Ruthie explained.

"Your mam died the same day your baby was born," Eliza said. "I'm sorry for looking in your Bible, but it just didn't make sense. What happened to your baby?"

Ruthie didn't know how to respond. After a few moments' hesitation, she said, "She was given to a couple whose own baby girl had died. They gave her all the love she needed."

"Did you miss her?"

"Every day!" Ruthie tried her hardest, but was unable to prevent her whole body from shaking as she sobbed.

"Did you ever see her?" Eliza questioned. "I hope you did."

Ruthie found it impossible to speak. How should she answer this?

Suddenly, Mrs. Turley's words about Ruthie and Eliza looking like mother and daughter came into Eliza's mind. "What's her name?" she asked with some urgency.

When Ruthie still couldn't speak, Eliza persisted, "Who did you give her to? Who are her parents now?"

Ruthie lifted her head and saw the realisation in Eliza's eyes. "I'm sorry, Eliza," she sobbed. "I think you know the answer."

"It… can't be me!" Eliza too began to cry. "Mam was my mam and Dad is my dad. Everyone says I'm like Dad! Lily is like Mam, but I'm like Dad! You're wrong!"

Eliza made to rise, but Ruthie wouldn't release her hand.

"Listen, Eliza," Ruthie began. "Your mam will always be your mam. She was the best mother you could've had. Your dad is the best dad too."

"But I look like Dad! I am like Dad."

"That's because you are still related to him. Eliza, the man who attacked me was your grandfather."

"No! I hate him!" Eliza's voice raised and Ruthie got unsteadily to her feet, moving to her daughter's side to enfold her in her arms.

"I'm sorry, Eliza. I should never have told you. I promised your dad I wouldn't, and I got that wrong too."

"I made you tell me," Eliza admitted through her tears.

"Nothing has to change. I can still be Auntie Ruthie to you and Lily."

"But you're really my mam," Eliza sniffed. "Lily isn't my sister anymore. It's all changed."

"Lily is still your sister and always will be."

"Why didn't we ever see you?" Eliza asked.

"I couldn't. You were with your parents and Lily."

"But why did Dad take us to you the night of the air-raid?"

"Because he wanted to get you both away from your grandfather. He didn't think you were safe there."

"But he wasn't my grandfather. Is that why he used to hit me?"

"He didn't know you were his child. He was a cruel man. Eliza, I have to ask you, did he ever try anything with you, like he did to me?"

"I think he was going to once," Eliza said quietly. "He used to come into our room at night and I'd pretend to be asleep. He'd have no clothes on. Then one night, not long before Dad came back, he came to the bed and got in there with us. I was really scared and tried telling him to go away. He was really drunk. He was trying to get closer to me, but then Lily woke up. The smell of the drink was really strong, and it made her sick! It went everywhere! All over her, all over me, and all over him. It was disgusting, but it made him go away. He was really angry and tried hitting Lily, but I threw a shoe at him. He ran out of the room really mad then. I wanted to take Lily and run away, but she wasn't well, and I didn't want to take her out in the cold. Then Dad came home."

"I thank the Lord Eddie came home when he did." Ruthie sighed. "I'm also thankful Lily was sick when she was. I'm sorry that happened to you, Eliza."

"I wish I hadn't checked in the bibles," Eliza sighed. "If I hadn't, everything would still be the same. Now everything is different."

"I'm so sorry," Ruthie apologised again.

"Do we have to tell anyone?" Eliza asked.

"Not if you don't want to."

"Who else knows?"

"Only your dad and me, and now you."

"I don't want anyone else to know," Eliza stated. "I'm going back to bed now." She got to her feet, pulling away from Ruthie.

Ruthie watched her disappear up the stairs, before sinking down in the rocking chair by the stove. There was no way she could go to bed now, she'd might as well sit here all night. She really had let them all down.

11

"Dear-o, Ruthie!" Mr. Turley exclaimed as he came into the kitchen and lit the lamp. "Whatever be you doing there?"

"What's the matter, Bill?" Mrs. Turley sounded concerned as she followed her husband into the room.

Ruthie sat up quickly, almost squashing her foot under the front rocker of the chair.

"Did you sleep there all night?" Mrs. Turley asked, assessing the situation.

"I'm sorry, I must have fallen asleep here," Ruthie tried to explain as she hurried to stand. She must look a right state after sleeping in her clothes all night.

"I knew it was too much to expect four of you to share that bed," Ada apologised. "I'm sure we can make up another bed of sorts in your room."

"No, it's alright, there's no need for that. I'll go out and give Mr. Turley a hand."

"Don't reckon you 'ad much sleep in that chair," Mrs. Turley observed, as Ruthie retrieved her coat and followed Bill out of the house.

Breakfast time was quiet, the excitement over the snow having long since gone. There hadn't been any more overnight, but the previous snowfall still lay thick on the ground. The trees had lost most of their covering of white, and the yard was now scattered with footprints. Ruthie noted the contrast to the previous morning. So much had happened in the last twenty-four hours. Everything looked bright and cheerful yesterday, but now it was dark and dreary.

Lily and Elsie chattered as they ate, but Eliza was silent. Even the Turleys weren't their usual talkative selves.

Ruthie hardly listened as Mr. Turley read from his Bible. She'd enjoyed that part of the day, but this would be the last time she would be here for it. She couldn't think of that, so just didn't listen. It was too difficult.

Lily and Elsie skipped off to school, while Eliza trailed behind them. Yet another complete contrast to how the girls usually left the house.

Once they were alone, Ruthie turned to Mrs. Turley and announced, "It's time I was gone. I'm going to do my bit for the war. I know the girls will be safe here with you and Mr. Turley. I'll pack my things and leave today."

"What's all this about, Ruthie?"

Ruthie hadn't expected such a direct question. "I need to do my bit," she repeated.

"You're doing that here. Mr. Turley needs your help on the farm, and I need your help too. Not to mention Eliza and Lily."

"I know you will look after them. They are safe here."

"But that wasn't what we agreed. The girls' dad said you would be staying here with them. That's what he wanted."

"He wanted to make sure they would be safe, and I know they will be. Just look at how you helped Elsie."

"Sit down, Ruthie." Mrs. Turley pulled out a chair and sat down, indicating Ruthie should do the same.

"I really should be going," Ruthie protested.

"Not until you tell me what's really going on. Something happened last night with you and Eliza. I saw the way you avoided each other, and again this morning. Come on," she spoke gently, "it can't be that bad, can it?"

"It is!" Ruthie failed to hold back her emotions, and her tears burst forth.

Ada rose, hurried around the table, and put her arms around her.

Ruthie surprised herself when she rested her head on Mrs. Turley's shoulder and cried like she hadn't in years. When she finally stopped, she pulled away, trying to apologise. "I'm sorry. It doesn't matter."

"I think it does matter. Tell me all about it. I'm a good listener. If you still want to leave when we're finished, I won't stop you, although I don't want to see you go."

Sitting at the table alongside this kind, caring, older woman, Ruthie wondered where to begin. She supposed she did owe Mrs. Turley an explanation, and it would be better if someone understood what Eliza was going through. She hesitated, trying to work out where to start. "Eliza is my daughter," she began. Ada didn't seem surprised, so Ruthie continued, "Eddie and I were best friends growing up. He lived with his mam and dad downstairs, and I lived with mine upstairs. His mam died, then my dad. We were always there for one another and did everything together. His dad was the most cruel man I knew. He used to hit Eddie and everything. Eddie used to come up to our place when his dad had been drinking, but sometimes he couldn't get away in time. They found it hard to keep the house clean, and Mam didn't earn much, so I did a bit of work for the Davies men. His dad started looking at me funny and following me around. I didn't like it, but I never thought anything else would happen. Then one day, I was doing the cleaning. I always tried to do it when he was out. He came back and was really drunk. Eddie was at work, so there was only me and his dad in the house. He dragged me into the bedroom, and you can guess the rest. It was Eddie's bedroom too, so that made it even worse. I didn't go there after that. I was so ashamed, and I wouldn't see Eddie either. Then, over a year later, Gareth, that's Eddie's father, was waiting for me one night out the back of the house. I couldn't get away from him. After that, I found out I was having a baby." Ruthie paused here, unsure of how to continue.

"That can't have been easy for you," Mrs. Turley said thoughtfully.

"I didn't tell anyone. I decided that once the baby was born, I'd take it to an orphanage. Then there was the flu going around. Mam got it and I was looking after her. The baby came early, and Mam died, all on the same day. I got the flu as well, so didn't know how I'd get the baby to the orphanage. Then Eddie came round. He wanted Mam to go and see to his wife, Lizzie. She also had the flu, and their new baby girl wasn't doing well either. Lizzie was never strong. I told him Mam was dead, and I asked him to take my little girl to the orphanage. He was surprised I had a child. He kept saying he didn't know I was seeing anyone. I told him I wasn't, and he took my baby. That was the last I knew of her, until the night before we came here."

"But Eddie said they were both his daughters. How did he find her?"

"When he went back to check on Lizzie and their daughter, the baby was dead. He wanted Lizzie to keep fighting, so put my baby in her arms. She never knew it wasn't her child."

"And that's why you got the birthdays muddled up last night."

Ruthie nodded. "That's when it all went wrong. Eliza was already suspicious of me. We should never have said I was their mam's half-sister. Lizzie would never have turned away from anyone, and Eliza couldn't understand why I'd suddenly appeared. It seems she got to checking in her mam's Bible last night. She looked in mine, too. I never thought anyone would see what I wrote in there. I'd written in the date of my daughter's birth. There was no name. Eliza came and asked me about it, so I had to tell her the truth. Eddie and I agreed they didn't need to know, but Eliza knew something wasn't right."

"What did you tell her?"

"I said she was my daughter and that she'd had the best parents she could've had with Eddie and Lizzie. I told her who her real father was and how it had happened. I was afraid he'd done the same to her. It seems he tried once. If they'd been there any longer, he would have. I didn't tell her I'd asked Eddie to leave her at the orphanage. I feel ashamed that I wanted him to do that, but I didn't know what else to do. If I could've chosen anyone to take her in, it would have been Eddie and Lizzie. I've let Eddie down, and I've let Eliza down too. I made it sound like I chose her parents, but I didn't. I have no right to be a mother. I fooled myself into thinking I could look after the girls and do for Lizzie what she'd done for me, but I can't. I'm no good."

"You are good with them, I've seen it. I know you love those girls… and their father."

Ruthie's head shot up, and she stared open-mouthed at Mrs. Turley.

"I saw it the day you all came here. Don't worry, your secret is safe with me. But Ruthie, Eliza and Lily need you, and I think you need them."

"I do, but I can't. They're better off without me. I gave Eliza away, not knowing where she would end up, or even if she'd be loved. I've been on my own ever since, and that's the way I should stay."

"But God knew. He placed her in a loving family, and now he's giving you the chance to be a part of that loving family as well. You were separated from your child for a time, but now you are reunited. God doesn't want you to be alone, Ruthie."

"But she deserves better than me. I don't know anything about being a mother."

"You love her, that's the main thing. The rest will come in time. You are being given a second chance."

"I don't deserve one. I gave her away, Mrs. Turley, I gave my little girl away!"

"I'd say we can do away with you calling us Mr. and Mrs. Turley. It's Ada and Bill." Ada got to her feet and went to pour them each a mug of rather stewed tea from the pot. Sitting back down, she placed one of the mugs in front of Ruthie, before she said, "God has given you this second chance. He is a God of second chances. Eddie is a praying man. I could tell that when he was here. I can also see that's how he and Lizzie brought the girls up. Eddie was led to you that night. He wouldn't have left the girls with just anyone. I believe God led him to you. It seems to me that you've been punishing yourself ever since you gave your baby away. God doesn't want that for you. We all make mistakes, Ruthie, some bigger than others, but we all make them. You made the only choice you could at the time. Who did you have to help you bring up a baby? Who would've looked after her while you were out working to get enough money to feed her?"

"There was no one. Mam was the only family I had."

"You did your best, Ruthie."

"I'm not a good person." Ruthie's eyes were fixed on the table.

"We are all sinners, that's why God sent Jesus. We were talking about that the other day, weren't we? Jesus took on the sins of everyone and died on the cross in our place. We are all sinners, Ruthie, but when we put our trust in Jesus, our sins are forgiven."

"But my sin is too big to be forgiven."

"Sin is sin. No matter how big or small, a sin is a sin and Jesus paid the price for all of them. He wouldn't want you to punish yourself and deny yourself love for the rest of your life. Jesus is offering you a new start. A way of being part of Eliza's life and a way of beginning a new life in him."

"But what about Eliza? I'm sure she hates me."

"Eliza is confused, which is understandable, but I'm sure she doesn't hate you. The two of you are so much alike. If you leave now, that will be harder on her. She will understand why you couldn't look after her before, but she won't see why you are leaving now. They've lost all that's familiar to them, they need you."

"You really think I should stay?"

"Put yourself in Eliza's place. She's just discovered you are her mother."

"I see what you mean." Ruthie lifted her head to make eye-contact with Ada.

"So will you stay?"

Ruthie hesitated before she said, "I owe it to Eliza. I suppose if I go now, she'll think I never wanted her."

"It may be difficult with Eliza for a while, but in time, I expect she'll come round. Now everything's out in the open, she may feel more settled. I'm sure it wasn't easy for you, pretending to be their auntie."

"It wasn't. I thought it was all I'd ever have though, and I wanted to do whatever I could to keep them safe. That's still what I want. Will you help me, Mrs. Turley… I mean Ada?"

"Yes, I'll help you, but it may be wise to tell Bill as well."

"But… he'll think…"

"He won't judge you any more than I have. If you really don't want to, I won't tell him, but I can assure you, he will only want to help."

"Alright. Would you tell him?"

"Yes, I'll tell him. How about you make a start on the dinner here and I'll go out with Bill? I can talk to him while we work."

"Thank you. I've broken a promise to Eliza though. I said we'd continue pretending I was her auntie if that's what she wanted. I only told you the truth because I was going to leave, and I wanted someone to understand what she was going through."

"You can still go on saying that if that's what you both decide. Bill and I won't say a word about it to anyone, including Eliza. Hopefully, she'll talk to me about what she's feeling. Oh!" Ada's hand flew to her mouth.

"What is it?" Ruthie asked.

"Just after you all arrived, Eliza told me she didn't know if you were really her auntie. I told her that there was no doubt you were related. I said you and her look so much alike, you could be mother and daughter. I'm sorry, Ruthie, if I put ideas into her head."

"You didn't do anything wrong. I think she would have still gone looking for evidence in the Bibles. Maybe it's better she knows the truth after all. Well, most of it anyway. I don't want her ever finding out I was planning to send her to an orphanage."

"She won't hear it from me," Ada reassured her. "Now, I'll go and see what Bill's up to. I hope he doesn't want to be movin' the bull again!"

12

"Go on Lily, you and Elsie go on home. I'll be there in a bit!" Eliza spoke angrily.

"But Eliza, you always walk home with me." Lily seemed confused.

"You've got Elsie to walk with. Go on! I'm walking with Florence and Stella."

Lily and Elsie reluctantly left the older girls and began the short walk back to the farm, jumping over the heaps of snow left at the side of the road as they went.

"What be wrong with you, Eliza?" Florence asked in surprise, looking at her friend. "You 'aven't been with us all day."

"Yeah, she even got a question wrong, and that's a bloomin' first!" Stella exclaimed.

"I don't know, just wasn't concentrating, I suppose."

"All day?" Florence inquired. "It's usually me who's looking out the window."

"Did you look in the Bibles?" Stella asked bluntly. "Oh! You weren't on the way before your mum and dad were married, were you? You know, like me sister was."

"Don't be silly!" Eliza snapped. "You talk some rubbish, Stella."

"Alright, alright! I was only askin'. So did you look?"

"Mind your own business!" Eliza said grumpily, kicking a pile of snow and scattering it across the road.

"I be 'ungry," Florence announced. "We ought to get 'ome, Stella."

"You're always bloomin' 'ungry. Come on then. Oh!" Stella stopped and stared open-mouthed at the young man striding towards them. "'Aven't seen 'im before!" she exclaimed in awe.

"Come on, never mind 'im. Probably another evacuee, I expect," Florence grumbled.

"'E can't be! 'E weren't in school, were 'e?" Stella stated.

As he approached, the three girls became more intrigued. Both Eliza and Florence intended passing him with only a brief greeting, but Stella had other ideas.

"'Ello! Nice to meet ya!" she said confidently. "I'm Stella, and these are me friends, Florence, and Eliza."

"Oh, good afternoon. It's a pleasure to meet you. What a charming place this is."

"What's your name?" Stella asked. "Are you an evacuee? Me and Eliza are, well, she sort of is."

"Please excuse me, I didn't introduce myself. My name is Sebastian Westfield, but you can call me Seb. I'm also an evacuee of sorts. My tutor and I arrived a few days ago. We're staying in a cottage on a farm."

"You're a bit posh, ain't ya!"

"Oh!" Seb laughed the strangest laugh any of the girls had ever heard. Quickly composing himself, he went on, "Father wouldn't have me talk any other way. He was determined I mustn't talk like the common Londoners."

"'Ey! I'm a bloomin' Londoner! What's wrong with the way I talk?" Stella glared at him.

"I do apologise! I didn't mean to offend you. I was just saying what they said to me. Father insists I must follow him into his business, and one must speak correctly, you know. Now he insists I mustn't start talking like the country bumpkins around here."

"She's one of them!" Stella exclaimed, pointing to Florence. "You've been and gone and insulted 'er an' all now!"

"Who be you calling a country bumpkin, Stella?" Florence stamped her foot.

"'E was!" Stella insisted.

"I say! I don't suppose you could help me? It seems I've got myself a bit lost!" Seb enquired. "I'm looking for the Turley farm."

"I should say you be lost!" Florence exclaimed. "You've passed that back down the road."

"What ya goin' there for?" Stella asked.

"One of the farm hands sent me. I've been going around from farm to farm for what feels like hours, but no one's got what I'm asking for."

"What is it you're after?" Eliza asked. "I'm staying at the Turley farm, so I might know if Mr. Turley has it."

"I'd be awfully grateful if you could tell me. You might be able to save me a journey. These roads are ghastly!"

Eliza looked at the shoes the boy was wearing. No one wore shoes like that around here, especially not in the snow. "What is it you need?" she asked again.

"The hand asked me to go and borrow the bucket to milk the bull," Seb told them.

There was a snort of laughter from Florence, and Eliza and Stella both turned their attention to her.

"What's wrong with you?" Stella asked.

Florence only shook her head.

"Where you been so far?" Stella turned back to Seb.

He listed about five different farms, then ended by saying, "I just don't want to go back without it."

A sudden realisation hit Eliza. Someone was having Seb on! She knew you couldn't milk a bull, and by the look of her, Florence knew what they were up to as well. "I'd go back and tell him you found the bucket and milked the bull yourself," she advised.

"What! Me?" Seb exclaimed in disbelief. "I wouldn't go near that bull, let alone milk it!"

"I've never seen your dad milk the bull," Stella said thoughtfully to Florence.

"That's because 'im don't!" Florence burst out laughing.

"I say, I don't know what's so funny here, but I need to know where I can get that bucket."

Eliza was laughing too now, as she explained, "You can't milk a bull. Reckon that farm hand saw you coming."

"Oh! I get it!" Stella broke into a wide grin. "You only milk the girl cows, don't ya!"

"Oh no!" Seb suddenly realised his mistake. "That farm hand was beastly! All those farmers too! They kept sending me from one place to another, saying someone else had the bucket. Whatever would Father say if he knew I'd been taken for a fool by a simple farm hand!"

"Like I said, just tell him you got the bucket and did it yourself," Eliza urged. "The last laugh will be on him then, because he'll know you found him out."

"But all those farmers!" Seb protested.

"You be not the first, and you won't be the last. Looks like those country bumpkins got one up on you!" Florence stated. "Come on, time we got 'ome. I told you, I'm 'ungry!"

Leaving Seb standing in the road, the three girls continued on their way.

"I thought 'e was s'posed to be clever, talkin' like that and all, but 'e weren't, were 'e?" Stella sighed.

"I think it was mean of the farmhand and the farmers to make fun like that," Eliza stated.

"'Im thinks 'im's better than us!" Florence said indignantly.

"I don't suppose he knows much about the country." Eliza tried to defend Seb.

"You 'aven't fallen for 'im, 'ave ya?" Stella sounded shocked.

"No, but it can't be very nice being stuck in a cottage with a tutor. Imagine having to live with your teacher all the time!"

"Yeah! Maybe 'e 'as to do schoolwork all day! I saw 'is sort in London. They didn't live where I did, they 'ad big 'ouses and all. Don't s'pose 'e 'ad to share a bed with a load of other kids and the bloomin' bedbugs!"

"Bedbugs!" Florence exclaimed, scratching her shoulder. "You didn't bring them with you, did you?"

"Perhaps they didn't like the bombs either!" Stella laughed. "I dunno! Your mum gave me a good bath when I got here! Washed all me bloomin' clothes too! Did you 'ave them in Cardiff, Eliza?"

"Some places did, but we didn't. Mam made sure of that! No fleas either! I was glad when Mrs. Turley said bedbugs and fleas weren't allowed in her house! I'd better be getting back! They'll be wondering where I am! I'll see you tomorrow!" Eliza called, breaking into a run and racing ahead of her two friends.

Eliza ran into the house with a lighter heart than she'd had all day. "I'm sorry I'm late. I was talking to Florence and Stella, then this boy called Seb came along. He has to live with his tutor on one of the farms, and the farm hand had sent him out to borrow the bucket to milk the bull. He'd been to loads of different farms, but they kept sending him to the next one. He was coming here next. I realised they were having him on, but didn't know how to tell him. Me and Florence sort of told him between us that you don't milk the bull. I think Florence was going to let him keep asking at first, but he didn't have the kind of boots on for walking around here. I told him to tell the farm hand he'd got the bucket and milked the bull himself!"

Laughter erupted in the kitchen as the Turleys, Ruthie, and the girls listened to Eliza's story.

"Where was the bucket?" Elsie asked innocently.

"He didn't need it," Mrs. Turley explained. "Someone was playing an unkind joke on him."

"You took ages to get home," Lily said accusingly. "Auntie Ruthie was worried. Mr. Turley was going to come and find you. I said me and Elsie would go, but he said it was too late."

Eliza hung her head in shame. "I'm sorry I was late."

"I'll be getting back outside," Bill announced.

"Lily and Elsie, come and help me see if the hens have laid any more eggs," Ada said, moving the two younger girls towards the door.

"Oh no!" Elsie stopped in her tracks. "I dropped an egg and…"

"One dropped egg won't matter here. Come on, you've nothing to be frightened of," Ada reassured her, as she and the younger girls left the kitchen.

Mother and daughter stood looking at one another. "I didn't mean to make you worried," Eliza apologised.

"I was afraid you might not come back after what happened last night," Ruthie said with concern.

"I did think about running away," Eliza spoke honestly.

"I'm glad you didn't. Eliza, I know this is going to be hard for you, but we can find a way through. You know more about praying than I do, but I think if we both pray, we can work this out."

"How did you know I was thinking about running away?"

Ruthie sighed. "Like it or not, Eliza, you and I are very much alike. Sometimes I feel like running away from things when I'm afraid." On a lighter note, Ruthie added, "I'm glad you told Seb the truth about the bucket. Your mam and dad have brought you girls up with good morals. That was quick thinking, telling him to say he'd already milked the bull."

"Did you want to run away when I asked you all those questions last night?" Eliza asked.

"I did for a while, but I'm not going anywhere. I want to be here with you and Lily."

"Because Dad asked you to be here with us?"

"I intend to keep my word to him, yes, but more than that, I want to get to know you. I'm going to do whatever I can for both of you. I haven't had any family around since my mam died. I didn't know how much I'd missed that until I came here with you girls."

"Shall I help lay the table?"

"Yes please." Ruthie smiled at her. It seemed Eliza was as good at changing the subject when things got difficult as she herself was.

13

The rain had been falling hard all day. The snow had melted, and the yard had turned into a sea of mud. As it was a Saturday, Eliza was helping Bill and Ruthie on the farm, while Lily and Elsie worked alongside Ada in the kitchen.

"This is better than the other farm!" Elsie exclaimed as she concentrated on peeling a potato. "I haven't been shut in the cellar once here."

"And neither will you be. No one has ever been shut in our cellar here, Elsie, and no one ever will. Mr. Turley and I have two boys, and believe me, they got into some trouble at times, but they were never locked in the cellar, or anywhere else, for that matter."

"My mum didn't shut me in anywhere. I want to see my mum. When will they find her?"

"I don't know, Elsie love. I know they're doing all they can to look for her."

"Stella at school said my mum might be dead, but I told her she was wrong."

"That wasn't nice of Stella to say that to Elsie, was it, Mrs. Turley?" Lily put in.

"It wasn't very kind of her, no. We shouldn't go around saying things like that when we don't know what's happened," Ada agreed.

"Do you think my mum's dead?" Elsie looked directly at her.

Ada sighed. "I really don't know, love. I know there's a lot of confusion in London, because of all the raids, but perhaps she's just had to move somewhere else. I'm sure they'll find out soon."

The door opened and Eliza entered the kitchen. It was clear for all to see that she wasn't happy.

"Come in to warm up, have you, Eliza?" Ada asked, smiling at her.

"You can help us," Lily offered.

"I wanted to help move the cows," Eliza muttered.

"They're big and scary!" Lily exclaimed.

"Why couldn't you help?" Elsie questioned.

"It's dangerous moving the cows when you're not used to them," Mrs. Turley explained kindly.

"That's what she said!" Eliza grumbled as she removed her coat and held out her hands towards the stove.

"Who? Do you mean Auntie Ruthie?" Lily asked.

"Yes! She hasn't lived here any longer than I have. Why can she move the cows, and not me? Why is she telling me what I can and can't do?"

"Ruthie has been here as long as you, but she's been working with the animals every day. She has learnt a lot about them and how to read them. She wanted you to be safe," Ada told her firmly. "I'm sure Mr. Turley said the same thing."

Eliza's sigh told her that indeed Mr. Turley was of the same opinion.

"Can I go and read my book from school?" Eliza asked.

"Of course. You can bring it downstairs and read by the fire if you like. It's warmer in here."

"It's alright, I'll read it upstairs," Eliza said as she hurried from the room.

Eliza went to sit in the windowsill of the bedroom she shared with Lily, Elsie, and Ruthie. She didn't know what to call her anymore. She'd found it hard to call her Auntie Ruthie before, but now it was even harder. How could she be her mother? She knew it was true, but she didn't want it to be. How could her parents have lied to her all these years? It wasn't fair. Nothing would ever be the same again. If Mam had never died, she would never have known. If Dad hadn't gone away, Mam wouldn't have died. If it hadn't been for the war, Dad wouldn't have gone away. She'd never really thought about not looking like their mam. Lily looked just like her. She'd always supposed she looked like her dad… well, she did in a way… but it wasn't because of her dad, it was because of the man she'd presumed was her grandfather. The thought of him being her father made her feel sick. She'd almost been sick the other day just thinking about it.

Why had she told Florence and Stella what she was wondering? If she hadn't, Stella wouldn't have given her the idea of looking in the Bibles. Then she would never have found out. Would that be better? Probably not. She wished she could get it all straight in her mind.

Why did Auntie Ruthie, or whoever she was, have to be so nice? Lily was always saying, Auntie Ruthie this, and Auntie Ruthie that. Why couldn't she just leave them alone?

Lily entered the room, asking, "Eliza, will you read your book to me, please?"

"I thought you were helping Mrs. Turley."

"I've finished that. Eliza, why don't you want to read to me anymore?"

"I've got other things to do!" Eliza said grumpily.

"But you always used to. Please Eliza? You said you would always read to me because Mam can't anymore."

"Leave me alone, Lily!" Eliza snapped.

Lily burst into tears. "Why are you being horrible? You used to be the best sister ever before we came here!"

"Because I'm not your sister!" Eliza shouted at her.

"Yes, you are! You are!" Lily shouted back.

"No! I'm not! Now go away and leave me alone!"

Lily ran from the room and down the stairs. Having heard the girls' raised voices, Ada was heading up there to see what was wrong. She caught Lily up in her arms and held her as she cried.

"What's wrong with Lily?" Elsie asked.

Mrs. Turley sat down in the rocking chair, the distraught child in her lap. "Tel me what happened, Lily. It's not like you and Eliza to argue."

"She said she's not my sister!" Lilly sobbed. "She won't read to me anymore. She said she would always read me books. Mam always did. Why did she say she isn't my sister?"

Ada sighed. How should she answer this one? "You and Eliza have had a lot of changes," she began. "I expect she will read to you again soon."

"Eliza never shouted at me before," Lily wailed.

"I'm sure she didn't mean to."

"I'll be your sister!" Elsie suggested eagerly. "I never had a sister before, and I think you'd be a really good sister."

"That's very kind of you, Elsie," Mrs. Turley said. "I tell you what, I've got a basket of rags. I'll get it out now. How about you both choose some? And I'll make a rag doll for each of you. You can choose some for a dress for her, too."

"My rag doll got lost on the way on the train," Elsie said sadly. "Could I really have another? I'll look after her. It wasn't my fault. Some boys took her off me and threw her up on the bit where all the cases were. I cried because Mum made her for me."

"That was really mean of the boys!" Lily said, glancing at her friend. "I'd like a rag doll too, please. You can make Elsie's first though, because hers got lost."

Ada got out the basket and left the girls searching through it. She climbed the stairs and entered the bedroom, where Eliza sat curled up on the floor, tears streaming down her face.

Lowering herself onto her knees beside her, Ada put an arm around the girl's shoulders. "Lily came downstairs very upset," she began, "And it looks like you're upset too. Would you like to tell me what it's all about?"

"I can't!" Eliza cried. "I just can't!"

Ada hesitated a moment before she tried again. "Lily said you told her you're not her sister. Why did you say that, Eliza?"

"Because…" Eliza shook her head. Then, reconsidering, she explained, "Lily isn't my sister, not really. Mam wasn't my mam and Dad's not my dad. Oh, Mrs. Turley, you were right when you said Auntie Ruthie and I had to be related because we look the same. She's really my mother!" Eliza leaned against Mrs. Turley, allowing the older woman to hold her while she cried.

When Eliza became a little calmer, Ada suggested, "Let's sit somewhere more comfortable."

The two stood, and keeping an arm around Eliza, Ada led her to the bed, where they sat down side by side.

"I imagine it was all quite a shock for you to find that out."

"I made her tell me," Eliza admitted. "I know I shouldn't have, but I looked in her Bible. There was a baby girl born two days after me. That's why she thought my birthday was the same as Elsie's. The thing is, she wasn't married. It wasn't her fault though. I know she's telling the truth because it was the man I thought was my grandfather. I never liked him, and he would've done the same to me sooner or later. Mam explained all those things before she died. I don't like to think that man is my father. Now I'm being horrible to everyone, and maybe I'm just like him."

"Oh Eliza, I don't know the man, but I don't think you're anything like him. The man you always called your father is a good person, isn't he?"

"Oh yes! He's the best dad."

"He's nothing like his father then."

Eliza considered Ada's statement, before she said, "No. I'd never thought of it like that."

"What do you know about how you came to be with your parents?"

"Ruthie said her and Dad used to be best friends. She said I had the best people to look after me, because she couldn't."

"That sounds fair enough. Now, when your dad needed to get you away from his father, he knew who to go to for help. Sounds like God was in that plan to me, doesn't it to you? You had your mam to keep you safe for as long as she was able, and your dad came back before any real harm was done by his father. Then he took you to Ruthie and the two of them brought you girls here. He wasn't going to take any chances with your safety, and he knew Ruthie already loved you and would keep you both safe. Just think, you and Lily might've ended up somewhere like Elsie did. You said yourself Lily was terrified of the bombs, and you only said the other day that she seemed better in the country than she was in Cardiff. It's all part of God's plan, Eliza, always remember that."

"Yes, I suppose you're right."

"I'm here if you want to talk at any time. Also, remember to talk to Jesus about it. He will always listen. Then remember to listen to what you're being told."

"Yes, thank you Mrs. Turley. I want to say sorry to Lily. I never made her cry before."

"Lily is a kind, forgiving girl, just like you. I'm sure she'll be alright, but she'll probably want an explanation about why you said she wasn't your sister."

"What should I tell her?"

"That's up to you."

"Mam and Dad always said it's not good to keep secrets."

"That's true. Perhaps you and Ruthie should decide together what to say. It doesn't matter if you and Lily aren't actual sisters. She'll still always be your sister, because that's how you grew up, just like the parents who brought you up can still be your mam and dad."

"I'll talk to Ruthie. I need to apologise to her as well. She didn't have to come here with me and Lily, but she did."

"I'm proud of you, Eliza. It's not always easy to apologise, especially when we're hurt and confused."

"I'll go and talk to Lily first." Eliza got to her feet.

"I've left her and Elsie choosing rags to make dolls. I said I'd make them one each."

"Could you show me how to make them, please? I'm not much good at sewing." Eliza almost smiled.

"We'll do them together, I'd like that." Ada was relieved the conversation had gone so well. She couldn't imagine how Eliza was feeling. It was such an unusual situation.

In the kitchen, Eliza went straight to where Lily was sitting on the floor by the basket. She knelt beside her and put her arms around her, cuddling the little girl tightly.

"I'm sorry I shouted at you, Lily. I shouldn't have done that. Mrs. Turley said you and Elsie are looking for material to make rag dolls. When you've found what you're looking for, I'll read to you if you still want me to."

"Will you read to Elsie too? She's never had a sister. You are my sister really, Eliza, aren't you?" Lily questioned with concern.

"I always have been haven't I? So you can't get rid of me now. And yes, of course I'll read to Elsie as well." Eliza did her best to sound convincing.

"Can me and Elsie pretend we are sisters too?" Lily asked.

"If you like, yes." Eliza smiled. She'd felt like she was losing everyone she cared about, but maybe it didn't matter so much after all if Lily wasn't her actual sister. In their minds they would always be sisters, and now it seemed they'd got Elsie too.

Eliza kept herself busy during the rest of the day. It wasn't until the younger girls were in bed that she finally got up the courage to speak to Ruthie.

As Ruthie left the room after saying goodnight to Lily and Elsie, she found Eliza sitting on the top of the stairs. "Are you alright, Eliza?" she asked cautiously.

"I need to talk to you," Eliza told her. "Can we talk here?"

14

"What you rushing off for, Eliza?" Stella enquired in disgust.

"I told Lily and Elsie I'd go back to the farm with them. We're going to meet the new man who was coming today."

"'Ow old is 'e? Reckon I might come too!" Stella brightened.

"I wouldn't get too excited. Mr. Turley said he'd been working on farms for years, so he's probably really old."

"Why ain't 'e in the war?"

"I've no idea. I suppose we'll find out soon enough."

"Still reckon we should 'ave a look. What you think, Floss?"

"Stop callin' me that. My name be Florence. You can go if you like, but I'm going 'ome to see what Mam's been cooking. Thanks to you droppin' your dinner in the puddle on the way to school this mornin', I'm starvin'! My belly's been rumblin' all afternoon."

"Never asked you to give me some of yours!" Stella snorted.

"I'd never've 'ad a minute's peace if I 'adn't. You coming with me, or not?"

"Alright, I'll come. S'pose I can meet this new fella another day."

Eliza said goodbye to her friends and hurried to catch up with the younger girls, who were skipping along the road, singing as they went.

Eliza stepped between them and took the hand of each girl. "Come on!" she exclaimed with a laugh. "We'll never get home with you two skipping all the way!" She burst into song, and Lily and Elsie soon joined her in a hymn they'd been singing the previous night.

In the weeks since she had spoken to Ruthie, telling her how confused she felt, Eliza had gradually come to accept that she had been blessed with two mothers. The realisation of this had made her feel more like singing and laughing again. Although she often still wanted to be the one to help Lily, she was learning that there was a need in both of their lives that Ruthie could fill.

They'd decided that Eliza would still call her Auntie Ruthie. After all, there was no need for anyone else to know what had happened. Mr. and Mrs. Turley knew, but that was alright. Eliza felt safe where she was now. She missed her mam still, but she knew she was with Jesus, and she would see her again one day. All it needed was for her dad to come home, and things would be as good as they were going to get. She knew he wasn't really her dad, but he'd always be her dad. Auntie Ruthie had said that was the best way to think of him.

They got home in record time, and Mrs. Turley greeted them warmly, as she always did.

"Is the new man here?" Elsie asked.

"Yes, Toby arrived this morning," Mrs. Turley replied. "You'll see him when he comes in for tea. We asked him to eat with us tonight as it's his first day here."

"Can't we go and say hello to him now?" Lily asked.

Mrs. Turley laughed. "I suppose you could go out to the barn if you're that keen."

"Where's he going to sleep?" Elsie enquired.

"Down at the farm next door. You two girls are very interested in our new hand."

"I won't be the newest one here anymore," Elsie stated. "I'll like not being the newest. You heard about my mum yet?" This was Elsie's usual question when she returned from school each day.

"I'm afraid not, Elsie. I'm sure we'll hear something soon."

The three girls made their way to the barn to introduce themselves to the new hand. They found him working alongside Mr. Turley, who greeted them cheerily. "School finished already? That means it won't be far off teatime then! I suppose you've come to meet our new hand? This is Toby." Turning to the man working alongside him, he said, "And these are our girls, Eliza, Lily, and Elsie."

Eliza liked the way Mr. Turley had referred to them. She didn't think Stella was going to be as impressed with this new hand as she'd hoped. He looked to be nearer to her dad's age, but he didn't appear particularly happy. When he moved, something didn't seem quite right.

"What you staring at?" His sharp tone surprised Eliza.

"I'm sorry, I didn't mean to. It's nice to meet you." Eliza spoke quickly.

"There!" Toby bent and pulled up his trouser leg. "Happy now? Never seen a wooden leg before?"

Elsie's mouth opened wide in surprise, before she asked, "Does it hurt?"

"Course not!" Toby snapped. "So now you've seen what you've come for, I'll be getting' on with my work."

"Hang on a minute Toby," Mr. Turley's voice was firm. "The girls didn't know about your leg. I saw no need to tell them. They most likely came to welcome you to the farm."

"Come on Lily, Elsie. Let's go and help Mrs. Turley," Eliza suggested, her voice shaking a little.

Lily gripped Eliza's hand tightly as they left the barn, Elsie running as fast as her legs could carry her ahead of them.

Once they reached the kitchen, Lily announced, "I don't think I like Toby."

"What happened out there?" Mrs. Turley asked the girls.

"I… he…" Eliza wasn't really sure how to answer.

"He thought we wanted to see his wooden leg," Elsie explained. "I didn't though. I didn't like it. Does it ever fall off? Me and Mum had a table and the leg sometimes fell off that."

"It won't fall off," Mrs. Turley reassured her, "but perhaps it's not very comfortable for him. I don't think he's had it too long, so I expect he's still getting used to it. Perhaps people have been unkind to him about it."

"But we weren't!" Lily insisted. "We only went to say hello."

"I'm sure Mr. Turley will tell him you were only meaning to be polite," Ada explained.

They were interrupted by a knock at the door. "Who could that be?" Mrs. Turley wondered aloud.

"Will Toby knock with his wooden leg?" Elsie asked fearfully, moving to hide behind Eliza.

Mrs. Turley answered the door, and a smartly dressed woman entered the kitchen. "Am I right in thinking Elsie Hopkins is staying here?" she asked.

"Yes, Elsie is here," Ada replied.

Stepping from behind Eliza, Elsie asked, "Have you found my mum? Is she coming to take me home?"

"I'm afraid we've had confirmation that Elsie's mother was killed in an air-raid," the woman said, ignoring Elsie's question. "I need to take her to an orphanage until we can find somewhere better for her. We've moved the ones we can out of the cities, so she'll be safe there."

"No!" Elsie cried. "Tell her Mrs. Turley, Mum's coming to get me!"

"If you can gather her things together, I'll take her now. We need to be on the train."

Elsie dropped to her knees and Eliza and Lily were on either side of her, holding her tightly as she cried.

"You can't go!" Lily cried with her.

"She can stay here." Mrs. Turley's voice was calm, but firm. "Mr. Turley and I talked about it, and we said that if Elsie's mother couldn't be found, we'd like to keep her here."

"But she's not an evacuee anymore. She must go to the orphanage. Now, if you will gather her things, otherwise I'll have to take her without them." The woman made to move towards Elsie, but Mrs. Turley stepped between them.

"Eliza, please go and get Mr. Turley," she said calmly.

Eliza pulled herself away from the two younger girls and made for the door. Out in the yard, she broke into a run and headed to the barn. "Mr. Turley! Mrs. Turley needs you at the house. Elsie's mam's dead and the lady's taking Elsie to an orphanage!" She spoke quickly.

Bill hurried to the house, and Ruthie came out to meet Eliza. Flinging her arms around her mother, Eliza cried, "I don't want them to put Elsie in an orphanage! Mrs. Turley said she can stay, but the lady said she's taking her!"

Ruthie was surprised at her own words as she spoke calmly. "I don't want to see her leave, either. Let's pray about it. Come on, I'll come back to the house with you. I can hear Elsie crying from here."

They crossed the yard and entered the house, where they both stood just inside the doorway, praying silently.

Ada was now sitting in the rocking chair with Elsie clinging to her, Lily standing protectively in front of them, while Bill was facing the woman, speaking firmly. "Elsie can stay with us. She's been through enough. You can't tell me you have places in orphanages for all those who're going to need them. Elsie is part of our family now. She belongs here."

"Have it your own way then, but you won't get a penny for having her here." The woman spoke irritably before heading for the door, pushing past Eliza and Ruthie.

"You can stop crying, Elsie, you can stay here. No one's going to take you anywhere," Ada said gently.

"My mum's not coming, is she?" Elsie sobbed.

"No, love, she isn't. I know you're going to miss her, but we'll look after you."

"I don't have a mam either," Lily said, "but you can be my sister."

Eliza stepped closer to Ruthie. Yes, she'd lost one mother, but she still had another. Sensing what Eliza was thinking, Ruthie took her daughter's hand and pulled her closer, both thankful they had one another.

Another knock on the door made them all jump. "Oh no! She's not come back to take me, has she?" Elsie squealed in fright.

When Ruthie turned to open the door, Eliza instantly recognised Seb standing on the doorstep. "Hello Seb," she greeted him. His shoes now looked in a worse state than they had previously.

"Hello. I say! I met you once before, didn't I?"

"Yes." Eliza smiled.

"How can we help you, young man?" Bill asked.

"Oh, I'm ever so sorry to bother you, sir, but I've been sent to borrow some sky hooks. I don't suppose you have any spare, do you?"

Eliza noticed the twinkle in Mr. Turley's eye. "You'd better come in."

"I really must get back with the sky hooks. If you don't have any, I'll have to find someone who does. This is the third farm I've been to so far."

"Let them wait for their sky hooks. Have a cup of tea with us and I'll find you some boots. Those city shoes of yours are no good around here."

"I don't know. I mean… Father bought me new shoes especially."

"I'm not sure he'd mind if he saw the state of them now."

"I would be awfully grateful. My feet are terribly cold. This mud soaks right through my shoes, but Father said they were the best money can buy."

"And I'm sure they are, but you need different shoes in the country to what you need in the city. My boys are away at war, and I'm sure one of their pairs of boots will fit you just fine."

"And the sky hooks? Do you have them, sir?"

"It seems someone has been having you on, young Seb. Take a look at that sky out there."

Seb turned and gazed out through the window, scanning the sky with intent.

Mr. Turley continued, "Do you see anywhere to hang a hook out there?"

"Oh bother! I don't suppose I do. That beastly hand has done it again!"

"I suggest you tell him that Mr. Turley said the sky conditions aren't right for sky hooks, and whoever wants to use them on a day like this, is a fool."

"I'll do that. Thank you, sir."

"If they send you off to get something again, you should come here first."

"Right you are, sir!" Seb nodded emphatically.

"Come and have that cup of tea and a bit of bread and drippin'," Mrs. Turley invited Seb to the table, "while Mr. Turley goes to find them boots."

15

"Oh look! 'im's coming this way again. I wonder what 'im's been sent to get this time!" Florence laughed as the five girls stood at the end of the track leading to the Turley farm.

"Seb!" Lily and Elsie ran towards him. "Are you coming to the farm?" Elsie asked eagerly.

"I say! Magnificent day, isn't it? I was just out for a stroll."

"A stroll!" Stella snorted as Seb stepped up to join them. "Who goes for a bloomin' stroll?"

"I'd finished my schoolwork, and my tutor is having his usual afternoon off, so I thought I'd take in the air."

"Does 'im think 'im's one of them barrage balloons?" Florence muttered under her breath.

"I'm missing my piano terribly," Seb admitted sadly. "I'd usually spend the afternoon practicing."

"We've got a piano at our house. Mrs. Turley plays hymns on it," Lily told him. "She plays other songs too, but I like the hymns best."

"A piano? Right there on the farm? I never saw it."

"Yes," Elsie spoke enthusiastically. "You only came in the kitchen though and it's not in there! It's in the other room."

"I'm sure Mrs. Turley would let you play it," Eliza put in. Mr. and Mrs. Turley had liked Seb. They had invited him to visit whenever he liked, so Eliza thought this might be an ideal opportunity.

"You play piano then, do ya?" Stella sounded interested. "Bet you play all that fancy music."

"There are some truly wonderful composers!" Seb spoke enthusiastically. "I might just take you up on that offer, Eliza."

"Can we come and 'ave a listen?" Stella asked. "I've never 'eard anyone play fancy music before."

"What about tea?" Florence sounded concerned.

"Mrs. Turley will have some bread to keep you going," Eliza reassured her friend.

"I say! Do you mean now?" Seb was shocked. "I mean, doesn't one need a formal invitation?"

"What's one of them look like?" Florence asked.

"Something posh people 'ave I expect, silly!" Stella shrugged.

"Come on, all of you, if you're coming," Eliza said, leading the way up the track.

"I say!" Eliza wondered what Seb was exclaiming at and turned to see Elsie dragging him along by the hand.

"You don't have to be frightened of coming here," Elsie reassured him. "They're nice. Where I was before wasn't nice. They shut me in the cellar and made me clean the floor when I dropped an egg."

"It's a good thing I wasn't there," Seb spoke easily to her. "I drop things all the time."

"Do you have a mum and a dad?" Elsie asked.

Seb hesitated before saying, "Father insists he must stay in London for business."

"What about your mum?" Elsie persisted.

"Mother isn't well." Seb spoke flatly.

"My mam wasn't well," Lily put in, taking his other hand. "She went to be with Jesus."

"My mum got killed by a bomb," Elsie explained, "but I don't know if she's with Jesus."

"With Jesus?" Seb was surprised. "One can't be with Jesus. He lived a long time ago! I read about him once."

"Mam is with Jesus!" Lily insisted. "I know, because she believed in him. I believe in Jesus too, so when I die, I'll see Mam again. I want to see Mam, but I don't want to die yet."

"I want my mum!" Elsie began to cry.

Eliza dropped back and took Elsie's other hand. "Come on Elsie, let's show Seb the piano."

"Don't understand all that about Jesus," Stella muttered. "I mean, 'ow can 'e be everywhere?"

"Because he's God!" Lily told her confidently. "Dad said that Jesus is with us and with him at the same time, and he's in the war."

"'Ow did 'im feed all them people with a bit of bread and fish, anyway?" Florence wondered aloud.

"You and your bloomin' belly!" Stella laughed.

It was a rather awkward and confused Seb the girls presented to Mrs. Turley.

"Seb is missing his piano. I hope you don't mind, but I said he could play yours," Eliza explained.

"I do apologise… I don't know what I was thinking. How rude of me to come without a proper invitation," Seb stammered.

"You had an invitation," Mrs. Turley smiled. "We said you can come here whenever you like, and Eliza invited you today. We don't have anything more proper than that here. Now come on, I'll show you the piano. Then how about I get you all some bread and drippin' to see you through until tea?"

Once seated, Seb tentatively tried the keys of the piano. After declaring it "a little out of tune, but not too bad," he began to play.

"Cor! 'e's good!" Stella exclaimed in awe. "Didn't 'ear anyone play like that when I walked past the pubs!"

"Nor in chapel!" Florence agreed in wonder.

"I never knew there was so much music to be found in that old piano," Mrs. Turley said thoughtfully, as beautiful melodies flowed from the instrument. "Without music too!"

Seb played piece after piece, each more beautiful than the one before it. Mrs. Turley pulled out her simple stack of music, but Seb didn't glance at it once. So engrossed were they in what they were hearing, and the way Seb's hands moved lightly over the keys, time got away from them. Even Florence forgot about the promised bread and dripping.

"Will you come and play the piano again?" Elsie asked, as Seb announced it was time he left.

"Please come and play again," Lily added.

"You'd be welcome to come any time," Ada told him. "It does me good to hear music like that."

"If you're quite sure? I've missed playing the piano dreadfully."

"You ever played an organ?" she asked.

"Once or twice, yes. Do you have one of those, too?"

"No, but we do in the chapel. I was thinking, we don't get much good music like that around here. How about putting on a concert? You know, to raise everyone's spirits."

"I say! What a splendid idea! Marvellous! My tutor plays the violin as well."

"We have the organ and the piano at the chapel, so you can take your pick. A violin would be nice too, I'm sure."

Seb set off with a lighter step, while Florence and Stella left at a run, knowing they would be late home.

"We'll be for it!" Florence said, as they raced down the track, passing Seb on their way.

At the tea table, there was much talk about Seb and the concert, which would soon take place.

"Perhaps he could give lessons to those who want to learn," Mrs. Turley suggested. "I can teach them a bit, and Mrs. Hale can too, but we can't play like he does."

"I want to learn the piano," Elsie grinned widely.

"Me too!" Lily agreed.

Eliza knew she would love to play the piano, but she didn't think she would ever play like Seb. Her mam had said she'd always wanted to learn, so maybe she should do it for her.

After they'd eaten, Mrs. Turley asked Elsie to help her with something, while Ruthie took Eliza and Lily aside. "We had a letter today," she told them.

"A letter? From Dad?" Lily could hardly contain her excitement.

"Yes, it's from your dad. I haven't opened it yet, because I thought we could all read it together. Eliza, would you like to open it?"

Eliza's hands shook slightly as she slit open the envelope and took out two folded pieces of paper. On the outside of one was written "Elizabeth and Liliana", while the other had Ruthie's name on it. Eliza handed Ruthie's to her, then unfolded the other.

"I'll leave you to read it to Lily, if you'd like," Ruthie offered.

Eliza scanned the page before she said, "It's alright, you can stay."

"What does Dad say?" Lily couldn't get any closer to Eliza and the letter if she tried.

Eliza read, "Dear Eliza and Lily. I hope you are enjoying living at the farm and have made lots of friends in school. I'm sorry I didn't stay longer, but I know Ruthie will look after you well. I'm alright. The food isn't as good as I expect Mrs. Turley is cooking for you. Mind you both help out as much as you can, and do as you're told. I miss you both and I'm praying for you all the time. I'll be back as soon as I can, but it might not be for a while. Don't worry about me. Remember, Jesus is with me, just like he's with you. God bless you both. Love Dad."

"When will he come home?" Lily was on the verge of tears.

"He'll be home as soon as he can," Ruthie told her, "but he has to do his bit for the war at the moment."

Eliza was also fighting back tears. She wanted her dad more than ever. She wanted to talk to him about what she'd learnt, but she couldn't tell him that in a letter. It would have to wait until he got home.

Ruthie read her own letter silently. Eddie thanked her again for going to the country with the girls. He also told her he was praying for her. There was no mention of the true situation, after all, you never knew whose hands a letter would get into. Ruthie wished she could thank Eddie for the gift he'd given her. She had her daughter back. Not only that, having his girls to care for was beginning to teach her how to love again, and how to receive it. Lily had been so loving right from the start, and Ruthie hadn't known how to give or accept her love. Elsie too had taken to calling her Auntie Ruthie. The little girl often cried in the night, and Ruthie had become used to comforting her and getting her back to sleep. Even she and Eliza were becoming closer. How she longed for the chance to thank Eddie for all he'd given her.

"I told Dad about Elsie being my friend when we last wrote to him," Lily said. "Didn't he get our letter?"

"Sometimes it takes a bit longer for letters to get through," Ruthie explained. "I'm sure he'll get your letter soon. He's probably already had it by now. He would have written this one a while ago."

"So he knows Elsie is my best friend now?" Lilly wanted to know.

"I expect so, yes."

"Elsie won't get any letters anymore," Lily said thoughtfully. "Dad won't die like Elsie's mum did, will he?"

"We'll keep praying for him to stay safe," Ruthie said. She didn't understand herself why some prayers were answered, while others didn't seem to be. She'd ask Mrs. Turley about that, she decided.

16

"Morning Ruthie. Can I help you with that?"

Ruthie sighed as Toby stepped up close beside her, where she was cleaning out the horses' stables. "Morning Toby. I can manage alright, thank you." She forced herself to add the thank you.

"I don't mind helping you at all. A lady like you shouldn't be doing that kind of work."

"I'm sure Mr. Turley has other things for you to do," Ruthie spoke coldly. Toby was always following her around, and she didn't like it. Something about him made her uncomfortable.

"I was wondering if you wanted to go to the pictures with me on Saturday? I'll ask old Bill if we can have the time off."

"No, Toby, I won't be going to the pictures with you. And if I want time off, I'll ask Mr. Turley myself."

"I can see you're an independent one. Don't know why you allowed yourself to get stuck with your sister's kids."

"I'm not stuck with them. I want to take care of the girls. Now, I've got work to do, and I'm sure you have too."

"Who's the fellow then?"

"What are you on about now?"

"If you won't go with me, who is it you want to be going with?"

"I'll not be going with anyone." Ruthie turned her back on Toby and began shovelling out the stalls more ferociously.

She was relieved when he left soon afterwards. She hadn't liked the man since the first day he'd arrived. There had been no need for the way he'd spoken to the girls when they'd come to meet him. It seemed he thought everyone was out to make fun of his leg. Perhaps some people had, but there was still no need for him to speak to people like he did. And why did he have such a fascination with her? She'd told him time and time again she had no intention of going to the pictures, or anywhere else with him, but Toby didn't like taking no for an answer. He usually left her alone when Bill was around, but as soon as she was by herself, he made his move. It reminded her too much of Gareth Davies. Toby wasn't likely to behave as Gareth had, but he was certainly making a nuisance of himself. Besides, if he were to try something on, surely she could fight off a man with a wooden leg.

"Bill! Bill! Where are you? Bill!" Ada's voice was unusually high-pitched.

Ruthie dropped her shovel and ran to see what was wrong. Ada stood in the doorway of the barn, her face colourless, and a piece of paper clutched in her hand. "What's wrong, Ada?" Ruthie asked, fearing the worst.

"Ada? What be the matter?" Bill hurried from behind the barn.

"Oh Bill! It's a telegram. It's John!"

"Is he…?" Bill reached his wife's side and took the telegram from her shaking hand.

"Killed in action!" Ada sobbed.

"I'm so sorry." Ruthie's words sounded inadequate as she spoke them. What else could she say? What could she do?

"He's gone, Bill, our John's gone. He won't be coming 'ome!"

"Ruthie, take Ada into the house and make her some tea, will you? I'll be there in a minute."

Ruthie wondered at Bill's request. Then she saw the tears in his eyes, and knew he needed to be alone. What was she to do? What was she to say? How would she feel if it were Eliza? But she'd hardly spent any time at all with Eliza. Ada had brought her son up from the day he was born. She'd been there for every part of his life. Ruthie took Ada's arm and led her towards the house. "I'll make us some tea," she heard herself saying.

In the kitchen, Ada sank down into a chair at the table, rested her head on her arms, and cried.

Ruthie tried speaking words of comfort as she made the tea, then sat down beside Ada. She didn't suppose her words made any sense. Ada always knew what to say to everyone else, she knew that only too well. Now Ada needed someone, and Ruthie felt ill-equipped for the role.

"Just listen."

Ruthie didn't know how she heard the words, but it seemed like the right advice. Ada didn't need her to say anything, she just needed her to listen.

"Always wanted to be out on the farm with Bill, he did. Followed Bill everywhere. We always knew the farm would be in good hands with him, but now he's never coming back. This war is senseless. All those lives lost! Where will it end? I just can't believe he's never going to walk through that door again and ask if I've been baking anything. I wonder if Joe knows. They joined up together, you know. What if he was with him? I hope Joe's not gone too. I don't know what I'll do if both my boys are gone."

Eventually Ada stopped her constant talking and turned to look at Ruthie. "I'm glad you're here," she said.

"Just let me know what I can do," Ruthie offered, unsure of what else she should say.

"Just having you here is enough. I knew Bill would have to go off on his own, that's his way, you know. I know John is with the Lord now. He gave his life to him when he was still a boy! He was baptised when he was fourteen. Always had a strong faith has John. He doesn't have to suffer in all the fighting anymore. I knew he was finding it hard. I could tell by his letters. Never liked to see anyone or anything hurt. 'Im and Joe only joined up because they thought they should do their bit for the country. They weren't keen to fight, like some of the men were. I know I'll see him again one day, but it's hard knowing that might not be for some time."

The door opened and Bill entered. Ruthie got to her feet and poured him a cup of tea, before making a hasty exit, leaving the two alone.

Ruthie's mind was not on what she was doing for the rest of that day. She nearly allowed one of the cows to stand on her foot, then she nearly left a gate open. Ada's words kept going around and around in her mind. Ada was certain John was now with Jesus, and that she would see him in heaven. Eliza and Lily had that same assurance about Lizzie. Could Ruthie know for certain that she'd see anyone she loved again? Her mam and dad didn't know Jesus. What did that mean? She didn't like the answer that came to mind. Eddie was in the war. What if he was killed? Eddie was sure of Jesus being his saviour. He would certainly go to be with the Lord, as Lizzie had. His girls were also certain of what they believed. What did she herself believe?

Ruthie sat down on a bale of straw. Did she believe in Jesus? Of course she did. Did he really take on the sins of everyone in the world and die on a cross? Yes. Ada had explained all that. Ruthie had found it difficult to get her head around at first, but she did believe it. Did Jesus rise from the dead? Yes. Again, she and Ada had discussed that. A new question came into her mind. Did she believe that if she, Ruthie Lewis, was the only person in the world, Jesus would have still taken on her sin, died on the cross, then rose again? That was more difficult. She had sinned a lot. She'd given up her baby and sent her to who knew where! Thankfully, Eddie and Lizzie had taken her in, but it might not have been that way. Eliza might have ended up anywhere. Now Ruthie was allowing her to believe that she intended her to go to Eddie and Lizzie when she gave her up. Would Eliza forgive her if she knew the truth? Probably not. So why would Jesus die for Ruthie Lewis when she was still sinning?

"Break time, is it? Mind if I join you?"

"I'm getting back to work." Ruthie stood up and walked quickly away from Toby. She didn't want to have another conversation with him today.

Ruthie was waiting for Eliza, Lily, and Elsie when they returned from school. She wanted to give them the news about John Turley before they got into the house. Taking them into the barn, where they all sat on some bales, Ruthie explained the arrival of the telegram earlier that day.

"Mr. and Mrs. Turley must be very sad," Eliza said. "How can we help them? I'll help get tea ready."

"Thank you, Eliza, I'm sure that will be appreciated."

"Why does everyone have to die?" Elsie asked, "I don't want anyone else to die. You won't die, will you, Auntie Ruthie? Or Mr. Turley? Or Mrs. Turley?"

"We hope we won't for a long time," Ruthie tried to reassure her.

"Mrs Turley said that John and Joe know Jesus," Lily said thoughtfully, "so John must be in heaven with Mam now. Dad won't get himself killed, will he? He's at the war too. Do you think he met John and Joe Turley?"

"I don't suppose he's met them, no," Ruthie replied, ignoring Lily's first question.

The four of them went together to the house, where Ada was busy preparing tea. Eliza immediately went to help her, while Lily and Elsie seemed unsure of what to do.

Ruthie was on the doorstep, about to make her way back to the barn, when she saw someone hurrying towards the house. When she recognised the telegram boy, she felt sick. How could Ada and Bill stand losing both sons on one day? Would it be better knowing they'd likely been side by side as their lives ended? Ruthie was completely unprepared for the boy's words as he stepped up to her.

"Telegram for Miss Ruthie Lewis," he said, handing her the paper.

Opening it with shaking hands, she read the words on the page. "Edward Davies. Missing in action."

It had to be a mistake. Was she in the middle of a nightmare? Eddie couldn't be missing. What did it mean, anyway? The telegram didn't say he was dead, just missing. Did that mean dead? She didn't know.

She wasn't aware of sitting down on the step until a voice broke into her thoughts. She looked up to see Toby standing over her, a strange look on his face. "Looks like bad news," he observed.

"It's Eddie. He's missing in action," Ruthie told him.

Ruthie didn't remember how she got inside the house. She found herself sitting in the rocking chair, Lily in her lap and Eliza kneeling by her side, tears streaming down their cheeks. It was all too much. First John Turley, Now Eddie. Eddie wasn't supposed to die. She'd loved Eddie all her life, but he'd never known it. Why had she pushed him away all those years ago? Now she'd never know how it felt to be truly loved. But Eddie would never have loved her. He knew all about what she'd done. She knew he would never love her the way she loved him, but just to know she'd see him again when he got back from the war was enough. Just to know she could talk to him and share stories about the girls. She'd imagined them reminiscing about their own childhoods, and the fun they'd had. She'd hoped too that he would tell her about Eliza's childhood. She would never have that chance now, not if Eddie was dead.

"I don't want Dad to be dead," Lily cried.

Ruthie noticed Ada was now holding the telegram. "We don't know, Lily love. It says he's missing."

"So, he might not be dead? They might just not know where he is." Eliza sounded hopeful.

"There is always that chance," Bill said thoughtfully.

"Maybe he's not dead! Perhaps Lily's dad and your John are hiding from the Germans!" Elsie offered.

"It seems there may be hope, but we just don't know. It said John was killed in action, but this says Eddie is missing." Ada paused and wiped the tears from her eyes. "We'll pray for Eddie now, shall we?"

"I want Jesus to make him not be missing," Lily sighed.

"Maybe Jesus couldn't find my mum," Elsie said hopefully. "I never asked him to look for her."

Ruthie's head hurt. Was it her fault Eddie was dead? Maybe if she hadn't agreed to come with the girls and begun to feel happy again, Eddie would be alright. And as for Jesus, how could he let good men die or be missing while she was still alive? She was aware of their voices as they prayed together, but didn't hear their words. The thought of never seeing Eddie again was just too much.

Somehow, they got through the rest of the evening. Ruthie was relieved when it was time to go to bed. She didn't have to think about trying to make any kind of conversation anymore. Lily and Elsie were now sleeping on a smaller bed Bill had made of wood. Ada had made up a mattress and covered it with blankets. The two younger girls had thought themselves the luckiest people in the village to have such a special bed made just for them. Ruthie looked down at where they lay, each with her rag doll tucked in beside her. She put out the lamp and turned to get into her own bed, next to Eliza.

Neither of them spoke as they lay side by side in the darkness. Ruthie knew she should have said more to try to comfort the girls, but she didn't know what.

She was surprised when Eliza reached across and slipped her hand into hers. "You miss him too, don't you? You were his best friend, so you knew him even before me and Lily did."

Eliza's kindness was too much for Ruthie. She held tightly to her daughter's hand, unable to speak as the tears sprang from her eyes and rolled down her face.

"I know if he's dead, he'll be with Jesus, and with Mam, but I'm praying he's still alive. If he is dead, will they try to put me and Lily in an orphanage, like they wanted to with Elsie? They don't know you're my mother, so they might try to take us away."

"I won't let them!" Ruthie found her voice. "Eliza, I'll do whatever it takes to keep you and Lily with me. I'll tell them you are my daughter if it helps."

"Then people would know, and they might talk about you," Eliza sounded concerned.

"They can talk all they like, as long as you and Lily stay with me. I'm not letting you go twice." Ruthie realised she meant every word. She'd do anything in her power to keep Eliza and Lily, anything at all.

17

"Oh, Ben! That's not fair! You're no good at hide and seek! You were supposed to let Lily find me!"

"He's the best at hide and seek!" Lily laughed, as Ben jumped around with excitement at having led her straight to where Elsie was hiding.

"He spoils the game!" Elsie complained.

"Why doesn't Ben go with whoever's hiding?" Bill suggested as he approached the girls and took in the situation.

"Do you think he would?" Elsie asked in surprise.

"You might as well try. He might be just as good at hiding as he is at seeking."

"It's my turn to hide, so Ben can come with me," Lily grinned. "You're not allowed to call him though, Elsie."

"Alright, I won't. I'll stand here and count to one hundred," Elsie agreed.

"Come on, Ben! I've got the best hiding place!" Lily called, as she ran across the yard, Ben close at her heels.

"Good day Mr. Turley, hello Elsie."

"Seb!" Elsie squealed. "Have you come to play the piano?"

"I was planning to ask Mrs. Turley if I might possibly play."

"We're always glad to hear you play that old piano, Seb. It's a shame I won't be able to listen today. I've got a lot of work to do. I suppose it's warm enough for you to have the window open in there though." Bill was pleased to see Seb.

"Right you are!"

"You can play hide and seek with us," Elsie suggested. "Ben's playing too now, but he has to hide with Lily because he's too good at finding us. You could be on my team. Eliza's gone with Florence and Stella. I'll never find Lily without Ben. She always has good hiding places."

"Oh… Ah… I've never played that," Seb said awkwardly.

"Never?" Elsie Exclaimed. "What did you play then?"

"Play? Well, I had a train set. I had books as well."

"Books! They aren't playing! What did you play outside?"

"Outside?" Seb was thoughtful. "I don't suppose I really played outside. I used to walk in the gardens to get fresh air."

"That's not playing. Why didn't you play?"

"I don't recall having anyone to play with."

"Then you have to play with me and Lily and Ben."

"Remember, Elsie, Seb is older than you," Bill reminded her. "He might not want to play games."

"How old are you?" Elsie enquired.

"I am fifteen years old," Seb stated proudly.

"That's not too old to play. Stella's fourteen, and she still plays with us. She's older than Eliza and Florence, but she's in the same class as them because her mum didn't send her to school, so she don't know nothing. Fifteen is only one more than fourteen, so you're not too old. Please, Seb, please help me find Lily and Ben."

"Oh, alright then. It is a jolly nice day today, so it will do me good to be in the air a little longer."

"How does air do you good?" Elsie asked.

"I…" Seb thought a moment. "I don't really know. I suppose it makes one feel good. Just listen to those birds, Elsie! Just smell that fresh air."

"It doesn't smell so good when Mr. Turley moves the cows!" Elsie giggled. Taking his hand, she said, "Come on, Let's find them. We mustn't call Ben though."

"Right you are!" Seb agreed, as he allowed himself to be led across the yard by Elsie.

***

Ruthie enjoyed what Bill Turley referred to as spring planting. They'd done the fields together, and now she was planting seeds in the garden near the house, where more vegetables than ever were to be grown.

"As long as we've got veg and meat, we'll be alright," Ada had said. "Enough for those who don't have the space to grow as well."

Ruthie still found herself thinking of Eddie almost every moment of the day. The whole family, as she now thought of them, prayed together each morning and evening for his safety. Three weeks after the arrival of the telegram, Ruthie had more peace about the situation. At first she'd felt guilty for that, but Ada had said she mustn't, as it was God's peace and a real gift from him.

Ruthie also felt that she and Eliza had drawn closer to one another over the weeks. They often talked together, Ruthie telling Eliza about the fun times she and Eddie had shared, and Eliza reminiscing about her childhood with her parents and Lily. It seemed to help both of them to remember good times.

Coming to the end of the seeds she had, Ruthie got to her feet and brushed off her hands. Spring was most definitely in the air she decided as she rounded the side of the house and crossed the yard towards the barn. She went inside and headed for the shelf where the seeds were stored. As she reached up to get them, she felt hands come around her waist.

Ruthie jumped, and turned to see who it was, instantly realising her mistake, as Toby's face appeared just inches from hers.

"No need to be frightened, Ruthie," Toby grinned. "Reckon you knew I'd follow you in here."

"Leave me alone, Toby!" Ruthie spoke firmly, trying to push him away.

"Am I not good enough for you? Think you're going to wait for someone with two legs of his own, do you?"

"I don't care how many legs you have!" Ruthie pushed hard at him.

"I'll prove I'm still a man. You can't refuse me, especially now the one you were waiting for is dead."

"I don't know what you're on about, Toby. Just go away!" Fear made her voice shake.

Toby's hand came over her mouth, while his other arm came around her, lifting her off her feet and dragging her around behind a stack of bales.

***

Lily crouched low, one arm around Ben to hold him in place. Ben could never resist going to see what other people were up to, so she had to hold him still, otherwise he'd help Elsie find her. Elsie wasn't very good at playing hide and seek, so perhaps she should have let Ben help her. She'd been hiding here for ages and Elsie hadn't come yet. She'd thought she'd heard Seb's voice, and wondered whether he'd come to play Mrs. Turley's piano. She could creep out of her hiding place and go to the house to listen to him play. Elsie wouldn't think of looking in there. She would be looking for her for ages. But no, that wouldn't work. Ben wasn't allowed in the house. The dog had to stay outside. She hoped Elsie would find her soon. She was taking too long. Maybe she should let Ben help Elsie after all.

Lily was considering this when she heard voices nearby. One was Toby, and she didn't like Toby. She was glad he didn't often eat in the house with them. The other was Auntie Ruthie. She sounded frightened. Auntie Ruthie was never frightened. Auntie Ruthie was as sad as she and Eliza were that their dad was missing, but she was never afraid.

Lily watched in fear as Toby pulled Auntie Ruthie around behind the bales. She could see the back of Toby, but she couldn't see Auntie Ruthie's face, because Toby was trying to squash her between himself and the bales. What was she going to do? She had to help Auntie Ruthie. "Leave her alone!" Lily screamed, letting go of Ben.

In one bound, the dog sprang from the top of the bales where they'd been hiding, landing right beside Toby and Auntie Ruthie. Ben barked and growled, then made a grab for Toby's leg. Lily couldn't remember if it was the wooden one or his real one.

Toby seemed to lose his balance, and let Ruthie go. She gave him a hard push, then ran towards Lily.

Ruthie held up her arms and the little girl slid down into them. As she glanced sideways, she saw Ben, using his teeth to keep Toby from following.

Ruthie held Lily tightly and ran from the barn, almost knocking Seb off his feet.

"I say! Something wrong?" Seb enquired.

"Lily! You were meant to be hiding!" Elsie exclaimed.

"Seb, please take the girls to the house and stay there," Ruthie said, trying to transfer Lily to the boy's arms.

"No, Auntie Ruthie! He was going to hurt you! Toby was hurting you!" Lily clung to her.

"Get that dog off me!" Toby's roar came from inside the barn.

"What's going on?" Bill Turley hurried from a different direction.

"Ben's got Toby by the leg," Ruthie explained breathlessly.

"He was hurting Auntie Ruthie!" Lily cried.

"What, Ben?" Bill was shocked.

"No! Toby!" Lily informed him emphatically. "Me and Ben were hiding, and I saw Toby pull Auntie Ruthie behind the bales. He was squashing her!"

Bill looked at Ruthie. "Has he been giving you trouble?"

Ruthie nodded.

Bill turned and, with a face like thunder, strode into the barn.

"I'm alright, Lily," Ruthie tried to reassure her. "You and Elsie go into the house with Seb. I'll be there now in a minute."

"Come on Lily," Seb encouraged, holding out his arms to her.

Lily allowed him to take her into his arms and Elsie followed as he strode towards the house.

Ruthie stood, rooted to the spot. If Lily and the dog hadn't been there, she knew only too well what would have happened. She'd underestimated Toby's strength. How had it almost happened again? Wasn't once enough?

She stood staring ahead of her, not seeing a thing. What would Bill do? Would Toby deny it? What if Bill believed him and thought she'd encouraged him? What if he thought she'd encouraged Gareth Davies?

"I say! Are you alright? Looks like you had quite a shock."

Ruthie turned to look at Seb.

"It's alright, I've left Lily and Elsie with Mrs. Turley."

"Thank you, Seb." Ruthie's voice sounded distant to her own ears.

"I… Ah… I know what happened," Seb said awkwardly. "I mean, I know Toby's sort. I… My… My father. I saw him once. With one of the kitchen staff. She was frightened and… I told Father to stop, but he wouldn't. He… said I had to learn how to be a man. That's not how to be a real man, though, is it? I don't want to be like him. I gave Meg… She was the girl… I gave Meg my allowance, so she could run away. Father went mad when he found out she was gone. Mother told me I'd done the right thing, though. That's when Father had her sent away… Mother, that is. Then he sent me here."

"That was kind of you, Seb. I'm sure Meg will always remember you for doing that."

Their conversation was interrupted as Bill and Toby emerged from the barn. Seb stepped closer to Ruthie as they approached.

"Toby's leaving," Bill stated.

Toby's head hung low as he passed them. Only for an instant did he turn to glare at Ruthie.

Once he was out of sight, Bill spoke again. "I'm sorry that happened to you here, Ruthie. I'd have got rid of him before if I'd known."

"I'm sorry you've lost a worker," Ruthie apologised.

"Never mind that," Bill said. "The main thing is, you and the girls are alright."

"I'll help!" Seb's words were enthusiastic. "I'll admit I don't know anything about farming, but I can learn. That's one thing I'm good at, learning."

"Thank you, Seb." Bill smiled at him. "Your help will be appreciated. What about your work with your tutor?"

“Oh, didn’t I tell you? Silly me. He’s left. I’ll most likely have to attend the village school now, but I’ll come and work before and after school. Do say I can.”

“I’ll be pleased to have your help!” Bill’s pleasure was genuine.

“I am learning, you know! That hand sent me over here today for a monkey-wrench. I told him I’d need to visit the zoo for one of those, and then I walked away.”

Bill smiled. It could wait until another day to tell Seb that a monkey-wrench did actually exist.

18

"Come on, Lily! We're last, and we'll be late for Seb's concert!" Elsie urged.

Lily dragged her feet as the two girls walked along hand in hand.

"What's the matter with you two?" Ruthie turned back, stopping to wait for them.

"Lily's being slow," Elsie sighed.

Ruthie took Lily's other hand, and they soon reached the chapel, where Eliza, Florence and Stella had been helping Ada set up for the evening. Bill held the door open for them, and they entered the building, where the pews were filling up with villagers, along with those from further afield, who'd all come to hear Seb's musical accomplishments.

"Why don't all these people come to chapel?" Elsie asked.

"I was wondering that myself," Bill smiled down at her.

Bill went to see if there was anything his wife needed, while Ruthie found an empty pew. She slid in first, sitting next to the wall at the far end. Lily clung to her hand, then climbed into her lap. Elsie sat close beside her.

Ruthie wondered if Lily might be coming down with something, as she hadn't seemed right all afternoon.

Eliza spotted them and hurried over, sitting down next to Elsie. "Everything's ready," she spoke excitedly. "There are so many people! Seb isn't even nervous!"

"He doesn't need to be nervous," Ruthie stated. "I've never heard anyone play like him before."

Eliza's two friends joined Florence's family in the pew in front of them, then Bill and Ada came to sit next to Eliza.

"'Ow's 'im going to play the piano and the organ?" an old farmer asked in the pew behind them. "'Im must 'ave long arms! They didn't even move the piano over by the organ!"

"You daft apeth!" his wife muttered. "'Im won't play the two at once."

"'Im ought to learn to spell! Just look at that 'e wrote up on the blackboard! 'Im borrowed it from the school, but none of that makes sense! 'Im wants to go to proper school!" their son commented.

"Mrs. Turley said it's foreign languages," the woman informed them.

"I 'ope 'e won't play none of that German stuff!" her husband sounded horrified.

"'Ow do you play the piano in another language?" the son asked thoughtfully.

"Daft apeth! The music don't be foreign, just the bloke who wrote it!" his mother told him.

The Minister stepped up to the front of the chapel and everyone fell silent. After welcoming them all, he introduced Seb, who had positioned himself at the organ. He then announced that they would begin the evening by singing the well-known hymn, *To God be the Glory.*

"Perhaps 'im forgot the fancy stuff!" the man behind muttered, as the organ boomed out the introduction and they all stood to sing.

Lily leaned against Ruthie as they stood along with all the others and joined in the hymn. Ruthie loved singing hymns. She remembered her mam singing them sometimes, which seemed strange to her now, as she didn't go to chapel. Her Bible also belonged to her mam. If it hadn't been for that Bible, Eliza may have never found out the truth. Ruthie couldn't believe there was ever a time when she'd been afraid to admit Eliza was her child. Still, only Eliza herself knew, along with Eddie, Bill, and Ada, but she felt so much lighter now she wasn't carrying the burden of secrecy.

The hymn ended and Lily curled back into Ruthie's lap. Seb then introduced his first piece to be played on the organ.

"What's 'im say?" the man behind asked in a none too quiet whisper.

"I dunno. 'Im wants to learn to talk properly!" his son replied.

"Shh!" the woman hissed.

The place fell silent as Seb began to play. Ruthie glanced at the faces of those around her. Bill, Ada, Eliza, and Elsie beamed with pride. They all saw Seb as one of their own now. He didn't live at the Turley farm, but spent every spare minute there, doing his best to help. He still got a lot of things wrong, but he was trying his hardest, and was indeed a quick learner. You couldn't fault Seb's enthusiasm. Ruthie had a great deal of respect for the boy. She admired him for what he'd done for the kitchen maid, Meg. Seb wasn't anything like his father, that was certain. She'd learnt that his father had had his mother put away, to keep her quiet. Seb was determined to take her out of the institution just as soon as he was old enough. He'd confided in Ruthie that he no longer wished to go into his father's business. He knew it was better not to tell him this quite yet, as the older man would surely punish him. Seb feared he would be sent away, like his mother. So, he continued to live at the cottage with the made his father had sent with him and the tutor. Now the tutor was gone, Seb was enjoying time in the village school. He was so well educated that the teacher had to get special work to challenge him, but Seb had found he enjoyed helping the other children. He'd told Ruthie, as they milked the cows side by side one morning, that he believed he might like to be a teacher.

The audience erupted into applause when the music ended. The second and third pieces were received equally well. After this, Seb moved to the piano, where he played a lively tune.

"'Ow does 'im 'ave enough fingers to play all them notes!" the son exclaimed.

"Shh!" his mother hissed.

The next piece was slower and the boy behind called out, "It's Away in a Manger!"

"It's what?" his father asked.

"Away in a Manger, isn't it, Dad?"

"Shh! You daft apeth! It be not Christmas!" his mother quieted him once more.

Piece after piece was well received by all. The young, awkward boy, who had at first gone from farm to farm, asking for the bucket to milk the bull, was now seen in a new light. Everyone had great respect for his musical talent.

All too soon, Seb played his final piece. He then led them in three more rousing hymns before the concert was over.

"Can we do it again?" Elsie asked Ada.

"I don't see why not, as long as Seb is happy to do it."

Lily was now almost asleep, so Bill offered to carry her home. Ruthie hoped she would be better by morning.

They all congratulated Seb and invited him back for hot cocoa. Florence and Stella had already accepted the invitation to share the treat, as they'd helped with the organising and setting up.

Ruthie put Lily straight to bed before joining the others in the kitchen.

"You should 'ave seen 'em when you started playin'!" Stella exclaimed. "Thought their eyes were gonna pop out their heads!"

"You should have heard the people behind us!" Eliza joined in. "I don't think they've heard music like that before. The boy wanted to know how you could play in another language! His mam had to tell him it was the composer who was foreign, not the music!"

"I thought we were going to 'ave refreshments after, you know, like we do at Christmas," Florence said.

"Sorry Florence," Ada smiled. "Would you like a bit of cake?"

"Oh, yes please! I 'aven't eaten for hours!"

"You 'ad your bloomin tea before the concert, same as I did!" Stella snorted.

"And that was hours ago!" Florence stated.

"It really was a wonderful concert, Seb," Bill congratulated him.

Seb beamed with delight. "I wanted to put on a good show! You know, I always wanted to do a concert near where I grew up. Father didn't like the idea, but Mother was all for it! She would have enjoyed this evening."

"Where is she?" Elsie asked. "Couldn't she have come?"

Seb sighed and immediately his smile disappeared. "I'm afraid Father decided she was unwell. She had to go to a hospital of sorts."

"Why?" Elsie enquired.

"You mean 'e 'ad 'er locked up?" Stella asked bluntly.

"I suppose that's it," Seb agreed sadly. "I'll get her out when I'm old enough! You see if I don't!" His determination was evident.

"Why did 'e do it?" Stella questioned. "Sounds like a right piece of work, does your old man!"

"I don't think we should question Seb about the details," Ruthie put in, already being aware of some of Seb's story, and not wishing him to be embarrassed.

"Well! There was a bloke down our street who 'ad 'is wife locked away. Turns out it weren't 'er what was mad after all, it was 'im!" Stella spoke emphatically.

"How did they get her out? Do tell, Stella?" Seb was genuinely interested.

"Dunno. 'E disappeared too, so no one knows what 'appened. You could break in there and get 'er out!" Stella was enthusiastic.

"Breaking in won't help anyone," Bill put in.

"When I'm of age, I'll take her to live with me!"

"What do you mean, of age?" Eliza asked.

"When I'm twenty-one."

"That's bloomin' years away!" Stella exclaimed in disgust. "She'll be mad by then if she ain't now!"

At Seb's defeated expression, Ruthie put in, "I'm sure that won't happen. Maybe they'll realise she shouldn't be there and release her themselves. They'll need all the places they can with people coming back from the war."

"I do hope so!" Seb was thoughtful.

"How about a few games?" Ada suggested, hoping to lighten the mood around the table.

"Oh yes!" Elsie squealed. "Can we?"

Bill got out his dominos and divided them into teams. Elsie insisted on being on Seb's team and a rather unusual game of dominos began, while Ada and Ruthie cleared away the mugs and plates.

They were all still laughing and joking when Ruthie went to check on Lily. Up in the little bed she shared with Elsie, Ruthie found her tossing and turning.

"Are you not feeling well, Lily?" she asked.

"My head hurts. It hurts when I swallow too." Lily complained.

Ruthie laid a hand on the child's forehead and concluded that she certainly had a fever. What was she to do? She was glad Ada would know. "I'll get Mrs. Turley," she told Lily.

"Don't go, Auntie Ruthie," Lily pleaded.

Ruthie bent and hugged Lily close. "I'll be back before you know it. Mrs. Turley will know how to get your fever down."

Lily reluctantly allowed her to leave, and she hurried down the stairs, just in time to say goodbye to Seb, who was leaving along with Florence and Stella.

"Lily seems to have a fever," Ruthie told Ada with concern.

Eliza was already hurrying towards the stairs, Elsie close behind her.

Up in the bedroom, Ada confirmed that Lily indeed had a high temperature. "She's definitely caught something. Perhaps she got it from someone at school."

Overhearing her words, Eliza said, "Mary and Betty, who sit by Lily and Elsie, were off yesterday and the day before, David and Brian too. Do you think Lily has the same as them?"

"It's possible, yes. If Lily's no better tomorrow, we'll get the doctor to have a look at her. Do you know what's wrong with the others?"

Eliza shook her head. "Will she be alright? Lily always catches everything. I thought she was better now we were here."

"We'll take good care of her," Ada promised. "May be better if you go in with Elsie tonight, Eliza. It's no good you all catching it."

Ruthie lifted a now sleeping Lily into her own bed, while Eliza and Elsie got into the smaller one.

"Come and wake me if you need me," Ada told Ruthie. "Went through all sorts with both my boys."

Ruthie sat on the bed beside Lily. How had the little girl become so unwell in such a short space of time? She should have known earlier that something was wrong. According to Eliza, Lily had been doing so much better since they'd moved to the country. Ruthie should have kept a closer eye on her. What would it do to Eddie if anything happened to Lily? Ruthie had to believe he was still out there somewhere. And what about Eliza? She and Lily were so close. Ruthie knew she'd do whatever she could for Lily. The little girl who had accepted and loved a complete stranger without hesitation meant a great deal to her. Yes, she loved her as if she were her own child. She loved Lily as she loved Eliza.

19

Ruthie didn't dare sleep that night. She did all she could to bring Lily's fever down, but by the morning, Lily was no better. In fact, she was much worse.

Eliza and Elsie went to chapel with Bill and Ada, running straight home afterwards to check how Lily was.

The doctor called during the afternoon, and confirmed Lily had scarlet fever. By evening, it was clear that Elsie was also coming down with it.

"Seems like half the school got it," Ada commented with a sigh.

When Seb arrived the following morning to do his usual work before school, it was evident that he was also unwell. Bill sent him straight home, and Ada insisted on walking with him, to make sure the maid knew how to take care of him.

Ruthie didn't leave the girls once during the next several days, and Eliza also insisted on helping to care for them. Ruthie was extremely glad of her help, especially when she also began to feel unwell. She hid her discomfort for as long as possible, but finally had to give in and climb into bed next to Lily.

As she lay there, Ruthie was aware of Eliza's love. Her daughter often prayed quietly when she thought they were all sleeping. Ruthie wondered if she'd imagined it the first time Eliza asked the Lord to heal her mother and sister, but after hearing the same prayer so many times, Ruthie knew she'd heard right.

Elsie was the first to recover, and Ruthie was glad when she also felt able to get up and about again.

“It’s only usually the young ones who get it,” Ada said with some surprise.

“I don’t think I had it as a child,” Ruthie told her. Ruthie didn’t understand why some people got it, while others didn’t, but she was relieved that Eliza had stayed healthy.

Once again, Ruthie took over caring for Lily. She was concerned with how weak the little girl still was after more than two weeks. Ruthie found herself praying constantly for the child, pleading that if anyone had to go to be with the Lord, it would be her, not Lily. She now felt strangely closer to God. Something had changed within her, and she believed Jesus loved her, despite all she’d done. She was unable to pinpoint the moment it had happened, but during the hours spent by Lily’s side, Ruthie had prayed like never before, and now she was experiencing a closeness to God.

Word came that Seb too was taking some time to recover, but he at least was slowly on the mend.

It was the end of the following week when Ada saw the telegram boy hurrying towards the house in the afternoon. Not Joe, please, Lord, not Joe, she prayed. However, the telegram was for Ruthie. She wondered what message it would bring. Surely it was news of Eddie, but would it be good or bad?

Ada was glad Eliza and Elsie were in the other room. She walked slowly upstairs and into the bedroom where Lily was sleeping, Ruthie sitting close by her side. “Ruthie, it seems you have some news about Eddie.”

Ruthie jumped to her feet and crossed the room to take the envelope from Ada. Her hands shook as she opened it, taking out the single sheet of paper.

Ada held her breath, watching Ruthie’s face as she read.

"He's alive!" Ruthie almost squealed. "Eddie's alive! He's back in England too!"

"Praise the Lord!" Ada exclaimed. "What an answer to prayer."

Ruthie's expression changed to one of disbelief before she said, "He's been hurt."

Lily's voice came weakly from the bed. "Auntie Ruthie, what is it?"

"Oh Lily! Such wonderful news!" Ruthie rushed to Lily's side and gathered her into her arms. "Your dad's been found. He's alive! He's back here, in England!"

"Is he coming here?" Lily enquired.

Ruthie hesitated, "He won't be coming for a little while, as he needs to get better first. He will come as soon as he can, I'm sure." Moving to the door, she called, "Eliza, Elsie! We have good news!"

The girls hurried up the stairs and into the room. "Is Lily better?" Elsie asked hopefully.

"I'm sure this news will help her get better," Ruthie smiled. "Eliza, it's Eddie, your dad. He's alive and back in the country."

"Really?" Eliza's smile couldn't have been wider.

"Really." Ruthie hugged her tightly.

"Is he coming here?" Eliza asked, as Lily had only minutes before.

Ruthie sat down on the edge of the bed and Eliza sat next to her. "They said your dad was hurt. That's why they didn't know where he was for so long. He's being looked after in a hospital right now, but there will be a letter coming soon to tell us more," she explained.

"Can we see him?" Eliza asked eagerly.

Oh, how Ruthie wanted to go straightaway to Eddie. She'd hardly dared to hope that she might be with him again. She'd thought it would be enough just to know he was alive. Now she couldn't wait to see him face to face, but she couldn't go anywhere yet. Lily needed her right now. Ruthie had been afraid she wouldn't know how to care for Lily, but it had come naturally to her. "Not yet," she told Eliza. "As soon as they say we can, and Lily is better, we will."

"They may not let the girls into a hospital," Ada said quietly.

"I suppose that makes sense. Let's pray he'll soon be out of hospital." Ruthie was thoughtful.

"Will you still go and see him, even if me and Lily aren't allowed?" Eliza asked.

Ruthie wanted nothing more than to visit Eddie. She thought carefully before answering, "Yes, I'll see him when I can. I can tell him all about what you and Lily have been doing. You can write letters to him as well."

Ruthie spent another sleepless night beside Lily, but the following day, the little girl seemed to have improved slightly.

"We'll soon see Dad!" Eliza kept telling her. "You have to get better, Lily."

Ruthie was relieved when Lily at last seemed more aware of her surroundings. At her worst, she hadn't known if it was her mam, Eliza, or Ruthie caring for her. She often cried for one or another of them, then didn't seem to know who was holding her.

Only a few months ago, Ruthie knew nothing about looking after children, but she couldn't fool herself into thinking that she'd become Eliza and Lily's mother. When Eddie came home, he would take the girls back and probably marry someone else. She wondered about the extent of his injuries. Would he be going back to fight? Or would his days in the army be over? She found herself hoping he wouldn't have to return to the army, then realised that would mean he had some sort of really bad injury.

What if he'd lost a leg, like Toby? She shivered at the recollection of Toby. No matter how many legs he had, Eddie would be nothing like Toby. Maybe he would have lost an arm, or have an injury to his face. Whatever it was, she would still love him. She would always love Eddie, but he would never know. He'd married Lizzie, sweet, gentle, Lizzie. She herself was nothing like Lizzie. She'd given up any hope of a life with Eddie when she'd pushed him away all those years ago.

A thought suddenly struck her. What if he wanted nothing to do with her once he was home? She'd served her purpose in looking after his daughters. It would serve her right if he pushed her away, as she had him. She couldn't imagine life without Eddie or the girls.

After several more days, Lily was able to come downstairs for a short while each morning. The other girls were back in school and Seb, who was now much better, had come to the farm to play the piano. His father had insisted he not return to the classroom, as the school was to blame for him catching scarlet fever. Seb had been eager to help on the farm again, but Bill insisted he must regain his strength first. They all doubted Seb had told his father he was doing manual labour.

Lily sat in one of the large chairs, watching Seb at the piano. He played his classical pieces, along with familiar hymns. He also played other simple songs, which he taught Lily to sing. Her voice was weak as she sang, but she held the tune perfectly.

After they'd finished, Seb declared Lily had the voice of an angel!

"She has the looks, and the name too!" Ruthie smiled.

Seb looked down at the child. She was still very pale, but her blonde hair glistened as the sun shone through the window. "Lily is rather an angelic name," he agreed.

"Liliana Grace," Ruthie informed him. "That's the name her mother chose."

"Well, Liliana Grace," Seb smiled down at her, "I never heard you sing before when all the others were here. I do believe you should sing in our next concert."

"Me?" Lily questioned, her eyes widening.

"Yes, you."

"Not on my own?"

"I'll be right there, playing the piano for you. You have a think about it. You are just what the village needs to raise their spirits."

"That's a wonderful idea!" Ada agreed. "Perhaps you can get something ready, you know, for when your dad comes home. You could do a concert here, as a sort of practice."

A hint of a smile crossed Lily's face. "I'd like that," she said. "I like being called Liliana Grace, too."

Ruthie was glad Seb and Ada had given Lily a reason to regain her strength. It had seemed that all the fight had gone out of her, but already her eyes seemed brighter.

Lily soon tired and Ruthie carried her back up to bed. When she returned downstairs, she thanked Seb. "You've given her something to work towards," she told him. "You're just what she needed."

"Really? I never had brothers or sisters, or any other children to play with," Seb admitted. "I rather like Lily, Eliza and Elsie too. Even Florence and Stella in a funny sort of way. I've never had friends before. All of you are my friends now."

"And we are glad to have you as our friend," Ada told him. "You're one of us now, my boy!"

"I rather like that!" Seb exclaimed. "Those farm hands have stopped sending me after things which don't exist anymore, too! I enjoy living in the country! I just wish Mother could be here, not in that awful place Father sent her to."

"We will keep praying for her," Ada told him.

"Father said God wasn't real," Seb spoke thoughtfully. "Just something for the weak to cling to. But I'm now wondering whether he might be wrong! You and Mr. Turley believe in God, and you are the strongest people I know! I'm afraid Father seems to be wrong about many things. And you know, I don't even mind if he disinherits me! He sent me to the country as a punishment of sorts, but it's the best thing he ever did!"

Neither Ada nor Ruthie knew how to answer Seb, but both blinked back their tears.

"It seems Seb was as lonely as I was before coming here," Ruthie said to Ada later that afternoon. "I would never have thought it though, not when I first met him. I always thought those with money had it all."

"Money can't buy love, nor happiness," Ada agreed.

It was the following morning that the postman brought more news of Eddie. Ruthie tried not to let her hands shake as she seated herself in the rocking chair to read his letter. Something was wrong, she could tell by the envelope. This wasn't Eddie's writing. She'd know his writing anywhere.

"What is it?" Ada asked.

"It's not Eddie's writing," Ruthie stated. "I'm almost afraid to read what's inside. What if he's so badly injured that he can't write for himself?"

"It's possible, but there's no guarantee he'll stay that way. Perhaps his hands were badly burnt or something.

Best thing to do is to read it. Then we can pray and ask for guidance."

Ruthie smiled at Ada's sensible and practical approach. If only she could be as Ada was. The Turleys were still obviously sad at the loss of John, as well as being concerned for Joe, but it didn't consume them. Please Lord, help me deal with whatever is in this letter, Ruthie prayed silently, before she opened the envelope, took out the paper and read.

"Dear Ruthie, by now, you will know that I am alive. I'm not really sure how true that is. It would have been better if I'd not survived. I can't write to you myself, as I can't see. The explosion caused me to go blind. I am no use to my girls anymore. They are talking of sending me to a place in Shropshire, where I can learn to do things without my eyes, but it's no use. Tell Eliza and Lily that I died after all. I don't want them to see me like this. I don't want anyone to see me like this. When I asked you to look after them, I knew you would love them and do what's best for them. Now I need you to help them forget me. They need more than I can give them. They need you. I'll continue to send money, but they don't need to know where it comes from. Please do this for me, Ruthie. Your friend, Eddie."

Ruthie felt sick. She hadn't expected this. This wasn't Eddie. What was she going to do? She knew what she wouldn't do. There was no way she would tell the girls that their father was dead. How could he say he didn't want to see them?

"What did he say, Ruthie? You're as white as a sheet!" Ada stood over her.

Ruthie was unable to speak, so handed her the letter. She covered her face with her hands and let the tears fall.

After reading, Ada let out a long sigh. "I didn't see this coming," she said honestly. "What are you going to do?"

"I'll not tell the girls he's dead. I'll wait until we know where he is, then I'll go to talk some sense into him. I won't let him do this, I won't! The girls need him, and he needs them. I'll make him see that! Having him home is what's best for them, whether he can see or not."

"Good for you," Ada smiled. "Maybe seeing you, or rather, hearing your voice, will be just what he needs. We'll help you in whatever way we can."

20

"Auntie Ruthie, where are you going?"

"I've got to go and speak to someone about something. I'll be back this evening."

"But you never go away all day. You will come back, won't you?"

Ruthie bent to hug Lily. "Of course I'll come back, and Auntie Ada will be here with you all day. You can help her in the kitchen."

"But you never said you were going before Eliza and Elsie went to school."

"I don't suppose I did. Now, Seb is going to teach you the piano again today. I expect you'll learn some more songs too. You'll be back at school soon, so you make the most of your music lessons. We want to see Liliana Grace on the stage."

"I have to do the practice concert when Dad comes home first. When will he come, Auntie Ruthie? Does he have to stay in hospital much longer?"

"I'm sure he'll come home soon. Now, I must go. See you later, Lily."

Ruthie hurried from the room, picking up her bag as she passed the table. She called goodbye to Ada, then left the house almost at a run.

It had been harder than she'd thought to leave Lily, but she knew the little girl was in safe hands with Ada. During the time the girls had been unwell, the Turleys had insisted Eliza, Lily, and Elsie call them Auntie Ada and Uncle Bill. "You're like family," Ada had said. Ruthie knew they cared for them all as though they were true relatives.

It had also been more difficult than Ruthie had imagined to not be truthful with Lily. She hadn't dared let on to Eliza that she'd be away all day, as Eliza was sure to suspect that it had something to do with their father. She hadn't expected so many questions from the usually quieter Lily.

So far, the girls didn't know about Eddie's blindness. She thought about telling them, but then Eliza would have wanted to read the letter she'd received from him. There was no way they would ever know that Eddie didn't want to see them. If Ruthie had her way today, she'd change his mind about that.

Ruthie had found out the name of the place Eddie was being sent to for rehabilitation. She'd then gone to the post office and called them every day, until they confirmed Eddie had arrived. She had also been told that he was refusing visitors, but she wasn't taking any notice of that.

Ruthie didn't have to wait long for the train. She found herself a seat in a mostly deserted carriage and set off on the first leg of her journey.

As soon as the train left the village, some of Ruthie's old fears returned. She hadn't realised how safe she'd felt over the last few months. She would never have imagined moving away from Cardiff, but was now certain she would never go back to a city to live. She'd found home, real home, in the country, with Bill and Ada Turley, along with Eliza, Lily, and Elsie. There, she felt safe and protected.

It was past dinner time when Ruthie finally reached her destination. She hurried from the station and followed the directions she'd been given.

Arriving at the building, she rang the bell. The door was opened by a man with severe scarring on his face and no eyes at all. Ruthie wondered if Eddie would look anything like him.

"I've come to visit Eddie Davies," Ruthie announced, doing her best to sound more confident than she felt.

"Oh yes, he's new here. I didn't think he wanted to see anyone."

"He'll see me," Ruthie said with determination.

"What shall I tell him your name is?"

"Ruthie Lewis. Tell him I must speak to him urgently. It concerns his daughters."

The man led Ruthie to a small side room, then left to find Eddie. It was some time before he reappeared. "I'm sorry," he said. "He insists he won't see you. Some men get like that, you know."

"Well," Ruthie spoke with forced courage, "I insist I must see him. Please pass on that message."

As the man left the room once more, Ruthie had an idea. Walking on tiptoes, she hurried after him. He won't know I'm behind him, she thought.

Along a corridor they went, through a door, then down another corridor. They passed several men on the way, but no one took any notice of her.

Ruthie thought she detected a smile on the man's face as he turned and knocked on a door.

"I said I'm not seeing anyone!"

Ruthie recognised Eddie's voice immediately, but he sounded more angry than she'd ever heard before.

"The lady insists she must see you," the man called through the door.

"I said no. Tell her to go home and forget I'm still alive."

Ruthie walked up beside the man. "Eddie Davies, you open this door now!" she demanded.

There was a chuckle from the man beside her, before he said, "You'll have to go quieter than you did just then, if you want to follow without being heard."

So, he knew I was there all along, Ruthie thought, before she turned the knob and opened the door. "I'll open it myself then!" she announced, marching into the room.

"I told you…"

"I know what you told me, Eddie, but I'm not taking any notice. Now, you listen to me. Eliza and Lily need you."

"I'm no good to them anymore. Can't you see that?"

Ruthie looked fully at Eddie, where he lay on the bed. He had bandages around his face and hands, and he appeared to have lost a great deal of weight.

"I see you, Eddie, and I know you can do whatever you put your mind to. The girls really need you."

"I told you to tell them I was dead."

"I'm not doing that."

"Do they know you're here?"

"No. I'm not telling them about that letter you got someone to write to me. I'll tell them when I get back tonight that you are as eager to see them as they are to see you."

"Ruthie! I'm telling you…"

"Lily had scarlet fever, you know."

"Is she alright?" Ruthie noticed the concern in Eddie's voice and wondered if there might be hope after all.

"We were afraid we were going to lose her, but she's slowly getting over it now," she said truthfully.

"And Eliza? Did she catch it?"

"No. She was fine. She helped me look after Lily, then helped look after me too when I caught it."

"You got it too?" Eddie sounded shocked and concerned.

"Yes. I got over it alright though. Lily wants to do a concert for you when you get home."

"You'll have to tell her that won't be happening."

"No, Eddie. You need to come home. So much has happened."

"What do you mean?"

Ruthie glanced back at the man who had led her to Eddie's room, still standing near the open door. Deciding she had no choice but to go on, Ruthie said, "Eliza knows the truth. She looked in the family Bibles, Lizzie's, and mine. She needs you, Eddie, she needs her father."

"How…? We agreed…"

"It's a long story, but she's coming to terms with it all. Eliza needs you, Eddie. They both do."

"I can't."

"You can, Eddie. You've always been strong."

"You were the strong one. I just took the easy options."

"You are strong. The girls need you."

"I can't be any use to them now. I'll never work in a factory again."

"Maybe not, but you can work on the farm."

"Me? On a farm?" Eddie almost laughed.

"I've learnt, and so can you. Bill Turley says there's work waiting for you."

"I don't know anything about farming."

"Then you can learn. They will teach you that here."

"How do you know that?"

"I asked a lot of questions, when I phoned to find out if you had arrived."

"Why, Ruthie? I broke my promise to you, then dragged you away from all you've ever known to look after my girls. Do you want to go back to Cardiff? Is that what it is? Don't you want to stay with them?"

"I love those girls, Eddie, both of them. You did me a favour by taking me away from Cardiff. I want to thank you for that. I'll do everything I can for Eliza and Lily, but they need you as well. Where's the Eddie Davies I knew years ago? He wouldn't give up on anything."

"He got blown up, lost his eyes, and will never be the same again."

"But the same Eddie is still in there. You have to fight, Eddie. Fight to get your life back. I'm not giving up on you now."

"I have no life. What good am I to my girls? I'll never see them grow up."

"You may not see them, but you can hear Lily sing. She's been practicing. Seb is teaching her the piano, too. And Eliza needs to talk to you. She doesn't know all the details, but she knows enough. They are both growing up, Eddie, and they need you. I've brought letters from them." Ruthie reached into her bag.

"Shall I find you some tea?" the man in the doorway asked.

"Please," Ruthie said, before Eddie had a chance to answer.

She opened out the first letter and sat down in the chair next to the bed. "This is from Lily," she began. "Dear Dad, I really miss you. I'm glad you're not dead, like Mr. and Mrs. Turley's son John. I hope you don't have to go to the war again. I want you to come home. Elsie, who lives with us, doesn't have a mum or a dad, so I said she could pretend you were her dad, too. Elsie is my friend. I'm learning to play the piano. Seb is teaching me, and he wants me to sing in a concert with him. He calls me Liliana Grace. Lots of love from Lily."

Ruthie hesitated only a moment before opening Eliza's letter. "Dear Dad, I miss you, and can't wait for you to be with us again. I know you've been hurt, and I hope you will soon be better. I like living here and you will too. Lily got scarlet fever, and I was really frightened. I kept praying for her and now she's getting better. Auntie Ruthie is looking after us. I know who she is now. You are still my dad though. Please write back soon. Love from Eliza."

"It's no good," Eddie sighed. "What will they think when they know I'm no use anymore?"

"They won't. You and Lizzie brought them up better than that. They just want you home, Eddie. I was serious about you working on the farm."

"You need to leave, Ruthie." Eddie's voice was quiet now. "This is all too much."

Ruthie had tears in her eyes as she reached out and put a hand on his arm. "I'll leave now, if you insist, but I'll be back. I'm going to tell the girls the truth as well."

As Ruthie turned to leave the room, she saw Eddie's shoulders shaking. Please Lord, she prayed silently, help him realise his life is worth living.

21

By the time Ruthie got off the train in the village, it was well past dark. Rain had been falling for the last couple of hours. Heavy rain, which seemed to blow at her in sheets as she made her way towards home.

The Turley farm really did feel like home now. If only Eddie would come, he'd feel it too. He'd realise how happy Eliza and Lily were, and that would surely help him recover, Ruthie thought, as she trudged along the muddy roads.

Ruthie had planned to be home hours before, but first she'd missed the train, then they'd been held up because of an air-raid. She had no idea of the time, but suspected it was past midnight.

Eventually, the turning to the farm came into sight. As she walked up the driveway, she wondered what would have gone through their minds when she hadn't come home as promised. Lily had been afraid she wouldn't come back, and her being so late would have most likely made her fears resurface. Eliza would certainly have questions. Ruthie decided she was going to tell them as much of the truth as possible, but was glad she wouldn't have to do it until the morning.

She was surprised to find a light on in the kitchen as she quietly opened the door.

"There you are. You must be soaked!" Ada came rushing towards her.

"You're still up! What's wrong? Is it Lily?" Ruthie gabbled, her teeth chattering as her whole body began to shake.

"I wasn't about to go to bed with you still out there on a night like this. Bill went to the station to meet the train, but it didn't come. Everyone is alright here. Come on, sit down and warm up."

Ruthie allowed Ada to take off her dripping coat and lead her to the chair, which had been pulled up close to the fire. It was warmer inside the house, so why was she shaking like this?

There was a noise from above, followed by hurried footsteps on the stairs. The three girls raced into the room, soon followed by Bill.

"Auntie Ruthie! I thought you weren't coming back!" Lily launched herself into Ruthie's arms.

"Come on, Lily, I told you she'd be back. Let her catch her breath a bit before you start climbing all over her," Ada spoke gently but firmly.

Ruthie settled Lily on her lap and wrapped her arms tightly around her. "I'm sorry I was so late, Lily. I didn't mean to frighten you. The train got delayed and there was nothing I could do."

Eliza stood close by Ruthie's side as she asked, "Where did you go?"

"You can leave the questions until tomorrow," Ada told her.

"It's alright." Ruthie reached out and drew Eliza down onto the arm of the chair. "I'll tell you all about it. I can see no one will sleep tonight unless I do."

"Where can I sit?" Elsie asked, putting her thumb into her mouth sulkily.

"There's enough room for you up here, Elsie. You can all warm me up!"

Elsie climbed up into the chair and settled herself, while Bill and Ada took seats opposite Ruthie.

"Eliza, Lily," Ruthie began, "I went to visit your dad."

"Is he coming home?" Lily squealed.

"Not yet. Now, let me start from the beginning. You know he was hurt in the war? Well, it seems his eyes were severely damaged. I'm afraid your dad can't see. He's blind."

"Blind?" Eliza questioned. "Dad's blind?"

"I'm afraid so. He's staying somewhere where they can help him do things without seeing. There are a lot of blind people there. They can do most things we can do. They teach them to make things out of wood, or do gardening, or look after animals."

"Seb said a blind man used to… make the piano have the right notes." Lily struggled to explain.

"Yes, I heard some blind people tune pianos." Ruthie smiled down at her.

"Will dad do that?" Lily asked.

"I don't think so. It would be good if he learnt to work on a farm, and maybe grow vegetables."

"Then he could come and live here!" Elsie bounced enthusiastically. "Lily said I can share her dad, because I don't have one."

"When will he come?" Eliza questioned quietly.

"Well, he has a lot to learn first. Remember, he has only recently been hurt. He has to learn to do all sorts of things again, like walking around and finding things."

"I'll help him!" Lily said. "I'll show him where things are."

"But how will he do it?" Eliza asked with concern. "How will he know where anything is? How will he find his way to places? What if he falls over things?" Tears filled her eyes.

"It will be difficult for him until he's used to it, but he will learn. A man who couldn't see anything at all opened the door to me and took me to your dad. He knew where to go, and which was his room. Your dad will have to do things differently, but he can do it. I think he will use a stick to find where things are. That's something else he will have to learn."

"How long will it take?" Eliza sobbed.

"I don't know, Eliza. He's very sad at the moment that he can't do the things he used to do."

"When can we see him?" Eliza continued her questioning.

"I don't know that either. We must all write lots of letters to him."

"But he won't see them!" Eliza sniffed.

"No, but someone will read them to him."

"Why can't we go now? I mean, not now in the middle of the night, but tomorrow?"

When Ruthie didn't answer immediately, Eliza continued, "Doesn't he want to see us?"

"Eddie loves you girls more than anything!" Ruthie said quickly. "He just needs a bit of time to get used to things."

"But you saw him," Eliza stated.

"He wasn't too happy about me turning up there, but I read him your letters. I didn't post them, I took them with me. He's glad you are getting better after the scarlet fever, Lily, and I told him how much help you were to us both, Eliza. He was happy to know you are both doing well."

"I want Dad. I want him to come home. Me and Seb will do music for him and make him happy again." Lily buried her face in Ruthie's shoulder.

"I think it's time you girls got some sleep." Ada got to her feet and caught Elsie's hand, while Bill came and lifted Lily into his arms.

When they had left the kitchen, Eliza slid down into the chair with Ruthie and clung tightly to her. "What if he never comes back? What if he doesn't want us anymore?"

"He loves you, Eliza. I think he's just feeling..." Ruthie struggled to find the right words. "I think he's feeling like he won't be a good father, now he's blind."

"But he is! He's the best!"

"I know, so we'll have to keep telling him that. It will be alright, Eliza, we just have to give him time."

"I just want to see him. It doesn't matter if he can't see me."

"We'll pray. God can help him realise we need him here."

"Auntie Ruthie," Eliza hesitated before continuing, "if he does come back, will you still stay here?"

"There's nowhere else I'd rather be." Ruthie did her best to reassure her. "I love you and Lily. I want to be wherever you girls are."

"Will... will Dad be angry that I know the truth? Will he still want me, now he doesn't have to pretend he's my dad anymore?"

"Oh Eliza! Of course he still wants you. Your dad loves you as much as he loves Lily. I hope you don't mind, but I told him how you learnt the truth."

"Was he angry that I looked in the Bibles?"

"He wasn't angry with you at all. He loves you, remember that."

"Sometimes I feel like... well, that I'm not being fair to Mam."

"How do you mean?"

"I still think of her all the time, and I still love her, but I'm glad you are my mam and I love you as well. Do you think she would be angry with me? God might be angry as well."

"I didn't know Lizzie well, but I don't think she'd be angry. She loved you and Lily so much. I don't reckon God would be angry, either. He loves us all, doesn't he? I mean, he loves everyone in the world, and that's a lot of people, isn't it?"

"Yes, I suppose it is."

"So, if God can love us all, and he's the one who shows us how to love, I think he could make it that you can love more than one mother. You don't have to choose, Eliza."

Eliza held onto Ruthie tightly as she asked, "Can I just do it once?"

"What is it you want to do?"

"Could I call you Mum? Just once, while we're on our own? I mean… people in England say mum, don't they? So I could have a mam, and a mum."

"I'd like that." Ruthie could hardly speak through her tears.

"I love you, Mum!" Eliza said quickly, before wrapping her arms more tightly around Ruthie.

"And I love you, Eliza. I couldn't wish for a better daughter."

The two of them ascended the stairs, where Eliza climbed back into bed. Lily and Elsie were already sleeping soundly in the little bed nearby. Ruthie undressed and got in next to Eliza. The shaking was gradually subsiding. She'd never experienced anything like it before. It was as if once she'd got home, all the tension from the day came out. In a way, she was glad she'd got all the questions over with tonight. She knew there would be more, but felt she could answer them now. The hardest bit had been telling the girls their father was blind. Now they just had to convince him they still wanted and needed him at the farm. If only he knew how much.

22

"Seb, tell me a story about the blind man who used to make the notes right on your piano," Lily urged.

Seb shifted awkwardly on the kitchen chair, before he began, "Well, I didn't know him that well, Lily. Father didn't like me being in the room when the piano tuner was there, but let me think. I did speak to him sometimes. He would have a man with him who could drive him from house to house. Father said he was the best piano tuner around. I used to listen outside the window when he was tuning it. It took a dreadfully long time. One day I sneezed. It was awfully loud. He asked who was there, so I said it was me. I told him I only wanted to watch him tune the piano, and I hoped he didn't mind."

"What did he say?" Lily's eyes were wide.

"He said, 'Come on in, boy, and I'll show you how it's done'."

"Did you go in?"

"I did. I thought Father would say it was rude not to, since the piano tuner had asked me specifically. It was truly fascinating. When he'd finished, he began to play. The music was just splendid! Do you know what? He asked me to play as well."

"What did you do?"

"Well, I played. And would you believe it, he began playing along with me."

"You both played the piano? Like when you teach me?"

"Well, a bit like that, but I thought I should impress him, so I played the most difficult piece I knew. That's what Father would expect. And he knew that piece, too. I've never experienced anything quite like it since."

"Will Dad play the piano like that now he's blind?"

Seb smiled. "It takes a lot of years to play like that, Liliana Grace. Does your father enjoy music?"

"Oh, Dad used to sing, all the time."

"When he comes home, the two of you can sing together."

"When will he come, Seb?"

Seb was saved from answering her question, as the door burst open and Eliza, Elsie, Florence, and Stella hurried into the kitchen.

"Stella has to go home!" Elsie blurted out.

"You mean to London?" Seb looked shocked.

"Yeah. Back to bloomin' London with all its bombs and bedbugs. Don't see why I've gotta go. Me mum says I 'ave to go to work now, not school. I was just getting to like it an' all."

"When do you go?" Ada brought a plate of bread and dripping to the table and handed it around.

"Next week! I don't wanna go. I could run away and hide somewhere."

"I'm sure your mother is missing you," Ada said.

"Missin' the stuff I pinched from the market more like. The others were never as good as me."

"You can't do that! It's wrong to steal!" Elsie's eyes widened in surprise.

"Only the stuff they were chuckin' out!" Stella said defensively.

"Mum used to say that the people who nicked stuff from the markets were…"

"I'm sure Stella won't do it again, will you, Stella?" Ada interrupted Elsie.

"Well, if we're 'ungry, I'll 'ave to. Mum said I 'ad to come 'ere, so there was one less mouth to feed, so unless she's got rid of the rest of the kids, I suppose we'll be 'ungry."

"I don't have to go back to London, do I?" Elsie looked concerned.

"No. You're staying here with us, my girl," Ada told her.

"'Ow do you make your bread better than Mam's?" Florence enquired.

"You better not let her hear you say that," Ada smiled. "Want another piece, do you, Florence?"

"Can I? Thanks Mrs. Turley." Florence helped herself to another huge slice and took a bite. "I'll 'ave my room back to meself, but it will be funny without you there, Stella."

"You could come and see me in London, Flo!" Stella exclaimed.

"No! I don't want bedbugs!" Florence replied around another mouthful of bread. "And my name's Florence, not Flo, or Floss."

"Do you have to go home to your mum, Seb?" Elsie asked.

"I'm afraid I won't be seeing my mother any time soon. I do hope Father doesn't send for me, though."

"Do you know where your mother is?" Eliza questioned.

"Yes, but I'm not allowed to see her."

"What!" Stella snorted. "Says who?"

"Father, of course."

"That mean old bug… Sorry Mrs. Turley. Seb, why do you 'ave to listen to 'im?"

"Because… well, because he's Father, I suppose."

"That's stupid! You're almost old enough to go to the war. You can't let him tell you who you can and can't see."

"I'm not old enough for another couple of years yet," Seb insisted.

"Well, some pretend they're older than they are. Everyone knows that!" Stella snapped. "You 'ave to see her, Seb. What if where she is gets bombed or something?"

"Father said the institution she is in is right out of the way, so it shouldn't be a target for the Germans."

"Where is she? Where is the place?" Stella leaned forward eagerly.

"It's in Wales."

"We lived in Wales," Lily smiled up at him.

"We should look on Mr. Turley's map to see where it is!" Stella spoke quickly. "You know, to make sure it's not somewhere the Germans want to bomb."

"What you going to do if they are going to bomb it?" Florence asked.

"Shut up, Flo, and don't be so bloomin' daft. I just think Seb ought to know what kind of a place his mum's living in. Mrs. Turley, can we 'ave a look at Mr. Turley's map, please? It's kind of like doing school work, ain't it? I mean, learning about places."

"Yes Stella, I suppose it is. I'll go and get you the map now."

Soon, they were all studying the map and talking excitedly about the place in Wales where Seb's mother was now living. After only a few minutes, Lily and Elsie lost interest and went to play with their rag dolls. Then, a short time later, Eliza decided she should help outside on the farm, and Florence left for home, leaving Seb and Stella studying together.

Ada smiled to herself as she made her way outside to pick a cabbage for tea. It wouldn't be quite the same without Stella. Despite her upbringing, the girl had fitted in well. Life would seem quite dull without her. She would never be forgotten and Ada knew she would continue to pray for her, especially once she was back in London.

***

"So, what do you reckon, then? Is that a plan?"

"I say, Stella, I really don't know about all this."

"What's not to know?"

"Well, Father will be terribly angry."

"You said 'e don't go there, so 'ow's 'e gonna know?"

"Father knows everything."

"What's the worst 'e can do, beat you?"

"Father doesn't beat me, because people would ask questions. He might send me away. He might lock me up, like Mother."

"'E can't do that! Come on Seb, this could be your only chance. You gotta do it. I'll come with ya. 'E can't be mad with me, 'cos I'll be gone anyway. She'll think you don't care if you don't do it. 'Ow would you like it?"

"I don't suppose I would. Are you really sure, Stella?"

"Course I am. Don't be scared, Seb, it'll be alright. I know just what we gotta do. You leave it to me."

"Well, if you're absolutely certain."

"'Ow many times do I 'ave to tell ya! Trust me, Seb. You seen the time? I'd better go! Florence will 'ave eaten my bloomin' tea as well as 'ers else!"

"I say! It is getting late, isn't it? I'd better be going as well."

"You make sure to hold on to that bit of paper, mind!" Stella wagged her finger at him as she headed for the door.

Seb refolded the map tidily, then said goodbye to Mrs. Turley and the younger girls. He crossed the yard and called to Mr. Turley, Ruthie and Eliza, before heading off down the driveway, whistling as he went. You know, he thought to himself, if I were a girl, I would skip right now, like Lily and Elsie do.

23

"Where's Stella?" Eliza asked as she met Florence in their usual meeting place for their walk to school.

"I don't know. I thought she might have come to your house for something, because she wasn't at 'ome. She didn't even 'ave breakfast."

"She never came to our place this morning," Eliza said thoughtfully.

"Seb didn't come either!" Elsie put in, before running ahead to meet some other younger girls.

"She's right. Seb has been helping on the farm again in the mornings, and he didn't turn up today."

"'Er's got my coat and all. My winter one! I reckon 'er's gone daft, 'cos it's summer now and 'er's gonna be 'ot."

"Your coat? That will be too big for Stella!"

"What you saying, Eliza?"

"Sorry Florence, I didn't mean that. I just meant, why would she take your coat when she has one of her own?"

"Why does Stella do anything?" Florence grumbled.

"What did your mum and dad say?"

"They said she's being silly, because she has to go 'ome to London."

"But Seb has gone too. You don't think…?"

"What? They can't run off and get married, they aren't old enough!"

"No, silly! Seb wouldn't marry Stella! I mean, do you think they might have gone to see Seb's mother?"

"Oh!" Florence stopped in her tracks and turned fully to face Eliza. "They might. They were talking about where it was and looking at the map. Stella doesn't 'ave any money."

"Seb does. His father gives him an allowance."

"Then they might've gone. What we gonna do?"

"Nothing. We can't say anything to anyone. Just say Stella isn't well when we get to school."

"What about Elsie?"

"She won't say anything," Eliza reassured her.

***

"Cor, Seb! We did it! Excitin' ain't it!"

"We have indeed got onto the right train, without being discovered. I do believe we might actually pull this off after all."

"You didn't think I could do it, did ya?"

"I'd say it's an exceptionally good plan, Stella. Why do you have Florence's coat on, though?"

"Never mind that. Perhaps I'll look a bit older in it."

"It's too big for you."

"Give it a rest, Seb! What's it matter what I got on!" Stella turned towards the window for several minutes, before she turned back to Seb and asked, "What's your mum like?"

"She's the kindest person I know. You'll just love her, Stella."

"So why's she shut in that place?"

"Because she knew what Father was up to, and he didn't want her to tell anyone."

"So 'e 'ad 'er shut in there to keep 'er quiet?"

"Yes, I'd say that was about right."

"Why didn't she just tell 'im where to go?"

"No one tells my father where to go. He does the telling."

"So," Stella was thoughtful, "she doesn't get angry then?"

"No. The only times she got angry were when she found out what Father was doing, and also when they came to take her away."

"What did she do?"

"Nothing. They just stuck a needle in her and she went quiet and kind of floppy, like Lily and Elsie's rag dolls."

"What's 'er name, anyway?" Stella enquired.

"Selena. It's a beautiful name, don't you think?"

The journey seemed to last for hours, and they were both glad that Stella had thought to bring some food along.

"I say, Stella, you do think of everything!" Seb stated, as he bit into a sandwich.

They finally reached their destination and stepped off the train. "What you like with directions?" Stella asked. "You gotta remember the way back to the station."

"I was jolly good at navigating and finding places. It's all rather an adventure, isn't it? I always wanted a real adventure. Did you ever have an adventure, Stella?"

"Lots!" Stella snorted. "None you'd approve of, though, I don't suppose. I'm serious, mind Seb, you need to remember the way."

"Of course. But we'll be coming back together, won't we?"

"Course, but I don't 'ave to do it all!"

They found the institution relatively easily. Staring up at the dingy building with its iron bars at the windows, Stella exclaimed, "Cor! It's worse than I thought! Looks like the work'ouse!" She stumbled dramatically and fell to her knees.

"I say! Stella! Are you alright?" Seb bent to help her up.

"Me ankle!" Stella wailed dramatically. "Reckon I broke it!"

"Perhaps there's someone who could look at it for you. I'll ask."

"No! Don't do that! They might keep me there. Just let me lean on you. You'll 'ave to 'old me up!"

With Seb's arm around Stella, they made their way to the imposing iron gates. When Seb announced they were there to see his mother, a young man who looked as though he'd rather be anywhere else, let them in without hesitation.

After ringing the bell beside the heavy oak door, they were greeted by a stern-looking woman, who eyed them warily when Seb stated he was visiting his mother.

"Name?" she demanded.

"I'm Sebastian Westfield," Seb spoke confidently.

"Your mother's name?" she barked.

"Selena Westfield."

"She is to have no visitors," the woman said before making to close the door.

Having already discussed this possibility with Stella, Seb stepped forward, preventing her from closing the door. "You didn't receive word from my father you were to make an exception? He will be furious when he hears you disallowed me to spend time with my mother, for what is likely to be the last time. He's sending me to relatives in Canada, you see."

"Orders are orders," the woman said.

Seb sighed dramatically. "Father will be displeased. In fact, he'll be enraged. He sent word to say you were to allow me in to see her. I suppose he'll be moving her to a more… suitable establishment after this."

The woman sighed and opened the door. "There have been problems with the phone lines, all due to the war, you see. It is possible that the message did not get through to us. I will trust your word, young man. You may see her for a short while. Only you though."

"But I 'ave to go with 'im! I'm 'is maid!" Stella exclaimed.

The woman looked skeptically at Stella, but Seb put in, "It's true. She must come with me."

"Maid?" the woman enquired.

"Ah!" Realising how it appeared with his arm around Stella, Seb explained, "She hurt her ankle as we arrived here."

"I see. Well, as I'm in a good mood, you can both go in for a few minutes."

The woman pulled the door open, indicating they enter the dingy building.

Stella glanced about her at the plain walls and dirty-looking stone floors. She didn't like the look, nor the smell of the place. She'd heard about asylums like this, but hoped she'd never have to enter one. Now she was on a mission to help her friend.

Stella noted each turn they made. They passed several closed doors, before one was opened and they were led into a dimly lit room.

A scream from elsewhere in the building caused the woman to shake her head in frustration. "I'll be back in a few minutes. You'll likely not get a word out of her." She hurried away, leaving the door open.

Stella quickly closed the door, before turning towards the bed, where Seb was bending over the frail-looking figure lying motionless under a thin blanket.

"Mother…" Seb's voice shook slightly.

The woman's eyes flickered before she looked straight at her son.

"Mother, it's me, Seb. I… I came to see you."

"Seb?" her voice was weak.

"Oh Mother! What has he done to you?"

Stella stepped forward and smiled down at the slight woman. "Hello Mrs. Westfield, I'm Stella, Seb's friend. Bloomin awful place this, ain't it? Don't worry though, we're gonna get you out."

"Stella! You can't say that! That's cruel!"

"I mean it Seb. We're takin' 'er 'ome!" She flung off her coat and glanced about the room. "Forgot bloomin' shoes, didn't I!" she exclaimed, before she bent down and took off her own.

"Stella, what are you doing?"

"Get these on 'er! Quick, before that old bat comes back. Then, take 'er, and go. Put the hood up on the coat and they won't know who you've got your arm around."

"But… what about you?"

"I'll find me way out!" Stella pulled back the blanket and put an arm under Selena Westfield's shoulders, lifting her into a sitting position and thrusting her arms into Florence's coat.

"Stella, you're crazy! What about your ankle?" Seb enquired, his mouth agape.

"Nothing wrong with it! Just 'ad to look like you were leavin' the same way you come in. Now, get over 'ere and 'elp me!"

24

"Come on in Florence. I didn't expect to see you tonight. Stella not with you? Eliza will be in now in a minute. How about a bit of bread to keep you going?" Ada slid a slice of buttered bread towards Florence, who took it and bit into it eagerly.

"Mam sent me round here to find out if you'd seen Seb," Florence explained around her mouthful.

"No. I meant to go around to the cottage to see if he was alright, but I've been busy today. I hope he hasn't come down with anything."

"We think 'im's gone with Stella." Florence took another bite of bread, before going on, "'Er disappeared this morning. 'Er took my coat and all!"

"Where would the two of them be?" Ada enquired.

"Did Stella come back?" Elsie burst into the room, followed by Lily. "Eliza said I mustn't say anything in school, but I'm home now, aren't I, Auntie Ada?"

"Yes, Elsie, you're home. Now start from the beginning. Where do you suppose Seb and Stella have gone?"

"To see Seb's mother!" Florence stated. "Though why Stella 'ad to take my coat, I don't know."

Eliza entered from outside and looked guiltily down at the ground.

"What do you know about this, Eliza?" Ada turned to her.

"I didn't, I mean, I don't, not really. Florence said this morning that Stella was missing, and I said Seb didn't come here today either, so we reckoned they must have gone to visit Seb's mam. They were looking at the map, so we just thought…"

Ruthie and Bill now joined them.

"Did I hear that right?" Bill asked in surprise.

"I reckon you did," Ada sighed. "Did you catch on to what they were up to, Bill? They were asking you a lot of questions."

"I didn't think much of it at the time, but now you come to mention it… I'd say our Seb has found his common sense at last."

"Bill! Watch what you're saying! 'Im and Stella have gone off across the country, to who knows where, to see his mother in a…"

"It's not that far away, it's in Wales," Bill explained calmly. "I say good for him!"

"And if they don't let him in? Then what?"

"Then he'll know he tried. By the sounds of it, she shouldn't be locked away."

"But Bill! Seb isn't used to being alone out in the world. You know what happened when he first came here? He might get lost or something."

"He's got Stella with him. No one's going to get one over on him with her there. I think those two will make a good job of it between them."

"I hope he gets to spend time with her," Ruthie sighed. "He'll be disappointed if he doesn't."

***

There were shrieks and screams coming from all directions as Stella raced unseen along the corridor. She hadn't expected that much of a reaction, she'd only wanted to make a bit of a distraction.

Bursting through a door, she found herself in a dimly lit kitchen. Everything's so bloomin' dingy, she thought, before she noticed three pairs of eyes turn towards her.

"I'm sorry," she explained, "I didn't know where else to come. Don't suppose you could let me out the back way, could ya? I 'ad to run, I did!"

"Is she…?" The older woman stared at Stella, her eyes coming to rest on her bare feet.

"Never seen her before," a younger girl shook her head. "And they're not taking on any new ones."

"I was visiting," Stella began quickly, "and then it all went mad! Someone attacked me and even took my shoes! There were two of 'em together! I didn't know what they'd do next, so I ran. Please let me out. I don't wanna go back in there!"

"Go on," the older woman, whom Stella presumed to be the cook, shooed her towards the door. "We've got work to do."

Stella ran in the direction she'd pointed. She passed through a scullery, and then let herself out the back door. She allowed herself to sigh with relief before realising she was still fenced in.

After a quick scan of the high walls, she realised she wouldn't be able to climb them. There weren't even any trees near enough to help her. Stella swore under her breath. Of course, a hole like this wouldn't be easy to escape from. She'd just have to try her luck at the gate. But what if she was caught? She couldn't take that risk. The guard on the gate seemed half asleep, but she didn't suppose there were too many people going in and out of somewhere like this. Even he might look twice at a girl leaving with no shoes on her feet. Why hadn't she thought to bring spare ones? And why bring Florence's stupid coat? She knew why she'd brought that, in case Seb's mother was bigger, but who could be anything other than a virtual skeleton, living in a place like this?

Screams still came from within the building as Stella skirted the inside of the wall. As she neared the gate, she spotted a cart, its horse stamping impatiently as the driver spoke to the guard.

Without hesitation, Stella lifted the corner of the canvas covering the cart and climbed up, tucking herself out of sight.

At first Stella could see nothing, but gradually she made out her surroundings, almost screaming when she realised the object she was hiding next to was a coffin. She was sharing the cart with a dead person, probably a crazy one at that!

She was almost too afraid to breathe, lying there in the dusty cart. She hoped the man wouldn't look under the canvas before he left, but supposed he'd have no need to check on the occupant.

A terrifying thought struck her. What if they had more coffins to load up? No. The man looked like he was about to leave. She almost squealed as the cart suddenly lurched forward. She was letting her imagination get the better of her. She didn't have time to be dramatic now, she had to keep her mind on the task.

She held onto the coffin as they moved forward. The driver called goodbye to the guard, and the iron gate slammed behind them.

Stella waited until she felt them turn a corner, before daring to lift the edge of the canvas. She had to know where she was. Seeing that they were on a quiet country road, she lifted the canvas a little higher, sliding herself towards the back edge. It was as she was contemplating how to escape that they hit a bump in the road. Stella squealed as she felt herself falling through the air.

As she hit the ground, the driver let out a shout, and the horse picked up speed. As Stella scrambled to her feet, she watched the cart bouncing its way along the road away from her. She guessed the driver wanted to be rid of his occupant as soon as possible, especially if he'd heard her squeal!

Stella broke into a run, hopeful that she was going in the right direction. It wasn't long before she found herself on familiar ground. She easily made her way to the station, arriving just as a train pulled in. She soon spotted Seb and his mother, as, with his arm tightly around her, he half carried her onto the train. Stella followed them into the carriage and sank down opposite them.

"Cor! Me feet!" she exclaimed. "Gone and ruined my stockings, I 'ave!"

"I say, Stella! I'll buy you some new ones!" Seb grinned at her.

They were relieved when the train pulled out of the station. Stella even wondered if she glimpsed a smile from Selena.

"How did you do it, Stella? How did you get out?" Seb enquired.

"Never mind me, 'ow did you do it?"

"It was all rather straightforward. What with all the noise going on, I just said we must go, and we were let out straightaway. I can't imagine whatever started them all off like that!"

Stella grinned. "Strange, wasn't it? Just at the time we needed it."

"Stella? You didn't, did you?"

"I 'ad to! We never would've got out otherwise!" Stella then went on to tell of her escape.

As they changed trains, Stella became nervous that someone would suspect something when they saw her with no shoes, and Seb almost carrying his mother. She needn't have worried, as no one took the slightest bit of notice of them.

It was nearing midnight when they finally reached the village and stepped from the train.

"I say!" Seb stopped in his tracks, causing Stella to bump into the back of him. "What am I going to do with mother? I can't take her back to the cottage! That dreadful maid will have Father there right away!"

"I dunno." Stella was thoughtful as she yawned noisily. "Could you both hide out somewhere for the night?"

"There'll be no need for that."

They jumped as the voice spoke from beside them. "Ruthie! What are you doing here?" Stella squeaked.

"I could ask you the same question, but I can see for myself. Eliza was worried about the two of you… We all were. I said I'd come and see if you got off the last train, and it seems it's a good thing I did. It looks like you didn't just visit your mother, Seb."

"No… I… um… well… you see… Oh bother!"

"You won't make 'er go back there, will you, Ruthie? It's a bloomin' awful place and she don't belong there. Please, don't tell!" They were all surprised when Stella burst into tears.

"I don't think anyone will be going anywhere far tonight." Ruthie sighed. "Come on, you'd better come back to the Turleys' farm. I think that's the best thing for now."

Together, Seb and Ruthie carried Selena's slight form, Stella trailing behind them, still sniffing and hardly able to put one foot in front of the other.

They were all relieved when they entered the warmth of the Turleys' kitchen, where they lowered Selena into the large chair, while Stella collapsed in a heap on the mat by the fire. "My bloomin' feet!" she complained.

"Oh dear! What have I done! Father will be furious!" Seb shifted nervously from one foot to another. "Stella! Why did we do it? We were only going to visit!"

"Don't you bloomin' well blame me, Sebastian Westfield! We weren't gonna leave your mother in that dark, dingy prison! We 'ad to get 'er out! We'll just 'ave to keep 'er hidden."

"But how? He'll likely be on his way by now. He would have left once the maid realised I was missing."

"They didn't suspect you were missing until this evening," Ruthie told him. "The maid presumed you were here."

"I... won't go back!" Selena's voice came with more strength than they would have imagined.

"Alright." Ruthie turned from putting the kettle on and knelt by Selena's side. Taking her hand, she said gently, "We'll do what we can to make sure you don't. In the meantime, let's have a cup of tea."

"What's going on?" Ada entered the kitchen, shortly followed by Bill.

"Oh! Ah..." Seb swung around to face them. "Stella and I went to get Mother. Well, I had no idea we were going to bring her home, but we did."

"So I see!" Bill broke into a wide grin. "Good for you, lad!"

"She can't go back there! It's like a prison!" Stella explained. "You can't make 'er go!"

"We don't intend to," Bill turned to her, "but you'd better get back home. They've been wondering where you are!"

"Me feet are killin' me!" Stella complained.

Ada bent to inspect them. "They do look sore. I'll clean them up for you. What happened to your shoes?"

"She put them on Mother," Seb explained, "so she'd look like Stella did on the way in."

"Florence's coat too?" Ada smiled.

"I thought she'd be bigger," Stella sighed.

Ada bathed and bandaged Stella's feet before sending her home. "The door won't be locked," she told her, "so you'll get in. Don't expect them to be very happy, though."

"Maybe best to say you've been to see Seb's mother, but deny all knowledge of anything more at the moment," Bill said thoughtfully, as he watched Stella trying to get her bandaged feet into her shoes. "I don't know if taking someone from a place like that is a crime."

Seb also left with the same instructions. He hadn't been keen to leave his mother, but Ruthie and Ada assured him they'd keep her safe. Selena, obviously still sedated and worn out from the day's adventure, was sleeping soundly in the chair.

25

"It's alright, Selena, you're safe here." Ruthie reassured the woman, who was looking fearfully around the kitchen.

"Where am I? I was dreaming," Selena tried to explain.

"Seb brought you here last night. You came with him and his friend Stella on the train."

"I'm not locked in?"

"No. You are safe here. We are very fond of Seb. You've done an excellent job of bringing him up." Ruthie tried to make the frightened and confused woman feel more at ease.

"When I was allowed to," Selena sighed thoughtfully. "But what am I to do? Hector will be furious!"

"I'm sure he will, but as yet, he has no idea of where you are. We need to keep it that way for as long as possible. We have two young girls who may unintentionally let on you are here, so it would be best if we get you upstairs before they come down. How about a nice cup of tea first? We've got an hour or so."

"Thank you. Real tea? You won't put anything in it, will you?"

"No, of course I won't. I'll make us both a pot of tea. You can pour it yourself if you like." Ruthie pulled the kettle onto the stove.

"I must look a dreadful state!" Selena said. "I seem to remember wearing someone's shoes, along with a rather large coat."

"Yes. Stella took her shoes off and put them on you. It seems she borrowed her friend's coat for you to wear as well. Our Stella seems to think of everything."

"Is she your daughter?"

"No. She's an evacuee at a nearby farm. I'm staying here with my two nieces, Eliza and Lily. This farm belongs to Bill and Ada Turley. They are very kind people. Seb has been staying just down the road. I'm sure he'll be here as soon as possible."

"Hector! He will be furious with Seb! With me, too!" Panic filled Selena's voice.

"We'll keep him away as long as we can. As for Seb, he's going to admit to going to see you, but nothing after that. How did they get you out?"

"I don't really know. I remember that girl… Stella? She was putting the coat on me, and then Seb was half carrying me. I remember little else."

"I'm sure they'll fill in the details." Ruthie brought the teapot and two cups to the table. Seeing Selena's shaking hands, she suggested, "Shall I pour the tea? You can choose whichever cup you want."

Selena eventually managed to lift the cup to her lips, only spilling some of the tea. After her second cup, she asked, "How long was I there?"

"I don't know. I expect Seb can tell you more. I've been thinking though. Do you have any other family? I mean, family of your own?"

"My parents disowned me after I married Hector. They wrote and said they didn't want to hear from me again. My friend told me he was no good. If only I'd listened to her, but I thought she was jealous."

"Getting in contact with your parents has to be worth a try. Where do they live?"

"They live in Devon, but they will say it's what I deserved. I still find it difficult to believe all those things they wrote. Hector said it was for the best that I never saw them again."

"Do you think maybe they didn't write it? Could it have been Hector? No parent could turn away from their child if they knew what you've been through."

"Do you have children?"

Ruthie was surprised at Selena's question. After hesitating a moment, she said, "It's complicated. I have a daughter, but I didn't bring her up. When I found out she was in danger, I knew I had to do whatever I could to help her. I think we should try to contact your parents."

"Not the phone!" Selena put her cup down noisily on the table. "He'll have people listening."

"Alright, not on the phone," Ruthie agreed quickly. "If you know the address, we can work something out."

"Why do you want to help me?"

Ruthie wondered how to answer this question. "I've recently learned about the kindness of others. I've also learned of God's love for me. If he could give his life for me, surely I can do what I can for others. Seb means a lot to us, and he loves you very much. He has also been a great help with Lily. She was extremely ill, but Seb gave her hope and a purpose to get through it. He has been teaching her the piano and encouraging her to sing. He has promised to help her do a concert for her father when he comes home."

"Sebastian has always been a good boy. He seems so grown-up now."

"Yes. He's grown up a lot in the months we've known him."

When Bill and Ada joined them, they moved Selena up to their room. As quietly as possible, they helped her upstairs, where she instantly fell asleep on the bed.

When Seb bounded through the door as they were all sitting at the breakfast table, Bill held up his hand to stop him from speaking.

"Seb!" Lily squealed. "You came back! I thought you were gone forever!"

"I'm sorry, Liliana Grace. I just had something to do, that's all. I wouldn't go away without saying goodbye."

"Where did you go?" asked Elsie innocently.

"Never mind that now," Ada put in. "Eat your breakfast, else you'll be late for school."

Eliza glanced at Seb and smiled knowingly.

"I'm going back to school again on Monday," Lily told Seb.

"Marvellous!" he exclaimed. Lily missed so much school, and she was always so happy to be returning to the classroom.

When Eliza and Elsie left for school, Ada took Lily to see to the chickens. As soon as the door was closed, Seb jumped to his feet. "Where is Mother? What's happened?"

"It's alright," Ruthie put a hand on his arm. "She's upstairs resting. Eliza knows something's going on, but the less the younger girls know, the better."

"What's the situation with your father?" Bill asked.

"The maid was furious. She phoned Father and told him I was missing. What are we going to do? How can we keep Mother safe?"

"I understand why you did it, son, but you could be in a lot of trouble," Bill sighed.

"Your mother was telling me her parents live in Devon. Do you know anything about them?" Ruthie asked.

"Not a thing. Father forbade us to speak of them."

"She was also afraid of us trying to contact them by phone," Ruthie continued.

"Oh yes! Father paid people at the exchange to tell him what was said. Do you suppose he would do that here?"

Bill and Ruthie glanced at one another. "One of us will have to travel there," Ruthie said decisively.

"I'll go," Seb volunteered enthusiastically.

"No, Seb. It can't be you," Bill put in. "It would be too obvious. I reckon it should be Ruthie. I never take long train journeys, but no one will question Ruthie. What do you think?"

"Of course. Yes, I'll go."

"I'm afraid Father will come and take me away," Seb sounded defeated.

"If he does, we'll still do all we can for your mother, and we'll still keep praying for you," Bill tried to reassure him.

"I wish he'd just disinherit me. I don't want his money and his businesses. What's all that if I don't have a family like you all have?"

Neither of them knew how to answer.

Seb hurried upstairs to see his mother, while Ruthie and Bill went outside. Ruthie took Lily with her while she worked, on the pretense of her getting more fresh air, which would do her good. There was a lot to be done on the farm, especially if Ruthie was going to have to take time to travel to Devon. Could she get there and back in one day? What reception would she get? Were Selena's parents still alive?

It was later that afternoon, once the girls were all home from school, that the peace of the day was shattered. Ruthie was upstairs talking to Selena when she heard a commotion coming from the direction of the yard. Moving to the window, she looked out. Bill, Seb, and Eliza were being shouted at by the most angry-looking man she'd ever seen.

"Where is she?" he bellowed.

"It's Hector!" Selena's voice came out on a squeak.

Ruthie rushed to her side and Selena clung tightly to her.

The next thing they knew, the door flew open.

"There's an angry man, Auntie Ruthie, and he's shouting at Seb!" Lily burst into tears as she ran into the room. "He said he took his mam from somewhere… Oh!" Lily's eyes focused on Selena. "Is that…?"

"Lily," Ruthie spoke quickly, "you know how your dad brought you and Eliza here to keep you safe from your grandfather? Well, it's kind of the same."

"I can keep a secret." Lily moved to stand next to them. "I don't like that man. Seb is my friend, so I won't tell."

"You're a good girl, Lily. Now, you stay here with Selena, and I'll go and help Seb."

Ruthie disentangled herself from Selena's hold, and Lily climbed up on the bed beside her, taking her hand. "I'll look after you," she smiled up at her, "And Auntie Ruthie will look after Seb. Auntie Ruthie is good at looking after people."

26

"You've gone too far this time, boy!" Hector bellowed at his son.

"What's the problem?" Ruthie hurried to Seb's side. She could no longer see Eliza and guessed she had retreated from the angry man into the barn, where Elsie was likely already hiding.

"Where is she?" Hector ignored Ruthie's question and sprang forward, taking Seb by the shoulders and shaking him.

"Now you look here!" Bill stepped forward, trying to release Seb from Hector's hold. "Don't you come to my farm and treat Seb like that. He's a good boy."

"You stay out of it!" Hector briefly turned his anger on Bill, giving Seb the chance to pull away from his hold.

Ruthie guided the boy a few steps backwards and kept her arm around him as Hector once again turned on his son.

"Where is she?" he demanded. "I know you were there."

"Yes, I went there," Seb found his voice. "I went to visit my mother. It was an awful place, and I wish I had taken her from it, but I didn't. You're always telling me how stupid I am, so how do you think I would be capable of getting Mother out of such a place? There were guards on the gate and high walls and fences!"

Hector's face reddened as his anger increased. "How do you propose she got away, then? If you didn't get her out, who did? She couldn't have done it alone. She doesn't have the intelligence for that."

"Please don't insult my mother!" Seb raised his voice. "She should never have been put away in such a place! I'm glad she got away! I only wish I knew where she was, so I could be with her!"

"The woman is crazy! You know that yourself."

"No, she isn't. My mother is not crazy. You are the crazy one, Father! Cruel, too!"

Hector's hand shot out and hit Seb hard across the face. "No son of mine is ever going to speak to me like that!" he growled.

"I wish I wasn't your son," Seb stated calmly.

"You'll soon change your tune when I take away all your allowances. You think you can do alright without me, but we'll see. It will be too late then. Don't come crawling back to me. You are no longer a son of mine. You are as weak and pathetic as your mother! I'll find her, and I'll ensure she is put back where she belongs. I've a good mind to do the same with you! I no longer have a son! You will inherit nothing of mine."

With that, Hector turned and strode away. Only once he was out of sight did Seb turn and rest his head on Ruthie's shoulder, so no one would see his tears. Ruthie held him close, like the young boy he was. She wondered if he realised how different his life would be without the financial support of his father. Seb had lived such a sheltered life. Her prayer was that Selena's parents were still alive and willing to take their daughter and grandson into their home.

"Was he really your dad?" Elsie asked in amazement, as she and Eliza hurried out of the barn. "He was even worse than the farmer I lived with first."

"Eliza, Elsie, I need you two to help me," Bill said quietly. "We have a lot of work still to do in the barn before we eat, and Ruthie needs to see to Seb."

Neither of them spoke as Ruthie led Seb into the house. In the kitchen, she sat him at the table, while Ada soaked a flannel in cold water.

"Put this on your eye." She handed the flannel to Seb, who took it without a word.

"I'll go and check on your mother," Ruthie said, "then I'll be back. Don't worry, Seb, we'll help you both get through this."

Ruthie made her way up the stairs. When she entered Bill and Ada's bedroom, there was no sign of Lily or Selena. "Lily?" she questioned.

"Auntie Ruthie? Is he gone?" Lily's voice came from beneath the bed.

Ruthie got onto her knees and lifted the blankets which hung down the side of the bed. Lily and Selena were curled together on the floor.

"It's alright, Hector has gone. You are safe."

"Me and Seb's mam were scared," Lily burst into tears.

"It's alright, Lily," Ruthie reassured her once more. "He's gone. Seb is downstairs, and no one is going to let that man in. You need to come out from under the bed now."

"It's like when we were being bombed," Lily sniffed. "Me and Eliza hid under our bed."

"You don't have to hide anymore," Ruthie tried again, but there was no movement.

"Seb's mam is scared." Lily explained.

"Selena, you really are safe. Hector has gone. Seb is still here, and I think he could do with seeing you. You can come out now."

Still, they did not move, and Ruthie could see that Selena was holding tightly to Lily, preventing her from crawling out of the enclosed space.

"I'm going to get Seb." Ruthie got to her feet. "It really is safe now, Selena. You and Lily can come out. No one will hurt you."

When there was still no response from Selena, Ruthie left the room and hurried down to the kitchen. "Seb, will you come and talk to your mother, please? She and Lily are hiding under the bed, and I can't get them out."

Seb said nothing, but got to his feet and followed Ruthie up the stairs. As Ruthie re-entered the bedroom, she wondered, for the first time, if there really was something wrong with Selena. Had she put Lily in danger by leaving her alone with the woman?

"Selena, you are safe," Ruthie tried again. "Seb is here now, and he will tell you that there is nothing to be afraid of."

Seb got clumsily to his knees, lifting the blankets. "Mother, he's gone. Please come out."

When Selena still did not reply, Seb continued, "You're frightening Lily. Please Mother, I… I need you to get out from under there," his voice shook as he finished.

"We can get out now," Lily spoke gently. "Auntie Ruthie and Seb say so, so it must be safe. Auntie Ruthie or Seb don't tell lies."

"Please, Mother," Seb tried again, "you must come out."

"He'll send me back there." Selena's voice was strong as she spoke. "He'll send me back there and I'd rather die than that."

"He's gone, Selena," Ruthie told her. "Hector isn't here."

"No one is permitted to call him Hector, apart from me… and his so-called friends," Selena stated.

"Well, I could call him a lot worse!" Ruthie almost laughed. "We are not under his authority here. This is Bill and Ada Turley's farm, and they say who comes here, and they won't have Hector in this house."

"She's right, Mother. Mr. Turley made him release his hold on me. They are not frightened of him. He doesn't rule here."

Ada appeared in the doorway. "I expect you are all hungry. Bill and the girls will be in shortly for tea. It will be nice to all sit at the table together. You'll enjoy having your mother with us, won't you, Seb?"

"Oh! Yes, Mrs. Turley, very much so. It smells awfully good, too. Come along Mother, Mrs. Turley always makes good food."

"He makes them put sleeping drugs in it!" Selena stated.

"No one makes Mrs. Turley do anything," Seb reassured her. "Please mother, you and Lily need to get out now."

"Are the doors locked?" Selena asked.

"I'll lock the door to make sure no one comes in," Ada promised.

"But you will be able to unlock it and go out if you need to," Ruthie put in, remembering Selena's earlier concern about being locked in.

"We really are safe here," Seb reassured her.

"I'll go and get the tea on the table," Ada said. "See you all in a minute."

She returned to the kitchen, and Ruthie wondered what else to try. Then, thankfully, she heard movement.

"That's it, Mother!" Seb broke into a smile. "Let Lily go, then you can both get out."

Lily came scrambling from underneath the bed and threw herself into Ruthie's arms, clinging tightly to her.

Fearful Lily's reaction would make Selena more reluctant to leave her place of safety, Ruthie hurried from the room, calling, "We'll be downstairs, Seb and Selena."

However, instead of going straight downstairs, she went into the room she and the girls shared and sat down on the bed with Lily in her arms.

"That man was really scary!" Lily cried. "Seb's mam was really scared, and she's grown up!"

"Seb's father was very cruel to her. Mr. Turley won't let him in here, though. You don't need to be afraid, Lily. We're all here to keep you safe."

"Why is he so horrible?"

"Some people just are, Lily, but thankfully there are more nice people than horrible ones."

"Mine and Eliza's grandfather was mean. We didn't like him."

"Yes, I know he was."

"Did you know him, Auntie Ruthie?"

"A very long time ago, yes."

"Was he mean to you, too?"

"He was, but we don't have to worry about that anymore. Let's go down and have tea."

"Auntie Ruthie, how do people stop being mean?"

Ruthie thought for a few seconds before she answered, "I don't know, Lily. All we can do is pray that they will come to know Jesus and won't want to be unkind anymore."

"So, we need to pray for Seb's father and our grandfather."

"Yes, Lily, you are right. We must pray for them both." Ruthie wondered at Lily's childlike faith. She knew it was possible for cruel people to turn their lives around. Ruthie knew that faith like Lily's was the best kind to have, but she still had a long way to go herself to believe men like Gareth Davies and Hector Westfield could ever change and be forgiven.

27

"Caor! So you were here! I thought that man was making it all up! Seb, you were clever hiding your mum like that!" Elsie grinned at him.

"It's important no one knows she's here, Elsie," Bill said calmly.

"I won't tell anyone! It's like when the farmer was horrible to me and I came here. We all come here to be safe, don't we?"

Ruthie looked around the table and realised how true Elsie's words were. The Turley farm was a place of safety for each of them.

"Now we just need Dad to come home and we'll all be here!" Lily said innocently.

"I wish we could go and get Dad," Eliza added thoughtfully.

"We have to wait for him to be ready," Ada told them. "We'll keep praying that it won't be too long."

"I used to pray," Selena said quietly.

"I didn't know that." Seb smiled at his mother. "Everyone here has been teaching me about Jesus. I do believe he is real. I'm sure he must be, else we would never have got you here."

"How did you get here?" Elsie asked.

"Never mind that now, we're just pleased she is," Ada said quickly. They knew they could no longer hide Selena's presence from the younger girls, but the less they knew, the better.

"Sebastian, why do you eat here? You said you were living somewhere else," Selena questioned.

"Sebastian! I've never heard anyone call him Sebastian before!" Elsie giggled.

"Everyone here is very good to me," Seb explained. "The maid didn't enjoy preparing meals. Sometimes she didn't bother, but Mrs. Turley always said I could have tea here. Occasionally I eat at the cottage, but Mrs. Turley's cooking is better!"

They all laughed.

"We must reimburse you." Selena looked first at Ada, then at Bill.

"Don't be daft!" Ada said emphatically. "We love having him here. He helps us around the farm."

"You know, Mother, I really enjoy working on the farm. I'm not always particularly good at it, but Mr. Turley has taught me a lot. Some of the villagers showed me up for the fool I was when I first arrived, but the Turleys and everyone else here were good to me." Looking at Eliza, he asked, "Do you remember the day I first met you, Stella, and Florence? I had been sent to get the bucket to milk the bull! I'd been to several farms, but no one told me you can't milk a bull until you did. You were the first real friends I ever had."

"Am I your friend too, Seb?" Lily asked.

"Oh, yes, Liliana Grace. Mother, do you know this girl has the voice of an angel?"

"We're going to do a concert for Dad when he gets home," Lily told Selena. "You can come too if you like."

"I say! How about we do one for Mother?" Seb was enthusiastic.

"Can we?" Lily looked to Ruthie.

"Well, perhaps we could do with some entertainment," Ada answered.

"Can I sing too?" Elsie asked.

Seb smiled, then said, "I'm sure we can find something for you, Elsie. How about some of the hymns we usually sing on a Sunday evening?"

"I think that's a very good idea," Ada nodded.

The rest of the meal was punctuated by excited chatter about the musical evening to follow.

Once they'd eaten, Ada suggested they leave the washing-up until after the concert. Ruthie watched Selena as Seb began to play the piano. Gone was the terrified woman, and in her place, a proud mother. Seb played while Lily sang, and again for Elsie. He then accompanied himself in what Ruthie guessed were his mother's favourite songs. When Seb announced it was time for them to sing hymns together, they all moved to stand around the piano.

As they sang *What a Friend We Have in Jesus*, Eliza slipped her hand into Ruthie's. At the end of the final verse, Eliza said quietly, "Auntie Ruthie, I want to visit Dad. Do you think we could go together? Just me and you."

"I'd like that, Eliza. Let's get things with Selena sorted, then we'll see about it."

The evening passed quickly, and it was soon time for Seb to leave. He said goodbye to them all, reassured his mother that she was safe and that he would return in the morning, before unlocking the door.

"I'll walk back with you, son," Bill stated.

"Thank you." Selena smiled at the older man. "I don't like the idea of him being out there alone. Be careful, Hector is capable of anything."

Bill and Seb left the house, and after locking the door behind them, Ruthie helped Ada and Eliza to clear up the kitchen.

"Where are we all going to sleep?" Elsie asked.

"Selena can have my half of the bed," Eliza offered.

"You and I can sleep on the floor," Ruthie smiled at Eliza.

"I couldn't take your bed," Selena said in surprise.

"It's no problem. I'm afraid we'll all need to share the same room, but at least you can have the bed to yourself," Ruthie told her.

"We've often talked about building another bedroom, but somehow we never got around to it," Ada laughed. "I reckon we should've done it before the war."

"I'm happy to not be by myself," Selena said. "I've had too much time alone. I can understand why Seb enjoys spending so much time here. You've given him the kind of family life I could only dream of providing for him."

As Ruthie said goodnight to the two younger girls, she looked to where Selena was sleeping peacefully in the bed. Was it the effects of the medication she'd been forcefully given that made her seem a little different at times? Ruthie supposed it must have been, as this evening, no one would ever think there was anything wrong with Seb's mother.

As Ruthie made her way downstairs, she was surprised to hear Seb's voice, along with Bill's, coming from the kitchen.

"My clothes were all on the doorstep!" Seb was telling Ada and Eliza, "my books, too. The maid was gone, and the farmer said I can't stay in the cottage any longer, because Father had said so. I don't have anywhere to go. Mr. Turley told me to come here."

"Well well well. And yes, of course you can come here."

"I don't think we should be surprised," Bill sighed. "He did say he was cutting you off, and I suppose he thought that putting you out of the cottage was the place to start."

"What am I going to do? It's all my fault. I'm still as stupid now as when I came here."

Ruthie went to stand behind him, where he sat slumped over the table. Resting her hand on his shoulder, she said, "You are not stupid, Seb. Maybe you could've done things differently, but we have to go with what we've got now. Things might not be easy, but you don't have to do it alone."

"Yes, we will help you, and remember, God is always with you. No one can ever take him away from you. You just need to remember he's there," Ada added.

"But what about Mother? We can't keep her hidden here forever."

"No. I'm going tomorrow to visit her parents, your grandparents. We need to pray they are still in the same place and are willing to help," Ruthie explained.

"We'll keep the girls home from school tomorrow," Bill said. "I don't want to take any chances."

"You are wise," Seb sighed. "That man cannot be trusted. It wouldn't take much for Elsie to give us away by mistake."

"Stella was wise to stay away today," Bill said, sitting down opposite Seb.

"Do you suppose I was foolish?" Seb asked him.

"I don't honestly know. I mean, your father is not a man used to being crossed. We don't want to see you hurt, son. It was wrong of him to have your mother put away like he did, and I'd like to say there was a better way of getting her out of there, but I'm not sure there's anything that could've been done differently. We must pray for guidance now."

"He might come back here." Seb shifted awkwardly on the chair. "He doesn't give up easily. What if someone saw me and Stella with Mother? If he finds out the truth, he'll be furious!"

"We can't do anything about that now," Ada stated. "We just have to wait and see what happens."

"Mother is terrified of him, and so am I! What if he comes and I'm in the barn? What if he comes into the house and Mother is in here?"

"Your mother won't be alone. I'll keep her and the girls in here with me, and the doors will be locked. You can stay with Bill when you are outside."

"But… you see… Father has a gun. I saw him use it once… not on an animal."

"You mean he shot someone?" Eliza asked.

Seb nodded.

Bill sighed. "I'm sorry you had to see that. I've got a gun too, so I'll keep it with me. I'd rather not use it, but I will if I have to. Don't you worry, Seb, he might not even come here again. I don't suppose a man like him will want to stay around here for long."

28

Ruthie sat upright, wondering where she was. What was that banging?

"Auntie Ruthie, what is it? Is it that man again?" Lily questioned as she flung herself onto the makeshift bed on the floor.

Suddenly, it all came back to her. They were hiding Seb's mother in the Turley farmhouse. Seb had also been thrown out of the cottage where he'd been staying on the neighbouring farm and was sleeping downstairs.

"I'll go and see. It sounds like Bill is on his way down already."

"It's not Seb's dad, because the person at the door is too small," Eliza said as she stood looking out of the window.

"Keep Selena and the girls up here please, Eliza," Ruthie said, as she disentangled Lily and pulled a dressing gown on.

She and Ada descended the stairs together, both stopping in amazement as Bill exclaimed, "Stella? Whatever's wrong? Is there a fire?"

"No! they're sending me away in the mornin'. They were really mad with me and wouldn't let me come over yesterday. They said I couldn't even come to say goodbye, but I 'ad to. I waited until they were in bed and came then. Sorry it's so late. Florence took ages to go to sleep because she 'ad belly ache."

"I Say!" Seb stood in the doorway of the front room, staring in amazement at Stella. "You gave me an awful fright, Stella, I thought it was Father."

"I'm not like that bloomin mad-man! 'E came round to the farm askin' me all sorts of questions yesterday. Florence's mum and dad wouldn't let him do anythin' though, 'cos 'e insulted them! They said I 'ave to go 'ome first thing in the mornin'. 'Ere, why are you sleepin' 'ere, Seb?"

"Father had me evicted from the cottage, because I finally stood up to him."

"You didn't let 'im 'ave your mum, did you?"

"Of course not! Not after all the trouble we went to!"

"We? You didn't 'ave to 'ide on a cart with a dead person! It was brave of you, standing up to 'im, though. What you gonna do? Is your mum alright now?"

"Mother is fine. We are hoping to make contact with my grandparents."

"'E's still around 'ere, you know that, don't ya? Florence saw 'im. 'E was complainin' that there was nowhere decent to stay, but 'e used a load of words Florence didn't know, so she forgot 'em."

"We were hoping he'd gone back home," Bill put in. "Thanks for the warning, Stella."

"We're going to miss you, Stella," Ada moved to hug her.

"I'm gonna miss you all, too. I'll write though, 'cos I can now. I wanna come back one day."

"I'll get Eliza. I know she'll want to say goodbye." Ruthie turned and ascended the stairs again. She soon returned, followed by Eliza, Lily, Elsie, and Selena.

"We were all awake!" Elsie announced. "You scared us, Stella! We thought you were Seb's mean father again."

"I ain't 'im!" Stella laughed, reaching to hug Elsie.

"Auntie Ruthie says you're going home," tears came to Elsie's eyes. "I can't go home, because my mum's dead. I don't want you to go, Stella. You were nice to me when those big boys took my rag doll on the train when we all came here."

"I'm gonna write, Elsie. You'll be alright 'ere. You've got lots of people to look out for ya."

Next, Stella hugged Lily. "Keep singing, Lily," she told her.

"You'll miss the concert when Dad comes home," Lily sniffed.

"You can tell me all about it in a letter. You never know, you might be famous one day and come to London to sing on the stage."

"I'll really miss you," Eliza stepped forward. "You and Florence were so friendly when I started at school."

"I wanna know all what's 'appening! Keep an eye on Floss for me too. Make sure she don't eat everyone's dinner, now she won't be 'avin most of mine!"

They all laughed before Eliza led Lily and Elsie back up the stairs.

Stella turned to Selena. "You're lookin' better than you did the other day!"

"I don't know how I can thank you sufficiently, Stella. You and Seb saved my life."

"It weren't nothin'," Stella blinked rapidly.

"From what I've heard, because I don't honestly remember too much of it, you were extremely brave. You thought of everything, it seems."

"Apart from shoes. I've still got bloomin blisters! I should've asked Seb 'ow big you were, 'cos Florence's coat were big enough for you and me to fit in together!"

They all laughed, and Selena took Stella's hand. "I don't know what the future holds for Seb and me, but if there's anything I can ever do for you, Stella, I'll do it. We'll find a way of letting you know where we are, so don't hesitate to ask. We are eternally grateful to you."

For once, Stella seemed lost for words. She rubbed furiously at her eyes, before turning to Seb. "You look after 'er now we got 'er out, Seb. I 'ope you don't get into too much trouble." They briefly hugged one another.

Stepping back, Seb said, "I can never thank you enough, Stella. All of you here have been so kind to me. And you, Stella, have taught me to think for myself. I'll write when I can. I want to hear all about your family."

"I'll miss you too, Stella. Please write when you can," Ruthie hugged her. "You are very brave, and that will get you a long way. Don't let anyone change you."

"I wish I didn't 'ave to go. I wish me mum and me brothers and sisters could just come 'ere! The kids would love it! I'll tell 'em all about it. Bet they don't know milk comes from cows." She scratched her arm subconsciously before she continued, "I'm not lookin' forward to the bedbugs either! They ought to send them to fight the bloomin' Germans. That'd get rid of 'em! Bloomin' bedbugs are the only things that survive when places get bombed."

Bill and Ada said their goodbyes to Stella before she hurried off out into the night. Then Bill checked the door was securely locked, before he and his wife returned to bed.

"It's all going to be different," Seb sighed. "Stella is going, and who knows what will happen to me now."

"God will be with you no matter what happens, Seb," Ruthie tried to reassure him. "There may be difficult times ahead, but you won't be alone." She hesitated for a moment, wondering how much to say. "I lived my life not trusting or getting close to anyone for years, because of something that happened to me. I didn't think I would ever be happy again, but since I came here with Eliza and Lily, I've learnt how to live again. Seb, you will come across all sorts of people in your life, some good, and some bad. Don't ever shut the good ones out like I did."

Ruthie turned and walked quickly up the stairs. She got into her make-shift bed, thankful that Eliza was already sleeping. Why had she said all that to Seb? She knew it had been the right thing to do, though.

Ruthie lay still as she heard Selena enter the room. She didn't want her to ask any questions, not tonight.

The hours passed slowly as Ruthie lay as still as she could. Sleep would not come, and thoughts of the trip she had to make raced round and round in her mind. What had they all got themselves into? She knew nothing of Selena's parents… come to that, she knew very little about Selena. Seb and Stella hadn't acted wisely when they took her from the institution, but she couldn't blame them at all. What if Selena's parents were dead? What if they didn't want to be reacquainted with their daughter and grandson? They couldn't keep Selena hidden in the farmhouse forever. Sooner or later, Hector would be back. She didn't trust the man one bit. He reminded her of a more sophisticated version of Gareth Davies. He did whatever he wanted, with no concern for others. However, Hector had money and connections, so he was far more dangerous than Eddie's father had ever been.

The clock downstairs chimed four-thirty, and Ruthie decided to get up. The earlier she caught the train to Devon, the sooner she'd be home. She might not make it there and back in one day, it all depended on how the trains were running, and what kind of response she got from Selena's parents.

The station was deserted as Ruthie stood on the platform a short while later. She, Bill, and Ada had prayed together before she'd left on her mission.

Ruthie kept glancing around her, expecting to see Hector at any moment, and was relieved once she was finally on the train and it pulled out of the station.

The morning passed slowly. Ruthie went from thinking of the jobs she could be doing on the farm, to wondering what kind of reception she would receive from Selena's parents. She had been hoping to visit Eddie again soon, but Bill needed her help on the farm. Eliza was keen to see her father, and Ruthie thought it would do them both good. Maybe Eliza could make Eddie change his mind. Lily wouldn't like being left at home, but she wasn't going to take her all that way, especially if Eddie was as determined not to see them as he had previously been. Something like that could really set Lily back, and she was already so weak.

Ruthie finally reached her destination late in the afternoon. There was no way she was going to make it home that day. She kept praying that all was well and that Hector hadn't paid the Turley farm another visit. It had been agreed to keep the girls off school, as no one knew what lengths the man would go to.

From the train station, Ruthie took a bus, then found herself walking along a country lane. The birdsong all around her did little to ease her tension.

Finally, she reached the driveway of the house. She'd got directions back in the village, where she had been relieved to discover that Selena's parents were still alive and living at the same address.

Ruthie straightened her clothes as best she could, then walked towards the house. Everything appeared well looked after, which again seemed to be a good sign.

She hesitated briefly, looking up at the large building, before stepping up to the front door. Of course Selena would have come from a family with money. Why else would a man like Hector have been interested in her?

She rang the bell and heard it echoing in the hallway. When the door was quickly opened by a smiling young maid, Ruthie gave her name and asked to speak with Mr. and Mrs. Rotherham, concerning a private matter.

She was shown into a beautifully decorated sitting-room, where she stood awkwardly by the window, while the maid hurried away.

Samuel and Lavinia Rotherham soon entered the room. Ruthie could instantly see the resemblance between Selena and her mother. More surprising was how much Seb looked like his grandfather.

Introductions were made, and Ruthie was invited to take a seat.

"I'm afraid we don't recognise your name," Samuel Rotherham began, "so have no idea what this private matter concerns."

Ruthie twisted her hands nervously in her lap, before she began, "I'm afraid it concerns your daughter, Selena." Deciding it was best to get it all out in the open, she explained, "Hector had her locked away in an asylum for daring to stand up to him. Your grandson, Sebastian, and his friend, went alone to visit her, even though his father had forbidden him to even talk about her, let alone see her. They somehow took her out of the asylum, and she is now staying at the farm where I'm currently living. As you can imagine, Hector is furious, and Selena and Seb are terrified of him."

29

The sound of the ornate clock ticking seemed to intensify as Ruthie waited for some kind of response from Selena's parents.

It was Lavinia who broke the silence. "An asylum? Not an asylum!"

"I'm afraid so." Ruthie was suddenly very nervous. She had no idea what kind of people the Rotherhams really were. What if they didn't believe her? What if they threw her out without hearing the full story?

"You'd better start from the beginning," Samuel spoke quietly. "We were under a completely different impression altogether."

Ruthie took a deep breath, then began, "I don't know much, really. Seb… I mean Sebastian came to the village where I'm living. He had a tutor with him and was staying on a local farm. He is a little older than my eldest niece, but he became friendly with her and two other girls. The farmhands were making fun of him for not knowing the country ways, but Eliza and her friends wanted to help him. Seb started visiting us regularly at the farm, and often played the piano. One day, the farmhand tried to… well… tried to get too close to me. Seb was there when I told the farmer, and he stayed with me while Bill dismissed the man. Seb told me that Hector had done things like that with the servants. He didn't like how his father treated them, and Seb had given one girl money to get away. That's when his father had him sent to the country. He said his mother had tried to stand up to Hector, but he had her put in an asylum. He told us about how cruel his father was to both him and Selena."

Ruthie stopped and looked at the older couple. There were tears running down Lavinia's cheeks, while Samuel looked shocked.

"I'm sorry. I know this must be very difficult for you. Selena knows she disappointed you, but she is hoping you could reconsider how you feel and find it in your hearts to help her and Seb."

"Reconsider how we feel?" Samuel turned towards Ruthie in surprise. "In what way?"

"Well… about disowning her. I'm sorry, I didn't explain it properly. She asks you to forgive her for marrying Hector. She wants to make things right with you both. She understands why you needed to disown her and…"

"Disown her!" Lavinia exclaimed. "We never disowned Selena or Sebastian. We tried again and again to visit her, but she was never there. We wrote countless letters, but never received one in reply, not one! It was her who disowned us… or so we thought."

"Do you think…? I mean, is it possible…?" Samuel was unable to finish his question.

"I don't know how that all happened," Ruthie was confused. "But I do know that Hector is a cruel and controlling man. He came to the farm to search for her, but we had her hidden in the house. She is terrified of him. Seb is afraid of him as well, although he did his best to stand up to him. Do you suppose Hector could've not passed the letters on to Selena?"

Samuel stood up and began pacing the room. "Maybe Emmeline was right all along," he sighed.

"Seb was very brave," Ruthie continued. "He kept telling us how he wanted to get his mother out of that place, but his father had forbidden him to see her. So, he and Stella, one of the girls I told you about, went on the train. They somehow got in there and brought Selena out. It seems Seb threatened them with his father moving his mother elsewhere if they didn't let him in. Hector was probably paying a lot to keep her there. I can't imagine how they managed to get Selena out, but they somehow did, and they brought her back to the farm. Once the medication wore off, she began to talk a little about how things were for her. She has lived a difficult life with Hector. She is afraid of what will happen to Seb. The two of them are very close. They are united in their fear of Hector."

"Samuel, what are we going to do?" Lavinia clasped her hands tightly in her lap.

"We have been praying we'd hear from Selena for years, and whatever has gone on before, our prayer has been answered, and we have the opportunity to see her again," Samuel stated. "Emmeline said all along that Hector was a cruel man, and only after money. I don't suppose Sebastian ever got the money we sent him. If only Selena had listened to Emmeline. If only we had listened to her."

Lavinia explained, "Selena and Emmeline were the best of friends. The two girls were inseparable. Emmeline met Hector first, and it looked as though they would marry. Then they broke off their engagement, and Emmeline disappeared for several months. By the time she got back, Hector had his eye on Selena. Emmeline tried to warn her that Hector wasn't a good man, but Selena believed her friend to be jealous. Emmeline always asked about Selena, and I don't think she was jealous at all. How could we have been so blind? Hector told us so many stories about where our daughter was. I don't suppose now that any of them were true."

"Seb said that his father often used to lock him and his mother up in the attic," Ruthie said quietly. "They didn't have a life. Seb didn't have any friends until he came to our village. He didn't play when he was a child."

"We will go to them," Samuel stated. "We must go and bring them home. Where is this village?"

Ruthie explained, and it was agreed that Ruthie would travel with them as soon as possible.

"I will drive myself. No need to take a driver," Samuel decided. "How soon can you be ready, Lavinia?"

"Let's leave within the hour," Lavinia got to her feet. "I'll organise for the rooms to be aired, and this kind lady needs something to eat."

There was much activity during the next hour. Ruthie found herself presented with several large plates of food. How Eliza and Lily would enjoy hearing all about this place. Elsie thought the farmhouse was large, so what would she make of this one? It was easily five or six times the size of the Turleys' house. Probably more.

Ruthie felt tired as she climbed into the car with Samuel and Lavinia. Having established that she could read a map, the Rotherhams agreed she should sit in the front with Samuel.

"Are you sure you can drive all that distance, Samuel?" Lavinia asked.

"I'm certain. I've been driving myself since the beginning of the war."

"We used to have a driver," Lavinia explained. "We had several staff, but now we just have one girl who helps us inside, and our gardener keeps up the outside. He was too old to go to the war."

"Seb has been very helpful on the farm," Ruthie told them. "He didn't know anything about farming or working on the land when he first came, but he's a quick learner."

The journey was long, but eventually they drew near to the village. Ruthie found herself looking all around, in case Hector was about. The night was dark, and the blackouts made it impossible to see anything much.

Ruthie felt uneasy as they turned into the Turleys' yard. She told herself not to be silly, but she sensed there was someone watching them.

When Samuel stopped the car, Ruthie was glad to get out and stretch her legs. She left Samuel to assist his wife, while she hurried up to the door and knocked gently. "It's Ruthie," she called softly. She knew the door would be locked and that the Turleys would have been alerted by the car in the yard. They would all be wondering if it was Hector.

The door opened almost instantly, and Bill's smile of relief could be seen in the dim lamplight of the kitchen.

Samuel and Lavinia were right behind Ruthie now. They were just about to move into the house when a voice boomed beside them in the darkness, "I knew it! You tried to fool me, but you couldn't! No one fools me! Why else would they be here if their crazy daughter wasn't already inside?" Hector roared.

Ruthie rushed into the kitchen and pulled Lavinia with her, while Samuel stood his ground, and Bill, his gun in his hands, went out to join him.

Ada stood in the doorway, while Ruthie led a shaking Lavinia to a chair.

"He's back!" Seb hurried into the kitchen in his pyjamas. He stopped in his tracks when he realised Ruthie wasn't alone.

"Seb, this is your grandmother," she said calmly.

"I'm very pleased to meet you," Seb stepped towards Lavinia, holding out his hand.

Lavinia gripped it tightly and pulled him towards her. "Not as pleased as I am, Sebastian."

"Mother will be terrified," Seb stated. "I mean, knowing he's back."

Lavinia stood, still holding tightly to Seb's hand. "Then I should go to her. She needn't be afraid any longer."

When Seb looked a little unsure of what to do, Ruthie said, "I'll lead the way. The girls will be frightened too."

Up in the bedroom, they found the three girls crowded around Selena, who was visibly shaking.

"Auntie Ruthie!" Lily sprang from the bed and into Ruthie's arms. "He's here again! We didn't let Seb's mam go under the bed this time."

"He's not coming in," Ruthie spoke loud enough for them all to hear. "Selena, there's someone here to see you. Eliza, Elsie, you two come with me and Lily a minute."

Selena didn't seem to register her words. She just kept staring into space.

Eliza extracted herself from Selena's hold and pulled Elsie with her. They followed Ruthie out onto the landing, where they sat on the top of the stairs.

"What if he tries to come in?" Elsie cried.

"Uncle Bill and Seb's grandfather will stop him," Ruthie tried to reassure her.

Just then, a shot rang out.

"What was that?" Lily squealed in fright.

"I'll go and see." Ruthie tried to disentangle Lily's arms from around her neck, but the little girl was having none of it. Eventually, she managed to pass Lily to Eliza and hurried down the stairs.

In the kitchen, Ada was still standing in the doorway.

"What happened?" Ruthie asked.

"Bill had to shoot. Just in the air, mind you. That fool has run off now, but I reckon he might have gone the wrong way. Bill's gone after him. He thinks he's in the bull's field."

It was then that a shout filled the air, and Ruthie could instantly tell it was Hector in trouble.

"Get it off!" he bellowed.

"I'll help." Ruthie grabbed a lit lantern and hurried past Samuel, who was still standing just outside the door. She ran towards the bull's field, from where she could hear more shouts of protest from Hector.

Another shot rang out, and everything went quiet. What had happened now?

When Ruthie arrived in the field, she could see the lantern Bill had also taken with him.

"Bill!" her voice echoed across the field.

"Over here, Ruthie. It's safe to come. I've shot the bull."

Ruthie hurried towards Bill's voice. When she reached him, she found the bull lying dead on the ground, while Hector lay unmoving close beside it. "Is he…?"

"No," Bill shook his head. "We'll have to get him to the doctor."

When Ruthie turned, she saw Samuel and Seb hurrying towards them. "We need to get a board to put him on," she stated. "It seems he got on the wrong side of the bull. We must get him to a doctor."

The next few minutes were a blur as they worked together to find a suitable board and move Hector as carefully as possible onto it. Ada brought blankets, which they used to cover him. They then loaded him onto the back of the cart, as this was the easiest way of transporting him.

They rode in silence along the dark roads to the main part of the village, where Bill jumped down and hurried to knock hard on the door of the doctor's house.

They carried Hector inside, then left the room while the doctor and his wife looked at the wounded man.

Ruthie found Seb standing close beside her in the hallway.

"I don't like him," Seb said quietly, "but I don't wish him to die either."

"That's because you are a good person, Seb. The doctor will do all he can. I'm afraid your father met his match with the bull."

"What about the gun?" Seb asked.

"It was just a shot in the air," Samuel explained. "He was threatening to break his way into the house."

Ruthie looked from Seb to his grandfather. They really were alike.

Samuel stepped towards Seb and said awkwardly, "It's a pleasure to finally meet you, Sebastian. You are obviously a fine young man."

Seb brightened at his grandfather's compliment. "Pleased to meet you, sir," he said confidently.

30

"Did the bull really stamp all over him?" Elsie's eyes were wide with amazement.

"Yes. That's why I've always told you girls to keep out of the field when the bull is there," Bill explained.

"And Hector really is in hospital? He can't come back here?" Selena asked for the third time that morning.

"Yes, my dear," Samuel reassured his daughter. "Hector is in hospital. He won't be going anywhere for a long time, if ever."

"'Cos his legs were all broken," Elsie put in.

"Yes. It seems his back might be broken too. He can't hurt anyone again," Bill stated.

"Why is the bull not like the cows?" Elsie asked.

"The bull is the man cow!" Lily shook her head at her friend.

"Was he naughty before?" Elsie looked confused. "Is that why he got sent away to other farms?"

"He had to go to the other cows," Lily explained confidently. "Uncle Bill said the bull goes around the farms, so the cows have babies, and we all get milk."

"Cor! The bull was naughty then!" Elsie exclaimed. "There was a man down our street who gave lots of women babies, and they said he was really bad. I heard my mum talking about him. So which cow was the bull's wife? Will she be sad now he's dead?"

"That's what cows and bulls do," Lily sighed, sounding older than her years. "They don't get married."

"Who would like another piece of bread?" Ada carried a plate to the table. "I'm afraid we're out of bacon, but I can cook more eggs. The chickens are laying well."

"Would anyone like more tea?" Ruthie left the table to fetch the teapot. "Seb, are you ready for a second cup yet? You're usually the first to finish."

"Oh bother! I'm sorry. I'm rather slow this morning," Seb apologised.

Ruthie briefly touched his shoulder as she passed him. "You've got a lot on your mind. You were a great help last night, you know."

When Ruthie returned to the table, she looked around at the unusual gathering. Selena and her parents seemed happy enough, although it was evident they were all used to a different standard of living. Selena was still afraid that Hector would burst in at any moment, despite all their attempts to reassure her. Eliza and Lily were quiet, while Elsie was full of questions. Bill and Ada were doing their best to make everyone feel at home. It was only Seb who seemed somehow uncomfortable.

Bill read from the Bible as he always did. Then, when he prayed, Samuel and Lavinia added prayers of their own, thanking God for bringing Selena and Seb back to them.

When it was time for Bill and Ruthie to start on the day's work, Seb jumped to his feet, eagerly offering to help.

As the three of them left the house, Ruthie guessed the boy had something on his mind. She couldn't imagine what he was thinking after all he'd been through in the last few days.

It was as they entered the barn, he asked, "Was it my fault that my father was hurt?"

Ruthie gave him her full attention. Turning to face him, she said, "Not at all, Seb. You must never think that."

"I made him angry. I got Mother out of that place, but I just couldn't leave her there. I opposed him. If I hadn't, he wouldn't have come here. I just don't know what's right anymore."

"Of course you couldn't leave your mother in the asylum. It wasn't right that she was there. Your father was wrong to have her locked away like that. No one wanted him to get hurt, but he's still alive, and there's still time for him to turn his life around."

"Mother didn't have a life in that place, did she?"

"No, she didn't. I don't think either of you had much of a life with your father."

"That's true. I used to imagine everyone got shut in cupboards. I remember when Mother told me it wasn't right. When I own a house, I don't want an attic and I certainly don't want any cupboards. There won't be any rooms without windows either. I don't want anyone to be afraid under my roof."

"I don't think they could be, Seb. You are a good person. Your grandparents seem like good people, too."

Seb sighed. "I suppose they do, but it's all happened so quickly. The thing is, they are going to take Mother and me to live with them, but I don't know them. I don't really know Mother either, not like I know all of you."

"I understand. For what it's worth, their house seems very nice. And as for not knowing them, you didn't know us when you moved here, but now you're like part of the family."

"But that's just it. I want to stay here. I like being part of a family."

"And we'd love to have you, but your grandparents can give you so much more. Listen, Seb. I didn't know anyone when I first came here, so I do understand. You'll soon get to know them, just like I did with everyone here."

"But you knew Eliza and Lily," Seb said thoughtfully.

"No, I didn't. Their father brought them to me the night before we came here. He asked me to bring them to the country where it was safe. I didn't know them at all. Eddie knew it would be the right thing for all of us, and it was. Just like it will be the best thing for you and your mother to live with your grandparents. We'll write, Seb. We'll all miss you. I hope you'll come back and see us one day."

"Oh, I will! I'll come just as often as I can."

"I'll look forward to that. We all will." Ruthie reached out and hugged him. "You are a fine young man, Sebastian Westfield. Don't you ever forget it."

"Thank you, Ruthie. I wish I had an auntie like you."

They set to work side by side, Ruthie observing how confident Seb had become with the animals.

"I'll truly miss the farm," Seb reflected. "I wonder if there will be farms near my grandparents' house. I'd like to continue working on the land if I can."

"I don't know. It's a little way into the country, so there may be farms. I know you'd be a great help."

"Do you remember when I first arrived here? I daresay I looked a fool in those rather ridiculous shoes Father made me wear!" Seb laughed.

"They weren't very practical, were they?" Ruthie smiled along with him. "I didn't have the right shoes when I came here, either. I'm sure your grandparents will get you everything you need."

Once the morning tasks were completed, they returned to the house.

"Seb!" Lily threw herself into his arms. "What about the concert for my dad?" she cried. "If you're not here, we can't do it!"

"Oh dear! I'm sorry Lily. I'll do my best to come back, if I may?" he looked to his grandfather for permission.

"Of course you may come back," Samuel agreed. "It's important to keep your word."

"See, Liliana Grace, I'll come back. You keep practicing, alright?"

"I'll try, but it won't be the same. I wish you didn't have to go," Lily clung tightly to him. "Everyone goes, but no one comes back."

"Yes, they do, Lily," Lavinia said, gently. "Samuel and I have been praying for many years for Selena to return to us, and to have Seb in our lives, too. Now we are all together again. Sometimes things don't happen as quickly as we'd like them to, but never give up praying, and never lose hope."

Ruthie looked up and caught Eliza's eye. She knew only too well that some things took years to come right.

There seemed to be a great deal of activity in the house as Samuel, Lavinia, Selena, and Seb prepared to leave. Ada and Eliza prepared a basket of food for them to take on the journey, while Seb gathered up the belongings he'd brought from the cottage, and Selena put on one of Ada's dresses she'd altered for her.

"I will never forget your kindness," Selena said with tears in her eyes. "I never thought I'd escape Hector, or that dreadful institution, but I did. I couldn't have come to a better place. Thank you all for taking care of me. Thank you for all you did for Seb as well. I wasn't able to prepare him for the world, but you all did what you could for him. He could easily have been taken advantage of. You know, for years I was convinced God couldn't care about me at all, but I realise I may have been wrong. Things sort of fell into place, didn't they? I mean, if Seb hadn't been sent here, he and Stella would never have rescued me."

"And we would never have got our daughter and grandson back," Lavinia added.

With promises to write and visit soon, they went on their way. Samuel's last words were, "If there is ever anything we can do to help any of you, it would be our honour."

"I'm going to miss Seb," Eliza sighed. "It'll be strange without him and Stella."

"I know. We'll miss them both, but you still have Florence, and she'll be missing them as well."

"Yes, it's just… well, Seb and Stella are so different."

"They are that. It's hard when people leave, isn't it?" Ruthie put an arm around Eliza's shoulders. "Would you like to come and help me for the rest of the day? I'd enjoy your company."

"Yes, I'd like that." Eliza smiled. "Auntie Ruthie?"

"What is it, Eliza?"

"It's Lily and Elsie. They were talking about going to get Dad, like Seb and Stella went to get Seb's mother. I tried telling them they couldn't do that, that they're too young, but they don't understand why he doesn't come home, or even write letters. Lily thinks someone has locked him up in a place like Seb's mam."

"Oh dear," Ruthie sighed. "I'll talk to Lily."

"But she's right, in a way. Why doesn't Dad come home? I want to see him, whether he wants to see me or not. Please can I go?"

"Alright. But it won't be easy. Your dad has a lot to get used to, and it's difficult for him to accept there will be things he can't do like he did before. Let me catch up on a few things here, then we'll go just as soon as we can. Probably next week some time, if Bill says it's alright."

"Thank you! I can't wait to see him. I know you want to visit him again, too."

Ruthie chose to ignore Eliza's last statement. Instead, she said, "Don't be too disappointed if he doesn't seem as pleased to see you as you are him. He loves you really, it's just hard for him. I think a visit from you will be just what he needs."

"Will I need to pretend to be older to get in there?" Eliza enquired.

"You've been spending too much time with Stella! Whose coat are you going to borrow?" Ruthie teased, causing mother and daughter to laugh together.

31

"Why can't I go?" Lily cried. "I want to see Dad so much."

"I know you do, Lily, but you are too young. You and Elsie need to stay here and help Auntie Ada. Don't forget, I'm taking the cake you made especially for your dad. I'll make sure he knows you made it." Ruthie hugged the little girl. She knew how she would feel if others were going to visit Eddie without her.

"But he doesn't even write letters," Lily sighed.

"That's because he can't see!" Elsie shook her head at her friend. "I tried writing with my eyes shut, and it went all funny!"

"Why can Eliza go and not me?" Lily ignored Elsie's explanation.

"I've told you. It's because Eliza is older. Now, you girls be good, and we'll be back before you know it."

Ruthie hugged Lily once more, then Elsie, before joining Eliza where she waited outside.

"I feel mean going without Lily. I never left her behind before," Eliza said quietly.

"I know it's hard, but it's for the best. Come on, let's catch that train."

Once the train pulled out of the station, Eliza began looking around nervously.

"It's alright," Ruthie reassured her. "I felt like that myself the first time I left the village on a train."

Eliza moved closer to Ruthie. "We have to go into Wales, don't we?"

"Yes, but there will be so many people, no one will recognise either of us," Ruthie spoke confidently.

There were several delays, so it wasn't until late in the afternoon that they reached their destination. Eliza slipped her hand into Ruthie's as they walked up the driveway. They watched as several men worked on a garden, while others were going for a walk, using their sticks to navigate their way towards the road.

"Are they really all blind?" Eliza asked in a whisper.

"I think so, yes. Some of them certainly are," Ruthie said as she rang the doorbell.

When the door was opened, Ruthie informed the man that they'd come to see Eddie Davies. She watched Eliza as the girl realised that this man was also blind.

"He doesn't want to see anyone," the man said flatly.

"I've brought his daughter, so he must!" Ruthie insisted.

"He doesn't have to if he doesn't want to!" the man responded irritably.

"Is he in the same room?" Ruthie asked.

"Yes, but it doesn't matter, because I'm not letting you in." With that, the man slammed the door in their faces.

"What are we going to do?" Eliza burst into tears.

"Come on," Ruthie put an arm around Eliza's shoulders and led her away from the door. "I remember what was outside his window, so we'll just have to go that way."

She led Eliza around the side of the building, studying each window until she was satisfied she had the right one. To her surprise, the window was open, but it was too high up to allow her to see into the room.

"I think this is it. I'll lift you up, just to make sure," she said quietly to Eliza.

Eliza took hold of the windowsill, then, putting her foot on Ruthie's bent knee, she hoisted herself up. "It is!"

she giggled. "Dad," she called through the open window, "Me and Auntie Ruthie are here!"

"What?" Eddie's voice sounded surprised. "I said…"

"We're not taking no for an answer, Eddie. Are you going to let us in, or do we have to talk to you through the window?" Ruthie called.

"I… oh… go round to the door. I'll say it's alright, just this once," Eddie's reply came from within the room.

Ruthie lowered Eliza to the ground and together, they returned to the front door. This time, the man who had let Ruthie in on her previous visit was already standing there, holding the door open.

"Hello. We meet again," Ruthie said. "Eddie's daughter Eliza is also here with me."

"Eddie's a lucky man," he smiled. "You won't give up on him, will you?"

They followed him along the corridors to the door of Eddie's room, which was slightly ajar.

"Go on in," the man said. "I'll make you all some tea."

Ruthie pushed the door open, and Eliza gripped her arm. Together, they entered the room, where Eddie sat in a chair by the window.

"Hello Eddie," Ruthie spoke first.

"Hello Ruthie. Eliza?"

"Hello," Eliza's voice was little more than a whisper.

Ruthie noticed that Eddie no longer had bandages on his face, and that the area around his eyes was badly burnt.

"Lily made you a cake," Eliza found her voice. "She wanted to come with us."

"You can't bring her here," Eddie sighed. "Ruthie, whyever did you bring Eliza?"

"She wanted to see you. Don't you think she's had enough to deal with without you disappearing as well?"

"I want you to come home, Dad. Me and Lily both need you home. You'll like it at the Turleys' farm. They said me and Lily can call them Uncle Bill and Auntie Ada. Elsie calls them that, too."

"It sounds like you are settled there. That's good. You must understand why I can't come, Eliza."

"No. No I don't. Mum couldn't help dying, but you didn't die. Why won't you come back?"

"You have Ruthie to look after you."

"Here's the tea," the man announced as he carried a tray into the room.

Ruthie took the tray from him and placed it on a small table. "Thank you," she said.

"I'll just be next door if you need me," he told them, before leaving once more.

"Why do you stay in here?" Eliza asked. "There were lots of people outside and some in a big room playing games or something."

"No point," Eddie muttered.

"I'll cut some of Lily's cake, shall I?" Ruthie suggested. "I'll need to use the teaspoon for a knife, and we'll have to eat it off the saucers. We'd better not bother that kind man again."

Ruthie poured a cup of tea for each of them. She noticed that Eddie's hands shook slightly as he took the cup from her. She then did her best to cut pieces of the cake and handed out the saucers. "Lily enjoys working in the kitchen," she said. "Eliza, why don't you tell your dad about your friends and the things that have been happening?"

So, Eliza told Eddie about Florence, Stella, and Seb. She told of how Seb and Stella had gone to get Seb's mother out of the asylum and how Seb's father came to the farm and got hurt by the bull. "I'm going to miss Seb and Stella," she finished.

"They sound like good people," Eddie agreed.

"Elsie doesn't have parents anymore. Lily said she can share you. I've never known Lily have a friend before. She doesn't get so many things wrong with her now we're living on the farm. She caught scarlet fever, and I was really afraid."

"Ruthie told me how you looked after her and Lily. You're a good girl, Eliza."

"When will you come home, Dad? We all want you home. We really miss you, and I know you'll love it on the farm."

"That's enough, Eliza!" Eddie bellowed, making them both jump.

"No! Just because you don't have to pretend you are my dad, you're still Lily's! I thought you were the best dad a person could have, but you're not! You're as mean as your own father is!" Eliza shouted before she ran from the room.

"Why did you do that, Eddie?" Ruthie asked quietly.

"She doesn't understand." Eddie sounded defeated.

"And neither do I. Stop feeling sorry for yourself, Eddie Davies. All these men are getting on with their lives, so why can't you? You think long and hard about what Eliza said. Lizzie had no choice in what happened to her, but you do. Remember when you took us to the farm? You said you hoped the girls still had faith after losing their mother, then living with your father. They never gave up on God, Eddie, so you mustn't either. Lean on Jesus to get you through this, and let us help, too." With that, Ruthie got to her feet and left the room, closing the door noisily behind her.

She found Eliza in the next room, sitting with the man who had made the tea, along with three others. They all had paper in front of them, but there didn't seem to be any writing on it. On closer inspection, she saw that there were raised dots.

"I'm sorry!" Eliza ran to her and fell into her arms. "I didn't mean to say those things."

"I know." Ruthie held her tightly. Perhaps she shouldn't have brought her after all. She had really thought that Eliza being there would change Eddie's mind.

The sound of a man crying reached their ears. Ruthie had never heard it before, but she instantly knew it was Eddie. "We should go," she said. "We need to get the train."

"I'll make sure he's alright," the man reassured her. "Don't worry, he'll come around in the end."

"Could you tell him I didn't mean those horrible things I said?" Eliza sniffed.

"I'll do that, but I think he already knows."

Ruthie and Eliza made their way back to the train station in silence. Ruthie wanted to reassure her daughter, but she didn't know how. Maybe she was no good at being a mother after all.

The train was busy, but they found a seat in the corner of a carriage. Eliza rested her head on her mother's shoulder, trying to hide her tears. Ruthie held her close, whilst fighting back her own tears. She needed Eddie home just as much as the girls did. Her love for Eddie hadn't diminished over the years, it had grown.

32

"Your daughter looks worn out."

Ruthie tightened her arm around Eliza and looked up at the soldier who had spoken. "Yes, it's been a long day," she sighed. Their journey home was not proving straightforward. The first train had been held up for some time, meaning they had to wait several hours for their connection. Now they were at a standstill while they waited for an air-raid to finish. The black-outs were drawn, and the carriage was in darkness, except for the small torches with their beams covered by tissue paper carried by some of the service men and women. All Ruthie wanted was to get herself and Eliza home. The fact that, for this moment, she didn't need to pretend to be Eliza's aunt, and could allow this stranger to continue believing they were mother and daughter, was the only bright spot in the day.

The train eventually moved on. Ruthie guessed at the devastation the air-raid had caused by the number of fires she saw burning as she cautiously lifted a corner of the black-out. How had she stuck it in Cardiff all those months while the raids were a regular occurrence? The night Eddie had come to her door had been the worst of all.

The sky was light, and the birds were singing cheerfully by the time she and Eliza stepped off the train in the village.

"I'm going to write to Dad," Eliza said decisively, as they made their way home. "I'll do it as soon as I get in."

"Why don't you get some rest first?" Ruthie advised. Eliza hadn't spoken during the journey, but Ruthie knew she wasn't sleeping.

"I should do it straightaway. I was so unkind, and I need to put it right."

"You'll be able to think more clearly after some sleep. Maybe I shouldn't have taken you, Eliza. I really thought that seeing you would make him see sense."

"I wanted to go. I'm still glad I did, I think. What about school?" Eliza yawned.

"You don't need to go today. Lily and Elsie can go on their own."

"But you'll work on the farm."

"Yes, I expect I will." Ruthie yawned too.

"Lily will want to know what happened," Eliza sighed.

"They'll be going to school soon. We'll put her off until this evening, when we've had a chance to think about what to say."

Lily and Elsie were full of questions, but sensing all was not well, Ada sent them off, telling them they would hear all about it later.

Ruthie was thankful Ada knew how to handle all kinds of situations. She didn't know what to tell Lily. Perhaps she could ask the older woman for advice. She made to get a start on some work, however, Ada had other ideas, and both Ruthie and Eliza were ordered to get a few hours' rest.

By the time she'd undressed and got into bed, Eliza was already fast asleep. Ruthie knew she wouldn't be far behind her.

Ruthie awoke some time later and instantly knew she'd been sleeping for several hours, as the sun was now high in the sky. She wondered what had woken her so suddenly.

There was a noise coming from the yard. It sounded like a lorry. She got out of bed and walked to the window.

"What is it?" Eliza asked sleepily.

"It's a lorry. I didn't know Bill was expecting anything to be delivered."

They dressed quickly, then hurried downstairs.

"You won't believe it!" Ada rushed in from the yard. "It's a bull!"

"A bull?" mother and daughter questioned together.

"Yes. The finest bull I've ever seen!"

"Where did it come from?" Ruthie had her hand on the door handle.

"Selena's parents had it sent here, you know, to make up for the one Bill had to shoot. The man is most insistent that it's a gift from their family to ours. He says he has letters too! Go on out. I'll be there now in a minute with some tea."

Ruthie and Eliza went into the yard, where Bill and the smartly dressed stranger were unloading the bull from the lorry.

"He's a fine beast!" Bill stated, the widest smile on his face Ruthie had ever seen.

"Very gentle," the man agreed. "It had to be the best bull to be found. I take it you are satisfied with him?"

"Satisfied! I'm more than satisfied. I could never afford a bull of this quality!" Bill exclaimed. "Mr. Rotherham is an extremely generous man!"

"Samuel Rotherham insisted you should have the best," the man smiled.

The bull was easily led to his new home in the field. Ruthie could see for herself that this animal was well bred.

Ada brought out an abundance of tea, sandwiches, and cake, making Ruthie wonder how she could always produce a feast in no time at all. They took seats on the wall, from where they admired the bull as he explored his new surroundings, while the sun shone down on them all.

The man pulled out an envelope from his pocket, handing it to Bill. "Young Sebastian insisted I bring these letters for you."

The man was pleasant to talk to. He seemed to be well acquainted with Samuel and Lavinia Rotherham, and said how good it was to have Selena back with the family, as she had been missed terribly over the years, being their only child. He also said what a fine young man Sebastian was, and how many similarities there were between the boy and his grandfather, which was nothing short of a miracle, considering the two had only met for the first time just weeks before.

Ruthie could hardly wait to read Seb's letter. She'd been praying he was settling in well, and word from him would hopefully put her mind at rest.

The man had a long journey ahead of him, so he was soon on his way, a basket of Ada's bread, pies, and cakes by his side.

"Well, I wasn't expecting that!" Bill exclaimed. "Samuel Rotherham is a very generous man. A bull like this must've cost a fortune! And to have it brought all the way here."

"I think he's just pleased to have his daughter and grandson back," Ada smiled. "It really was good of him, though. Bill, with this bull, we'll have all the farmers wanting to borrow him!"

Bill picked up the envelope which he had placed on the wall beside him. "Let's see how our Seb is doing, before we get back to work," he suggested.

Ruthie took the folded piece of paper Bill handed to her. Straightening it out, she read, Dear Ruthie, I wanted to tell you how right you were. It's only been two weeks, but Grandmother and Grandfather are wonderful people! They are allowing me to go to the local school. Mother is doing well. She says she will write soon. She is helping Grandmother with many things at the church. There is a farmer in the village who needed extra help, so I've been going along and doing my best. Grandfather was a little surprised I wished to help on a farm, but I told him how I'd enjoyed working alongside you and Mr. Turley.

I have written to each of you, but please reassure Lily that I will keep my promise and return when her father comes home. Your friend, Seb.

"He says that his school is good, but he still misses the friends he made in our school," Eliza told them as she read her letter.

"The farmer he's helping is pleased with how much he already knew," Bill put in.

"He says they've got someone to cook for them at home, but her bread isn't as light as mine," Ada smiled. "It seems Selena wants to learn how to cook. Seb has asked me to send some recipes for her to try."

"He sounds happy, doesn't he," Ruthie added.

They folded away their letters and got to work, Eliza and Ruthie working side by side in the barn.

The day passed quickly, and soon the younger girls were racing into the yard. Ada called them straight into the house, so it wasn't until teatime that Ruthie and Eliza had to face Lily's questions about her father.

"When is Dad coming home?" she asked as soon as they were all eating.

"It won't be for some time as yet, I'm sorry. He still isn't well enough," Ruthie replied.

"Why? You said he'd get better!" Lily looked confused.

"And he will. Sometimes it takes longer than others. Your dad has a lot to get used to."

"But me and Elsie were pretending we couldn't see. We closed our eyes, and I only walked into the wall once."

"That's because I told you to stop the other times!" Elsie put in.

"When can I go to see Dad?" Lily asked.

"You have to wait, Lily," Eliza sighed.

Ruthie was wondering if Eliza had wished she'd waited, but she'd insisted earlier in the day that she was glad to have seen him. Eliza had taken the time to write a letter to her father earlier in the afternoon, and had gone straightaway to post it, before returning to help Ruthie.

"But you didn't wait! You went to see him!" Lily was becoming angry, which was most unlike her.

Ada, having heard all about the visit, said gently, "The thing is, Lily, children aren't allowed where he is at the moment, not young children anyway. You keep writing letters to your dad, that's the best thing you can do right now."

"But he doesn't write back!" Lily shook her head in frustration.

"But he has someone to read your letters to him, that's the most important thing," Bill said.

"He enjoyed the cake you made," Ruthie told her. At least this was the complete truth.

"I like baking," Lily replied flatly.

"What's the bull called?" Elsie asked, suddenly changing the subject.

"He hasn't got a name," Bill smiled.

"Why don't the animals all have names? I wouldn't like it if I didn't have a name."

“It’s different with animals, Elsie. We don’t give them names, because sometimes they don’t stay with us for long.”

“Ben has a name,” Elsie insisted.

“Ben is a dog, and he isn’t going anywhere,” Ada smiled. “We had to give Ben a name so we could call him to help with the sheep.”

“I think the bull needs a name,” Elsie chewed her fingernail thoughtfully. “He has to live on his own, so he should be called something.”

“Well, you girls have a think about it then. I suppose a fine bull like him deserves a name!” Bill laughed.

“Can I ask Florence to come for tea tomorrow, please?” Eliza asked. “She’s really missing Stella.”

“Yes, of course you can. Florence is welcome here any time,” Ada told her.

Lily was quiet for the rest of the evening, but she asked no more questions, for which they were all extremely thankful.

Life was finding a new normal at the Turley farm, although each member of the household hoped Eddie would soon join them.

33

As Ruthie crossed the yard, she smiled as she watched Lily and Elsie playing on the swing Bill had hung in a tree. As usual, Ben was keeping an eye on them, walking back and forth, wagging his tail furiously. Lily was laughing with Elsie, but Ruthie knew Lily was only pretending to be happy. In the two weeks since she and Eliza had visited Eddie, they hadn't been able to reassure the little girl that her dad would come home. In fact, they weren't even sure themselves if Eddie would ever return to them.

Ruthie lay awake night after night, wishing she knew what to do. It was hurting the girls, and she didn't know how to help them. His silence was hurting her too, and no one knew quite how much. Ada knew she had feelings for Eddie, but Ruthie couldn't even tell her friend how strong they were.

There were times when Ruthie was angry with Eddie. How could he cut his girls off like that? He hadn't even asked anyone to reply to Eliza's letter. Then she blamed herself. She'd pushed him too hard. She should have let him come round in his own time. Years ago, she'd been able to talk Eddie around in any situation. He'd get angry about something his father had done, but she could always calm him down. Why had she presumed she still had the right to speak to him in the same way? Too many years had passed. She'd been the one to push him away for so long. No wonder he didn't take too kindly to her interfering.

Ruthie was about to go into the field, where Bill was checking whether the hay was ready to be cut, when she heard a vehicle coming up the drive.

She turned to see a car she didn't recognise approaching, so waited to find out who it was.

Cars rarely arrived at the farm, so the girls jumped down from the swing and came to welcome the visitor.

Ruthie drew in a sharp breath as the car stopped. The driver's door opened, and a tall man stepped out, but her eyes were fixed on the figure who was opening the passenger door.

"Dad!" Lily cried, as Eddie stepped out of the car.

The back door opened, and Ruthie recognised the man who had twice let her in to visit Eddie. He smiled as he heard Lily greet her father.

"Dad! You came!" Lily threw herself against Eddie, clinging to his waist.

"Lily!" Eddie bent and lifted her into his arms, where she clung to his neck.

"I thought you weren't coming back!" Lily sobbed. "You didn't write for ever and ever! I thought you were dead, and they didn't want to tell me! Eliza and Auntie Ruthie wouldn't let me see you!"

Ruthie felt Elsie's hand slip into hers. "Do you think she'll still share him with me?" the little girl asked.

Ruthie squeezed Elsie's hand. "Yes, I know she will. Come on, let's go and say hello."

Ruthie walked forward, her legs shaking slightly. Eddie was really here! "Hello Eddie, it's good to see you." Turning to the man she'd previously met, she said, "Hello, we meet again! I'm sorry, I don't know your name, but I'm Ruthie."

"I remember you well," the man smiled, holding out his hand. "Have you learnt to follow people more quietly yet, when you don't want them to realise you're behind them? I'm Fred. I'm very pleased to meet you properly at last!"

Eddie was still talking to Lily, so Fred introduced the driver of the car as Malcolm.

Ruthie invited them all to the house, where Ada was now waiting on the doorstep to welcome them.

Fred took Malcolm's arm while Eddie lowered Lily to the ground.

"I'll tell you where to go, Dad," Lily said. "Me and Elsie can show you! Come on Elsie."

Elsie reluctantly released Ruthie's hand and moved to Eddie's other side. "Hello," she said, as she gently took hold of his free hand.

"It's nice to meet you, Elsie. Lily has told me all about you in her letters. I'm glad she's got such a good friend as you."

Cautiously, the two girls led Eddie towards the house, Malcolm and Ruthie making small suggestions as they guided him. Finally, they were all seated around the kitchen table.

"Elsie, run over to Florence's and get Eliza, would you, please?" Ruthie asked.

"Course I will!" Elsie jumped up and headed out of the house.

"It's so good that you're here, Eddie," Ruthie tried to keep her voice even.

"It's about time, I'd say. Wouldn't you?" he smiled awkwardly.

"You're here now, and that's all that matters," Ada said, bringing mugs of tea to the table. "It's good to see you again, Eddie."

"I'd better go and finish helping Bill," Ruthie said. "How long can you stay?"

"We were hoping there was somewhere to spend the night," Eddie explained. "We have to go back tomorrow, but we'd like to go to church here with you in the morning. We don't mind where we sleep. A barn will do if there's nowhere else."

"You won't be sleeping in any barn," Ada told them. "You can make some beds up on the floor in the room next to this one. There's plenty of blankets."

Ruthie was intending to leave the room when Bill entered. "I saw we had company," he said, grinning as he recognised Eddie. "You've earned the rest of today off, Ruthie."

"I'm happy to work," Ruthie heard herself say, although the last thing she actually wanted to do was leave the house now Eddie was here.

"I insist," Bill smiled at her.

Eddie told them how Malcolm had agreed to drive him on the long journey, and how Fred had been eager to join them.

"I have something I want to show you, Lily, although I think we'll wait until your sister is here, too."

"What is it?" Lily took her eyes off her father just long enough to question Fred.

"Your dad is learning to read and write braille, so we thought that maybe you girls could write him some letters."

"Braille? We don't know braille. Eliza's teacher told her about braille, but we don't know it."

"That's why I'm going to teach you," Fred grinned.

"Then we can write Dad letters!" Lily's excitement was evident.

"I'd much rather read letters from you than the books Fred gives me!" Eddie laughed good-naturedly.

"Why can't you stay now? Then we won't have to write letters?" Lily asked.

"Because I still have a lot to learn. I was a bit lazy at first, but now I'm learning everything just as quickly as I can."

"I'd say!" Malcolm put in. "Wish they all had your determination."

"I reckon learning braille is a wonderful idea," Ada said.

"Auntie Ruthie can learn too!" Lily suggested. "You'll write to Dad, won't you, Auntie Ruthie?"

"Yes, if he wants me to." Ruthie was irritated at how flat her voice sounded. She'd tried so hard to not appear too keen, she'd gone to the other extreme.

The door burst open and Eliza and Elsie ran in.

"Dad! You really are here!" Eliza had tears in her eyes. "I'm sorry I said all those horrible things. Did you get my letter?"

Eddie put out his hand and drew Eliza closer to him. "You have nothing to apologise for. I'm sorry I behaved as I did. It was a good telling off I needed!"

The afternoon passed quickly. Lily and Elsie insisted Eddie needed a tour around the farm, so Eliza, Ruthie, Malcolm, and Fred went along with them.

The younger girls each took one of Eddie's hands, leading him carefully around the yard.

"All the cows are in the field in front of us," Lily told him as they stopped by a fence, "but not Rotherham, because he's the bull."

"Rotherham? That's an unusual name for a bull," Eddie commented.

"Mr. Rotherham bought him for Uncle Bill," Elsie explained, "'cos the old bull got shot because Seb's dad got in its way, and it stood all over him."

"But Mr. Rotherham knew Uncle Bill needed a bull, so he bought him another. Seb and his mum have gone to live with Mr. and Mrs. Rotherham now. They're Seb's grandmother and grandfather. They have a really big house!" Lily continued.

"There's been a lot happening," Ruthie smiled.

"You'll meet Seb," Lily went on excitedly. "He's going to come back and we're going to do a concert for you. We'll have to write and tell him!"

They completed their tour of the farm, then made their way inside, where Fred began to teach Ruthie and all three girls the braille alphabet.

"It's hard," Elsie said thoughtfully.

"I'm going to learn it though, so I can write to dad!" Lily said confidently. "Seb says I'm good at learning things."

"I'm looking forward to meeting this Seb," Eddie smiled.

"I can't believe you're really here!" Eliza grinned. "This has been the best day ever!"

It was later that night, once the girls were in bed, that Ruthie and Eddie got a few minutes to themselves, Eddie having said he could do with a bit of fresh air.

"Not sure you'd really call the air on a farm fresh," Ruthie laughed, as they walked outside together and stood leaning against the barn.

"I want to thank you, Ruthie," Eddie said quietly.

"You've nothing to thank me for. Bringing the girls here was the best thing that's happened to me."

"I took you away from everything you knew and expected you to help me out, like you always used to."

"And I'm glad I was able to do so. Eddie, you gave me something I never thought I'd have. I never knew what happened to Eliza, and you made it possible for me to get to know her. I need to thank you and Lizzie for taking such good care of her."

"You're not angry that I did what I did?"

"No. I'm sorry your own little girl didn't make it, but I couldn't have chosen anyone better to take care of mine."

"Ruthie..." Eddie hesitated, "it wasn't just Eliza who made me change my mind. It was you as well. You didn't give up on me."

"I never would, Eddie." Ruthie looked straight at him. She wondered if she'd have the confidence to look at him that way if he could see her in return. With his eyes so badly damaged, it was more difficult to see what he was thinking, but she detected that if possible, he'd be looking at her the way he used to.

"You will write to me as well, won't you, Ruthie?"

"Yes, of course I will."

"And you'll stay when I get back? It's so good of Bill and Ada to say there's work for me here."

"I'll be here Eddie, I'm not going anywhere."

"I suppose we'd better go back inside," Eddie said. "It's been a long day."

Ruthie held out her arm for him to take, but found him holding her hand instead. She felt him squeeze it gently, before moving to take her arm. Did this mean anything? Was there really hope?

34

The next three months were filled with activity, but for Ruthie, they passed slowly. Eliza, Lily, and Elsie spent much of their spare time learning to read and write braille, then writing furiously on the braille slate and stylus Fred had left for them. Ruthie wondered if Eddie had expected the number of letters he received, but he always wrote back to each of the girls, answering many of their questions and commenting on the things they told him.

Ruthie had also learnt the braille alphabet. She'd sat at the kitchen table long after everyone else was in bed. Once she was sure she could do it, she wrote a letter to Eddie. She kept it very simple, telling him how things were going on the farm, but the reply she received could have almost come from the Eddie she'd known as a young girl.

Now the day had finally come when Eddie would arrive in the village. Conversions had begun on one of the smaller barns, as Bill had said that his workers needed proper accommodation. The barn was fairly near to the house, and Ruthie and Bill had created a path, making it easy for Eddie to get from place to place.

Everyone was up earlier than usual on the morning of Eddie's arrival. The house seemed fit to burst with excitement. Even the late September sun shone brightly for the occasion.

"Are you sure Seb will come for the concert?" Lily asked for what felt like the hundredth time.

"Yes, Seb will arrive tomorrow, ready for the following evening," Ruthie told her.

"And he's going to stay until Monday," Elsie added, predicting Lily's next question.

"I hope Dad likes the concert," Lily sighed.

"He will. Everyone else in the village too, I'd say," Ada smiled. "I'm glad we can have it in the chapel again. They all enjoyed Seb's music last time."

"I'm pleased Dad's coming home," Eliza said to Ruthie as they did the milking side by side, "but it will be different, won't it?"

"Yes, in some ways, it will. It'll be good to have an extra pair of hands to help."

"Will Dad really be able to work on the farm?"

"I expect there will be things he may not be able to do, but he's learnt a lot in the last few months. The more time goes on, the more he'll learn."

"Lily was afraid he'd end up in with the bull. You don't suppose he will, do you?"

"No. We will all have to remember to say when the bull is moved to a different field. We do that though anyway, don't we? We always make sure Lily and Elsie know."

"Yes, I suppose so. But how will he find his way around?"

"I don't have all the answers yet, but I know he'll do it. We'll all learn together. I expect he'll start out working in the garden. None of us can see the spuds when they're underground, can we?"

"I suppose not," Eliza giggled. "You don't think he'll want to leave, do you? I like living here."

"No, I don't. He's keen to do farm-work. It was good of Bill to offer him a job. I know the Turleys want us all to stay."

It was late morning when Malcolm pulled the car into the yard, with Eddie seated beside him.

"Where's Fred?" Elsie asked.

"He had to work today," Eddie explained, as he hugged all three girls.

"Come on in the warm for some tea and cake," Ada called.

Eddie took out a cane and positioned it in front of him.

"How can me and Elsie help you if you have that?" Lily asked.

"I'm afraid you'll have to take it in turns," Eddie explained. "This helps me find my way around."

Reluctantly, Elsie stepped back and allowed Lily to take her father's free hand.

Once they were all seated around the table, everyone seemed to speak at once.

"You should see what we did to the barn!" Eliza exclaimed. "There's a real bedroom in there now. Uncle Bill says we can help make the rest of it like a house when you decide how you want things."

"It sounds like you've been very busy," Eddie smiled. "Thank you."

"I don't reckon we're the only ones," Ada said, as she handed him a mug of tea.

"We'll help you find your way around," Lily told her father. "I'll see for you."

"That's very kind of you, Lily. I think I'm going to need quite a bit of help at first."

"We could make a map of the farm," Eliza exclaimed. "You know, out of stones and things."

"That's an excellent idea!" Malcolm complimented her.

"It is, Eliza. You've always been good at thinking up ways around problems. I think that will really help me," Eddie smiled at her.

The rest of the day flew by. Ruthie didn't find herself alone with Eddie, as the girls were always at his side.

The following day, Seb arrived. Eliza and Florence, accompanied by the two younger girls, were at the station to meet him.

"Seb! You came!" Lily squealed, flinging her arms around his waist. "Dad's home. He can't wait for the concert!"

"I say! It's good to see you all again!" Seb hugged first Lily, then Elsie, before he turned awkwardly to Eliza and Florence. "It's an awful shame Stella wasn't able to come for a visit, then we'd all be back together."

"'Er mam said 'er couldn't, cos 'er 'ad to work," Florence explained.

They walked together towards the Turley farm, each trying to catch up on the news of the last several months.

"There's Rotherham!" Elsie pointed to the bull in his field.

"I say! He is a fine chap, isn't he? Grandfather was most pleased about your choice of name. He said he'd never had a bull named after his family before."

"Elsie chose it," Lily grinned up at him.

"Well done, Elsie!" Seb exclaimed.

The house was filled with chatter that evening as they ate together around the table. Everyone was keen to hear what Seb had been up to in the months since he left the Turley farm, while Seb wanted to know all the news from the farm and the village.

"Father is still in hospital," he explained. "It seems he will never walk again. it hasn't softened him though, by all accounts. Grandfather went to visit him."

"And how is your mother?" Ada enquired.

"She is a different person! She did so want to come along with me, but she and Grandmother are doing such a lot at the church, organising various projects and events. I've never known Mother so happy! She even sings about the house."

"She could've sung in our concert!" Lily said thoughtfully.

"Indeed. I know where I get my love of music from now. I say, has anyone heard much from Stella?"

"She's very busy," Eliza explained. "She's working in a factory and looking after some of her brothers and sisters."

"They got sent back from where they were evacuated from too," Florence muttered.

"Oh dear. I do hope they will be safe in London."

The following day was equally busy. Seb spent most of it practicing with Lily. It had also been arranged that many of the children from the school would sing one of their favourite hymns.

It was finally time. Ruthie was the one to guide Eddie as they walked together to the chapel. The girls and Seb had gone on ahead, needing to make last-minute arrangements.

They entered the building, and Ruthie led Eddie to a spot fairly near the front, where Lily and Elsie had insisted he sit. "How are you feeling?" she asked quietly.

"Like everyone is looking at me," Eddie said self-consciously.

"They won't take the slightest bit of notice of you once Lily starts to sing," Ruthie tried to reassure him.

"I still can't believe it. Our Liliana Grace up there on a stage. Lizzie would have been so proud."

"She's looking lovely. She's wearing a pink gingham dress, and her hair is in plaits with ribbons that match her dress."

"Now I can imagine her better. Thanks, Ruthie."

The concert began, and the chapel fell silent as Seb made his way to the piano. They started with everyone singing *Blessed Assurance*, before Seb introduced "Miss Liliana Grace Davies."

Lily truly looked angelic as she stood there beside the piano. Seb played the introduction, and her voice rang out loud and clear. Not a hint of the shy little girl many of them knew.

The evening was a great success. Seb knew exactly how to keep everyone interested as he entertained them all with piece after piece, sometimes joined by Lily, who smiled throughout the entire performance.

By the time they left the chapel, the night was black. Ada had asked the girls to run on ahead to help put out the food she'd promised, leaving Ruthie and Eddie together once more.

As they walked along the lane, Eddie said, "I enjoyed your letters, Ruthie. I wondered whether you would write."

"I didn't know if you would want me to," she said hesitantly.

"I'm glad you did."

Ruthie wondered what, if anything, she should say. What was Eddie thinking? Was it possible that he had feelings for her? A sudden thought struck her. What if he did, but presumed she wouldn't be interested in him? How could she let him know she was?

Eddie broke into her thoughts as he said, "Ruthie, there's something I've got to ask you."

She could hardly breathe as she asked, "What is it?"

"Would you come with me back to Cardiff?"

"What?" the question came out as a squeak.

"Not to stay," Eddie reassured her quickly. "I mean, I need to do a few things… only… I can't go on my own, not now. The thing is, Ruthie, it's not really fair of me to ask you, but there's no one else to ask."

"What is it you need to do?" she asked in some confusion.

"I want to go to Lizzie's grave, and the place where our little girl was buried. I found out where the orphanage children were buried, then I found the fresh grave."

"I never thought to ask what happened to her. I'm sorry Eddie."

"It's alright. I didn't know what to do, so followed the plan you'd already made, only I knew there was nothing to be done for her."

"Yes, Eddie, I'll go with you."

"That's not all. I need to see my father."

"See him?" again Ruthie's voice was high pitched.

"Yes, to tell him I know everything. I… also need to forgive him for the way he treated me as a boy, how he treated my girls, and most of all, what he did to you." Feeling Ruthie's arm tense, he continued quickly, "I don't expect you to see him. You can leave me at the door. I know it will be harder for you to forgive him, but I've learnt a lot recently. Not just how to live without my sight, but about God's love for me. I've learnt the importance of forgiveness."

"Yes, Eddie, I understand. I'll still go. I know I should think and pray about forgiving him myself, but I don't know if I'm ready to do that yet."

"I understand. Thank you, Ruthie. It means a lot to me. You have always been there to help me out."

"You've always been there for me too," Ruthie said quietly, "even when I pushed you away."

They walked back to the farm in silence, each lost in their own thoughts. What had she been hoping he'd ask?

Not that she'd accompany him to Cardiff, but she knew she'd do anything Eddie asked of her.

35

It was several weeks before Eddie and Ruthie made the trip to Cardiff. Eddie explained the situation to Bill while they mended a fence together.

Bill insisted they should go as soon as possible. "Things can change quickly in wartime," he said. "Have you considered that your father might not be there?"

"Yes, it's quite possible. He never used the shelter, and most of the street was taken out the night we left, but I have to try. If he's gone, I'll ask about to find out if anyone knows what happened, but if they don't, I'll know I tried."

"That's fair enough," Bill agreed.

They decided not to tell the girls where they were going, only that they would be gone for the day. With a basket of food packed by Ada, Ruthie and Eddie set off for the station.

Ruthie felt increasingly uneasy the nearer they got to Cardiff. If anyone else had asked, she wouldn't have gone anywhere near the place, but this was for the man she loved. She'd told Eddie he'd have to go into his father's place alone, as the idea of coming face to face with Gareth filled her with dread.

"I understand," Eddie agreed. "I might change my mind myself as yet."

"But Eddie, what if he throws something at you? He was always good with his aim. You won't see to get out of the way."

"I know, but I'll just take the chance. I really appreciate you doing this, Ruthie. I realise it isn't easy for you."

Ruthie didn't know how to respond. No, it certainly wasn't easy going back to a place where she'd spent so many miserable years. She consoled herself that it was only for one day, then she'd never need to go there again. She could return to the farm, where everything seemed safer, and life was good.

The train neared Cardiff, and Ruthie stared out of the window at the devastation all around. "They've bombed a fair bit of it," she told Eddie. "It looks so different."

They got off the train and left the station. Ruthie stood for a while to get her bearings. "Where first?" she asked.

"The cemetery by the orphanage," Eddie's voice was quiet.

With Eddie holding her arm, Ruthie made her way through the streets until she found the place. "We're here," she said, as they reached the gate. "Where do we go once we're in the cemetery?"

Eddie had obviously been expecting this question, as he explained, "We need to follow the path around to the right. Keep going around the corner. About halfway along, you should see an old oak tree. Let me know when we're level with it."

Ruthie followed Eddie's directions, pleased to find the old oak was still standing. Once they were opposite it, she asked, "Where from here?"

"Turn to your left and walk between the graves. There is a wooden cross on the fourth one back."

Ruthie guided Eddie off the path onto the uneven ground. They moved between the graves towards where she could see the home-made wooden cross standing among the grass. Bending to look at it, she read the writing carved into it. Beth 29.11.1928-1.12.1928. "Eddie, it's here. You carved the cross?"

"Yes. Not the best of jobs, but she had to have something."

"You named her Beth," Ruthie stated.

"Yes. She was so small, so I thought she needed a name to fit. We'd talked about naming our baby after Lizzie, if it was a girl. They were both named after her, Eliza and Beth."

Ruthie couldn't stop the tears from falling. This child had only lived a matter of days, born to two parents who loved her, while her child had become strong. She hated the thought of Eddie and Lizzie's baby having not survived, but she was thankful her Eliza had been given the best possible chance. "Do you want me to leave you for a while?" she asked.

"You can stay," Eddie said quietly.

Ruthie took his hand and placed it on the cross before stepping back slightly. How hard it must have been for Eddie, never to be able to speak of the loss of his own child. She knew how that felt. She hadn't known whether her child had survived, not until Eddie had told her over twelve years later.

After some minutes, Eddie straightened up and turned back towards her. "I'm ready to leave," he said.

Ruthie could hardly see through her tears as she led him back to the path and out of the cemetery.

"Where next?" she asked once they were back in the street.

"I'd like to go to Lizzie's grave, if you don't mind." He gave the name of the cemetery, and they were on their way.

Finding Lizzie's grave was a little more difficult, as Eddie himself had only visited it once, but the simple wooden cross bearing her name was eventually found. "I want to mark it properly," Eddie explained. He drew a rough wooden cross out of his coat, saying, "I had a man at the centre to do it for me. I don't know how he did it without seeing. I just about managed Beth's when I could see."

"It's lovely," Ruthie looked down at the wood on which was carved "Elizabeth Jane Davies 5.9.1911-15.11.1940".

"They said he'd done a decent job, but it's good to hear it from you." Eddie bent and dug the cross into the ground. "I wish I could've given her something better, her and Beth."

Ruthie didn't know what to say. Instead, she took a few steps back. "I'll give you a few minutes."

Eddie spent some time kneeling on Lizzie's grave before he got to his feet and turned in Ruthie's direction.

They walked in silence until they were on the street once more.

"Do you want to eat now, or would you rather go to your father first?" Ruthie asked.

"I'd rather eat then go home, but I'd better do what I've come for. Let's get it over with."

Ruthie felt like her insides were in knots as they made their way towards the street where she'd grown up. Eddie had been right. Much of the area had been destroyed by bombs, likely because it wasn't far from the docks. She stopped in her tracks as she turned towards where she remembered the street. There were many piles of rubble, and only three houses still stood, the centre one being that where Gareth Davies lived. "The house is still standing," she heard herself say.

They picked their way through discarded bricks and other rubble until they reached the houses.

"The windows are boarded up. I can't tell whether anyone is still living here."

"They won't have got him to leave," Eddie said confidently. "If you don't mind, just take me to the door and stay nearby, if you can, in case I need to make a quick exit."

"I'm coming in with you," Ruthie surprised herself by saying.

"Are you sure?" Eddie asked in amazement.

"Yes. I've got to do it. I need to show him I'm not afraid of him anymore."

They stepped up to the door and Eddie turned the handle, not at all surprised when the door swung open and the smell of alcohol came out to meet them. "Dad!" he called.

"What the…?"

As they entered the dim room, Gareth Davies sat bolt upright in his bed.

"You're still here then," Eddie commented.

"Where else would I be?" Gareth barked. "What's happened to you? Stupid enough to get close to a bomb, were you?"

Ignoring his father's comments, Eddie explained, "I'm not in the army anymore. I've lost my sight."

"How the mighty have fallen!" Gareth almost laughed. Then, seeming to notice Ruthie, he turned his attention towards her. "So, he came running to you like he always did, did he?"

Before Ruthie had the chance to answer, Eddie began, "I went to Ruthie the night I last saw you. You were wrong when you presumed Eliza and Lily were dead.

I let you believe that, so you couldn't get your hands on them."

"You lying…!" Gareth reached for a bottle and threw it, but Ruthie grabbed a discarded broom, hitting it in mid-air before it had a chance to hurt anyone.

"I see you haven't changed," Eddie sighed. "I'll never understand why you treated me as you did, but I suppose you had your reasons. What I don't understand, though, is why you treated my girls so badly."

"Badly! You don't know the meaning of the word!"

"And why did you treat me as you did?" Ruthie added. "Eddie knows all about it."

For the first time ever, Ruthie watched the colour drain from Gareth Davies' face.

"She's right. I know everything. You should be ashamed of yourself, taking advantage of a young girl like that."

"I… she…"

"No excuses," Eddie said firmly. "You would've done the same to Eliza, wouldn't you?"

"I…" Gareth was again lost for words.

"Well, both girls are safe now," Ruthie said. "I used to be afraid of you, Gareth Davies, but not anymore. I feel sorry for you. You are here, all alone. You know nothing about love."

"Don't you go talking that Bible rubbish Lizzie got Eddie into!" Gareth growled.

"It's not rubbish," Eddie said calmly. "You still have a choice, Dad. You can still turn to Jesus and ask for forgiveness."

Gareth roared as he swung himself out of bed and lunged towards them. Ruthie grabbed Eddie's arm, but he stood firm.

"You can't hurt us anymore," Eddie stated. "I won't be coming back again, so this is the last you'll see of us."

With that, he turned towards the door, Ruthie close at his side, leaving Gareth standing, half-dressed, in the middle of the room.

They were at the end of what had once been their street before Eddie asked, "Are you alright, Ruthie?"

"Yes, I think so. Are you?"

"Yes. How about we see if there's any of the park left and eat our food there?"

They were soon in the park, where Ruthie found an empty bench. They sat side by side as she opened the basket and took out the contents.

"There's cheese and pickle, or corned beef and pickle," Ruthie began.

Eddie stopped her by putting his hand over hers. "Ruthie, if I don't say this now, I might never have the courage to do it again." When her hand relaxed, he went on, "You and I have known one another all our lives. When we were young, I always thought we'd marry. Then you didn't seem to want me around and I married Lizzie. I loved Lizzie, but I never stopped loving you. I still do. If you can never feel the same way about me, what with me not being able to see and that, I'll not mention it again. But Ruthie, I still love you. Is there any chance…?"

"Eddie!" Ruthie turned to look fully at him. "I always imagined we'd marry too. The years I pushed you away were the hardest of my life. Now you're back, I'm hardly able to think of anything else. I imagined it would be enough just to know you were still alive, but I don't want us to ever be apart again."

"You really mean that? What about my being blind?"

"That doesn't make the slightest bit of difference to me. You are still Eddie Davies, the man I've always loved."

"Oh, Ruthie!" Eddie pulled her into his arms. "I can't believe it!"

"You'd better believe it," Ruthie said, as Eddie bent to kiss her. She'd wondered what it would be like to kiss Eddie all those years ago, but now she found it more pleasant than she'd ever imagined.

"Let's not waste any more time, Ruthie. Will you marry me?"

"Yes, Eddie, of course I will." Ruthie giggled as she said, "I wonder if Bill and Ada saw this coming! They kept saying how you needed to wait to finish the barn until you knew what you wanted."

"And now we can do it together. You, me, and our girls."

"Yes. But Eddie, about our girls."

"What about them? Do you reckon they'll be happy?"

"Oh yes, I'm sure they will. But what about Elsie? Bill and Ada have kept her on, but I don't know if they'll be allowed to adopt her, with them being older."

"Well, we can't have her going off anywhere else, can we? If Elsie wants to become part of our family, then that's fine by me. Eliza and Lily would have plenty to say if we didn't take her as well!"

"Oh Eddie, I never thought I could be this happy!" Ruthie exclaimed.

"Or me! Now I'm so happy, I could burst!"

"Well, we'd better eat Ada's sandwiches before we do!" Ruthie laughed. She'd wasted so many long years merely existing, but now she was about to begin the life she'd always longed for.

Acknowledgements

This book would never have been published if it wasn't for the encouragement of some wonderful friends and sisters in Christ. After reading some of my fiction writing, both Alex Banwell and Nozipho Khanda, convinced me that what I had written was worth sharing with others.

In 2009, when God blessed me with a wonderful friend who I truly think of as my sister, Alex introduced me to Christian fiction. This was a real blessing, as reading about how God works in people's lives helped me understand how to apply what I was reading in the Bible to my own life.

Alex has been there at every stage of this book, from reading the first draft of each chapter, to spending many hours editing it alongside me, putting up with my sometimes unconventional style of doing things. Without her dedication and patience, the characters would still be confined to my computer. I really can't thank her enough.

I'm hugely grateful to Gwynneth Weaver for proof-reading the text and pointing out my missed capital letters, as well as her other suggestions for improvement. When you know the characters inside-out, you don't always see when something isn't clear to the reader.

I also wish to thank Sandie Worrell for designing the cover. Sandie really understood what I had in mind, then worked along with the Lord to create something far better than I could ever have imagined.

And last, but certainly not least, if it wasn't for my Lord and Saviour Jesus Christ, there wouldn't be anything to write. He gave me the idea and the words to turn it into something which, if I've listened correctly, reflects his love, and glorifies Him.

About the Author

Lorraine Beard has lived all her life in the Forest of Dean. She sings and plays baritone ukulele as part of the church worship group, as well as writing some of her own songs. She has enjoyed writing throughout her life, but presumed her thoughts and ideas would only ever be for her own enjoyment. However, after her first venture into self-publishing with Book of Smiles, Lou decided to give others the opportunity to get to know the characters she has created and knows so well.

When she's not writing, she enjoys reading, baking, knitting, and most of all, spending time with friends.
If you wish to contact her, you can email:

lorrainebeardauthor@gmail.com

Cyfres BlinG

@ebol

Men entro!

Elgan Philip Davies

Cyhoeddwyd yn 2010 gan Atebol Cyfyngedig, Adeiladau'r Fagwyr,
Llanfihangel Genau'r Glyn, Aberystwyth, Ceredigion SY24 5AQ
01970 832 172
www.atebol.com

ISBN: 978-1-907004-50-6

Golygwyd gan Eirian Jones a Glyn Saunders Jones
Dyluniwyd gan Stiwdio Ceri Jones, stiwdio@ceri-talybont.com
Noddwyd gan Lywodraeth Cynulliad Cymru
Argraffwyd gan Wasg Gomer, Llandysul, Ceredigion

Cydnabyddiaethau
Hoffai'r awduron a'r cyhoeddwr ddiolch i'r canlynol am eu caniatâd i atgynhyrchu'r lluniau a'r deunydd hawlfraint yn y llyfr hwn.

Getty Images: tud. 16
Mary Evans Picture Library: tud. 18 (y ddau lun)
Photo Library Wales: tud. 19 (top); tud. 29 (gwaelod)

Cynnwys

Menter ydy bywyd

Mae bywyd yn antur ac mae mentro yn rhan o fywyd bob dydd. Dydy mentro ddim yn rhywbeth sydd ond yn perthyn i chwaraeon mentrus a pheryglus.

Meddylia am ddiwrnod arferol yn dy fywyd. Faint o bethau mentrus wyt ti'n eu gwneud neu a allai ddigwydd i ti?

- Croesi'r ffordd
- Beicio
- Teithio mewn car
- Chwaraeon
- Dringo ysgol
- Gwersi technoleg yn yr ysgol
- Defnyddio cynnyrch glanhau
- Chwarae gydag anifeiliaid anwes
- Coginio

Mae'r rhain yn rhan o fywyd bob dydd, ond eto sydd ag elfen o fenter yn perthyn iddyn nhw. Ond petai pobl yn poeni am beryglon bywyd bob dydd, fyddai neb yn codi o'r gwely yn y bore!

Wps! Dal dy afael!

Ar gefn dy feic …

ond mae yna bethau y gellir eu gwneud i leihau’r risg:

- Edrych i’r ddau gyfeiriad cyn croesi’r ffordd
- Gwisgo helmed
- Gwisgo dillad pwrpasol a defnyddio’r offer cywir
- Canolbwyntio a pheidio rhuthro

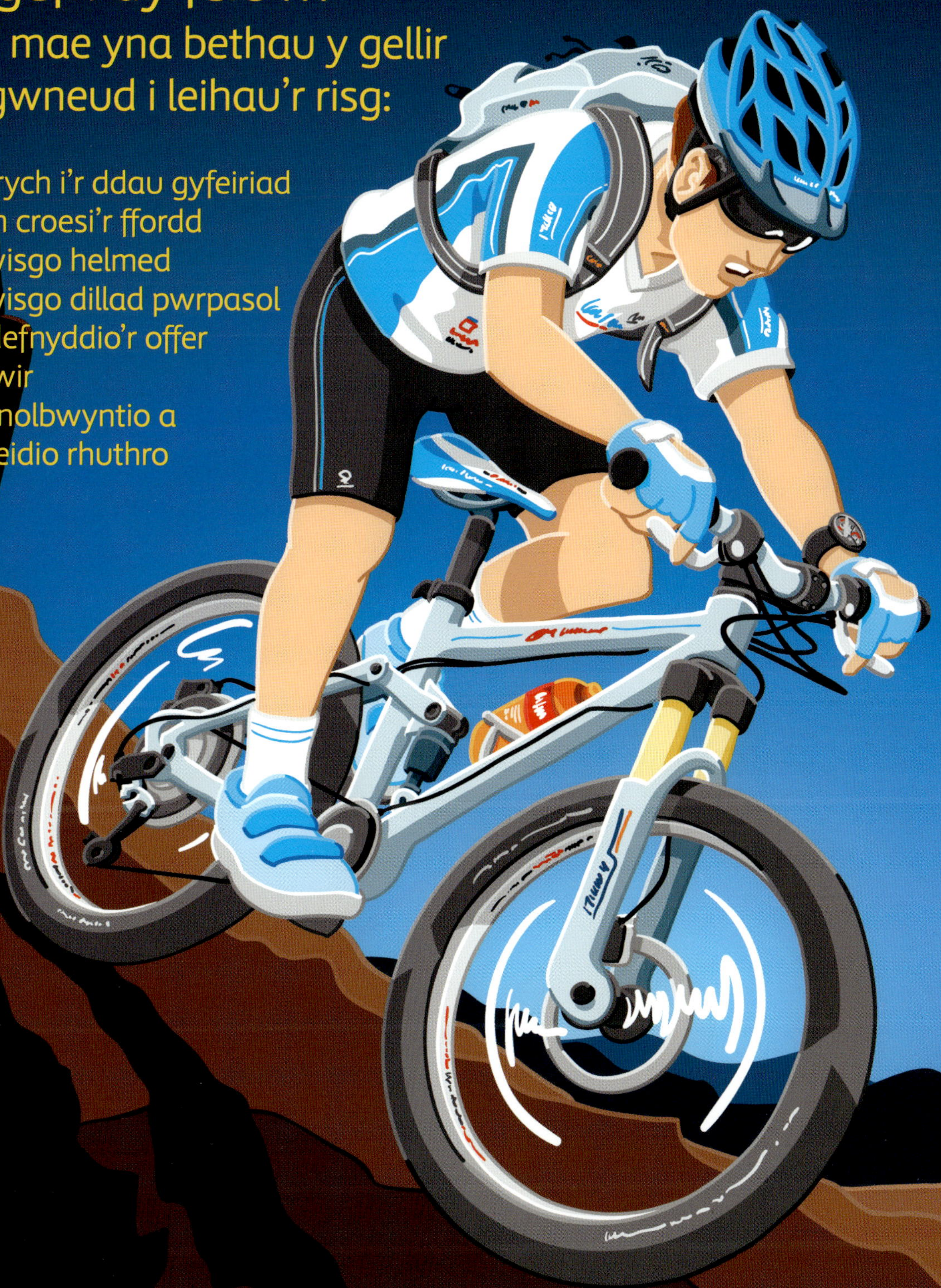

Wyt ti'n berson mentrus?

Mae rhai pobl yn fwy hyderus na'i gilydd. Mae'r hyder hwn yn gallu eu gwneud yn fwy mentrus. Maen nhw'n dweud eu bod nhw am fyw bywyd i'r eithaf a bod gwneud rhywbeth mentrus, peryglus, yn golygu eu bod nhw'n fyw. I rai mae byw ar ymyl y dibyn yn gwneud iddyn nhw werthfawrogi bywyd yn fwy.

Ond weithiau mae rhai pobl sy wedi blino ar fywyd yn mentro'u bywydau yn y gobaith o deimlo'n hapus. Neu mae rhywun yn eu herio i wneud rhywbeth mentrus sydd yn wirion.

Pa un wyt ti?

Wyt ti'n *adrenalin junkie*?

- Wyt ti'n hoff o gymryd rhan mewn chwaraeon mentrus, e.e. naid bynji, neidio o awyren?

Shaun White

Neu'n berson esgeulus?

- Wyt ti'n berson sy'n gwneud rhywbeth heb boeni am y canlyniadau?

Wyt ti'n berson nerfus neu ansicr?

- Oes ofn uchder arnat ti? Neu oes arnat ti ofn mynd mewn lifft? Neu wyt ti'n berson sy'n pwyso a mesur cyn mentro?

Mae'r ffin rhwng bod yn hyderus a mentro yn un denau. Hynny ydy, rhwng bod yn siŵr o'r hyn rwyt yn ei wneud neu dim ond gobeithio'r gorau, rhwng llwyddo a methu, rhwng byw a marw – ac mae'r canlyniadau yn gallu bod mor wahanol.

Mae pobl swil neu ansicr yn gallu cymryd risg i ddianc rhag problemau, neu am eu bod nhw am i bobl gymryd sylw ohonyn nhw. Mae eraill yn mentro er mwyn goroesi ofn neu ffobia.

Mae mentro heb feddwl am y canlyniadau yn achosi niwed neu anaf i ti, neu i eraill.

Beth am ystyried y canlynol?

- Gyrru'n wyllt a diofal
- Gyrru dan ddylanwad alcohol neu gyffuriau, neu mynd mewn car gyda gyrrwr dan ddylanwad alcohol
- Beicio tra'n gwrando ar gerddoriaeth trwy ffonau clust
- Ymladd, neu ddechrau ffeit

Beth ydy'r peryglon?
Beth allai ddigwydd?
Pwy allai gael niwed?

Gyrru ac anfon neges testun yr un pryd

Teithio'n beryglus mewn car

Unwaith mae rhywun yn pasio'i brawf gyrru mae yna berygl i griw o bobl ifanc lwytho i mewn i gar a mynd am 'sbin'. Mae yna demtasiwn i'r gyrrwr ei ddangos ei hun, neu i'w ffrindiau ei ddenu i yrru'n gyflym. Heb fod yn yrrwr profiadol, mae hyn yn gallu arwain at ddamwain.

Dydy pawb ddim yn ystyried y peryglon iddyn nhw'u hunain nac i eraill. Dyna pam mae cymdeithas wedi creu rheolau sy'n rheoli oedran gyrwyr neu gyflymder gyrru.

Cadw'n heini!

Does dim amheuaeth bod cadw'n heini yn sylfaen dda i fywyd. Y rheswm mwyaf amlwg ydy **iechyd corfforol**, lle mae campau fel nofio, dringo, sgïo a beicio yn rhoi **egni** *(stamina)* i ti ac yn dy wneud yn gryf. Mae campau eraill fel gymnasteg, tennis, dawnsio a ioga yn dy wneud yn ystwyth.

Ond mae yna resymau da eraill dros gadw'n brysur ac mae'r rheini'n ymwneud â'r meddwl yn hytrach na'r corff.

Pan fyddi di'n gwneud rhywbeth corfforol mae'r corff yn rhyddhau **endorffin** sy'n gwneud i ti deimlo'n dda. Maen nhw'n help i ysgafnhau unrhyw deimladau o fod o dan bwysau ac yn help i gysgu.

Mae yna elfen o fentro wrth gymryd rhan mewn unrhyw fath o chwaraeon. Mae perygl o gael anaf wrth ddawnsio yn ogystal â bocsio.

Mae **adrenalin** yn rhan bwysig o unrhyw gamp. Y cyffro o gystadlu yn erbyn tîm arall neu yn erbyn yr elfennau pan yn hwylio neu ddringo. Mae adrenalin yn cael ei gynhyrchu'n naturiol gan y corff mewn sefyllfaoedd cyffrous.

Pan mae adrenalin yn cael ei gynhyrchu mae'n cynyddu curiadau'r galon, yn lledu'r **rhydweliau** a'r pibellau aer ac yn cynyddu lefel y siwgr yn y gwaed. Mae hyn yn gwella perfformiad y corff am gyfnodau byr.

Does dim gwahaniaeth os ydy'r sefyllfaoedd hynny yn fater o fywyd neu farwolaeth, neu'n rhedeg am y llinell i sgorio cais. Yr un yw'r cyffro a'r un yw ymateb y corff.

Mae'r term *adrenalin junkie* yn cael ei ddefnyddio am rywun sy'n 'gaeth' i adrenalin ac yn gorfod cael y wefr mae'r hormon yn ei roi i'r corff. Un ffordd o wneud i hynny ddigwydd ydy dy roi dy hun mewn sefyllfa o gyffro a pherygl. Ac os nad yw chwaraeon arferol yn dy fodloni, beth am roi cynnig ar **chwaraeon eithafol**?

Mentro! Mentro!

Tra bod rhai yn mwynhau cymryd rhan mewn chwaraeon, mae eraill yn chwilio am weithgareddau mwy mentrus. Mae'r rhain yn cael eu galw'n chwaraeon eithafol.

Er bod llawer ohonyn nhw'n seiliedig ar chwaraeon a champau traddodiadol, mae elfen newydd yn perthyn iddyn nhw sy'n eu gwneud yn beryglus. Maen nhw'n cynnwys elfen o gyflymder, uchder ac ymdrech gorfforol. Oherwydd hyn dydyn nhw ddim yn gampau sy'n cael eu cymeradwyo gan bawb.

Campau i unigolion yn hytrach nag i dimau ydy'r rhain, gyda'r campwyr yn cystadlu nid yn unig yn erbyn campwyr eraill ond hefyd yn erbyn rhwystrau fel mynyddoedd ac afonydd, neu dywydd garw, eira, tonnau'r môr a gwyntoedd cryf.

Waw! Dyma beth ydy camp!

Dyma rai o'r campau eithafol:

- beicio BMX
- neidio â pharasiwt
- **paragleidio**
- rafftio dŵr gwyn
- sgïo eithafol
- canŵio
- **neidio BASE**
- eirafyrddio *(snowboarding)*
- sglefrfyrddio *(skateboarding)*
- **ceubyllu** *(potholing)*

Rafftio dŵr gwyn

Mae'r campau yma'n dod yn fwy poblogaidd wrth i bobl chwilio am ffyrdd gwahanol o deimlo cyffro ac antur.

Mae rhai yn credu bod y chwaraeon hyn yn cymryd lle anturio i wledydd pell, neu hwylio rownd yr Horn ac ati.

Paragleidio – neidio o ben clogwyn

Gwthio drwy agen gul yn y graig

Ond beth bynnag ydy'r gamp, mae'n rhaid cymryd gofal er mwyn eich diogelwch eich hun a diogelwch eraill.

Er bod cymryd rhan mewn chwaraeon mentrus ac eithafol yn gallu bod yn hwyl, mae sicrhau eich bod yn ddiogel yn bwysig.

Cyn neidio o awyren gyda pharasiwt mae neidwyr yn cael gwers ar sut i neidio a glanio'n ddiogel, ac mae'n rhaid neidio gyda hyfforddwr.

Parcour – Mentro yn y ddinas

Camp sydd wedi tyfu dros y blynyddoedd ydy **parcour**. Camp sy'n digwydd mewn ardaloedd trefol ydy *parcour*. Nod y gamp hon ydy eich dysgu i ddygymod ag unrhyw rwystrau rydych yn dod ar eu traws, gan feithrin sgiliau fel neidio, dringo a glanio.

Can mlynedd yn ôl roedd swyddog morwrol Ffrengig o'r enw George Hébert wedi rhyfeddu at ffitrwydd a sgiliau naturiol brodorion gwledydd Affrica, ac fe ddechreuodd ymarferion naturiol tebyg i hyfforddi morwyr.

Ond Ffrancwr arall o'r enw David Belle a drodd hynny'n gamp pan ddechreuodd Belle a rhai o'i ffrindiau ymarfer *parcour* gan ddefnyddio unrhyw beth oedd yn rhan o'r amgylchedd trefol. Yr unig beth roedden nhw'n ei bwysleisio oedd bod yn rhaid i'r *traceur*, sef yr enw ar bwy bynnag sy'n dilyn y gamp, fod yn ddiogel.

Bod yn ddiogel!

Ond o'r holl gampau hyn, efallai mai'r un sy wedi dal dychymyg pobl fwyaf ydy'r naid bynji.

Mae Seland Newydd yn gartref i'r naid bynji. Cafwyd y neidio bynji cyntaf yn Queenstown yn 1988, gyda'r neidwyr yn neidio 43m o Bont Kawarau. Dyna oedd dechrau twristiaeth antur yn Seland Newydd. Erbyn hyn ceir neidiau bynji mewn gwledydd ar draws y byd.

Ond nid rhywbeth modern ydy neidio o'r math yma gan fod y gamp i'w gweld mewn gwledydd eraill. Mae trigolion Vanuatu, gwlad fechan o ryw 82 o ynysoedd yn ne'r Cefnfor Tawel, wedi bod yn cymryd rhan mewn camp a elwir yn 'ddeifio tir' ers canrifoedd. Ar Ynys Pentecost perfformir y gamp adeg y cynhaeaf er mwyn i'r dynion ddangos eu dewrder.

Codir tŵr o bren, ac mae'r neidwyr yn cysgu wrth droed y tŵr hyd nes y bydd y neidio'n dechrau, er mwyn cadw ysbrydion drwg i ffwrdd. Mae'r dynion yn clymu gwinwydd *(vines)* i'w pigyrnau – nid rhaff bynji fel yn y neidio bynji modern! Mae paratoi'r gwinwydd yn hollbwysig rhag i'r neidiwr fwrw ei ben ar y llawr, neu fwrw i mewn i'r tŵr os yw'r rhaff yn rhy fyr. Mae angen i ben y neidiwr gyffwrdd â'r tir, ond nid bwrw'r tir gan achosi niwed i'r neidiwr.

Cyn neidio
Wrth neidio bynji, mae hyfforddwr yno er mwyn clymu'r rhaff yn ddiogel. Maen nhw'n sicrhau bod yr offer yn ddiogel.

Mae'r rheolau diogelwch yn cynnwys:

- Bod yn ffit ac nid yn ordrwm yn ôl oedran, taldra a rhyw
- Bod o leiaf yn 18 oed
- Bod neidwyr yn cael eu pwyso a'u rhoi mewn harnais pwrpasol
- Bod yr harnais yn cael ei gysylltu â'r rhaff bynji
- Bod rhywun yn eu harwain allan i'r platfform neidio
- Gadael i'r neidwyr neidio pan fyddan nhw'n barod

Defnyddio'r offer cywir
Mewn pêl-rwyd a chriced does dim hawl gan eich **gwrthwynebwyr** eich cyffwrdd na'ch taclo. Ond mae dal yn bosibl cael cyswllt anuniongyrchol, e.e. cael eich taro gan y bêl pan ydych yn batio, neu hyd yn oed wrth faesu; dyna pam mae rhai maeswyr, yn ogystal â'r batwyr, yn gwisgo helmed a phadiau.

Mae hefyd perygl o gael eich anafu wrth redeg yn y campau hyn, e.e. llithro neu droi eich troed.

Ond mae'n amlwg bod y perygl o gael anaf yn uwch mewn chwaraeon cyffwrdd. Mae chwaraeon fel rygbi a phêl-droed yn gorfforol iawn, a thaclo caled yn medru bod yn rhan o'r campau. I osgoi anafiadau difrifol mae'n bwysig cynhesu cyn chwarae, a gwisgo'r offer cywir, e.e. padiau ar y coesau ac amddiffyn y dannedd.

Ond mewn bocsio, pwrpas y gamp ydy sgorio pwyntiau yn erbyn eich gwrthwynebydd.

Mae llwyddiant a phoblogrwydd bocswyr fel Joe Calzaghe a Nathan Cleverly yn gallu apelio at fechgyn sy ddim yn hoffi gemau tîm.

Mae nifer o bobl ifanc, yn enwedig merched, yn dechrau gyda *boxercise* ac yna am ddysgu mwy am y gamp a datblygu mwy o sgiliau. Oherwydd y poblogrwydd ymhlith pobl ifanc mae'n rhaid sicrhau diogelwch pawb sy'n cymryd rhan. Ond nid rhywbeth diweddar ydy'r gofal hyn am focswyr.

Cadw at y rheolau ...

Mae'r cymdeithasau sy'n rheoli chwaraeon am i bawb fwynhau drwy gymryd rhan, ond ar yr un pryd maen nhw am i bawb fod yn ddiogel.

Mae nifer yn meddwl fod bocsio yn gamp beryglus. Ond mae rheolau pendant sy'n gwneud y gamp mor ddiogel â phosib. Mae bocsio yn hen gamp sy'n boblogaidd mewn nifer o ddiwylliannau. Mae yna luniau o'r gamp ar gael sy dros 4 mil o flynyddoedd oed.

Am ganrifoedd nid oedd unrhyw fath o reolau ynglŷn â sut y dylai **gornestau** gael eu cynnal. Doedd dim rhaid i'r bocswyr fod yr un pwysau, ac nid oedd hyd pendant i'r rowndiau. O ganlyniad cafodd nifer eu lladd, yn enwedig yn ystod y 18 ganrif pan oedden nhw'n ymladd am arian mawr.

Lluniwyd y rheolau cyntaf yn 1743. Yn 1867 gwnaed rheolau pellach a ddaeth i'w hadnabod fel Rheolau Queensberry. Mae'r rhain yn dal yn berthnasol heddiw. Erbyn hyn mae bocsio'n un o gampau mwyaf poblogaidd y Gemau Olympaidd.

Rhai rheolau bocsio

- Dylai'r sgwâr fesur 7.3m x 7.3m.
- Dim dal eich gwrthwynebydd.
- Pob rownd i fod yn dair munud, gyda munud o egwyl rhwng pob rownd.
- Os bydd rhywun yn disgyn i'r llawr mae'n cael deg eiliad i ddod ato'i hun.
- Os bydd bocsiwr yn taro'i wrthwynebydd tra bod hwnnw ar lawr fe fydd yn colli'r ornest.
- Ni ddylid gwisgo esgidiau â phigau.

Mae rheolau ychwanegol ar gyfer bocswyr amatur, sef eu bod yn gwisgo helmed ysgafn o ledr a bod gan ferched hawl i wisgo dilledyn i amddiffyn y frest.

Dringo

Edmund Hillary a Tenzing Norgay

Concro mynydd Everest yn 1953

Ond mae hen gampau yn dal yn boblogaidd. Mae cysylltiad arbennig rhwng Cymru a'r gamp o ddringo.

Ganwyd y daearyddwr a'r tirfesurydd George Everest yng Nghrughywel, Powys, yn 1790. Everest oedd yn gyfrifol am fesur a mapio dros 2,440 cilometr yn India a Nepal ac fe enwyd y mynydd uchaf yn y byd ar ei ôl.

Ym Mhen y Gwryd, yn ardal yr Wyddfa, y bu Edmund Hillary a'i gyd-ddringwyr yn hyfforddi cyn mentro i ddringo mynydd Everest yn 1953. Ymhlith y tîm roedd y Cymro Charles Evans ac ef a dringwr arall oedd i fod i ddringo i gopa Everest gyntaf, ond oherwydd y tywydd drwg bu'n rhaid iddyn nhw droi yn ôl. Tri diwrnod yn ddiweddarach llwyddodd Edmund Hillary a Tenzing Norgay i gyrraedd y copa.

Yn 1995 cyrhaeddodd Cymro gopa Everest am y tro cyntaf pan lwyddodd Caradog Jones, o Bontrhydfendigaid, Ceredigion, i gyrraedd y copa.

Mae Eric Jones, dringwr ac anturiaethwr sy wedi bod yn mentro ar sawl cyfandir, yn dod o Dremadog, Gwynedd.

Eric Jones ar y graig yn ymyl ei gartref yn Nhremadog

Mae Eric hefyd wedi dringo mynydd Everest ac yn gwybod pa mor bwysig ydy diogelwch. Mae'n rhaid cael offer da a digon o amser i baratoi ymlaen llaw, ond mae Eric hefyd yn cynghori unrhyw un sy am ddringo mynyddoedd uchel lle mae'r aer yn denau, i beidio â rhuthro i gyflawni'r gamp ac i beidio â dringo mwy na 2000 o droedfeddi bob dydd. Mae blinder yn gallu bod yn gymaint o berygl â'r mynyddoedd.

Ac mae diogelwch yr un mor bwysig wrth ddringo clogwyni sy'n llawer is nag Everest.

Dringwr ifanc, dawnus a chyffrous sy'n defnyddio cyn lleied â phosib o offer wrth ddringo ydy Ioan Doyle o Fethesda.

Mae dull Ioan o ddringo yn dibynnu'n llwyr ar nerth bysedd ei draed a bysedd ei ddwylo wrth iddo wthio a thynnu ei hun i fyny o agen gul i hollt denau. Mae'n edrych yn ffordd tu hwnt o beryglus i fentro i'r clogwyni serth, llyfn, heb raffau, ond mae'r math yma o ddringo yn gwthio sgiliau Ioan i'r eithaf. Mae Ioan yn llwyr ddibynnol ar ei allu ef ei hun – a dyna ydy'r pleser mae'n ei gael o'r gamp.

Ti bia'r dewis

Mae gan bawb ohonom ddewis beth ydym ni am ei wneud. Mae yna sawl dewis ...

Ti sydd i ddewis ...

Ymuno â Chlwb neu Gymdeithas
e.e. drama, gwyddbwyll
Manteision
- gwneud ffrindiau newydd
- dysgu sgiliau newydd

Mynd i Goleg
Manteision
- datblygiad personol
- dysgu mwy am bwnc rwyt yn ei hoffi
- dechrau bod yn annibynnol

Gweithio
Manteision
- ennill cyflog
- gosod sylfaen i yrfa
- rheoli amser hamdden a gweithio

Teithio o Gwmpas y Byd
Manteision
- cyfarfod â phobl
- dysgu ieithoedd a gweld sut mae pobl eraill yn byw
- gwneud penderfyniadau drosot dy hun

Mae'r rhain yn cynnig cyfle i ddysgu rhywbeth newydd. Mae'r rhain yn help i fagu hyder. Maen nhw'n dysgu rhywun sut i fod yn annibynnol, yn cynnig cyfle i gyfarfod â phobl a gwneud ffrindiau newydd.

Ond eto mae angen cymryd gofal cyn mentro. Mae angen pwyso a mesur y manteision yn erbyn yr anfanteision.

Fel mae'n ddoeth i ymchwilio i gamp cyn dechrau ei chwarae, mae hi hefyd yn bwysig darganfod gwybodaeth am y coleg, cymdeithas, gwaith ac ati i weld os ydyn nhw'n dy siwtio di.

Ti sydd i ddewis ...

Ymuno â Chlwb neu Gymdeithas

Anfanteision

- pawb yn adnabod ei gilydd yn barod a thithau'n cael dy adael ar dy ben dy hun
- colli cysylltiad â hen ffrindiau

Mynd i Goleg

Anfanteision

- mynd i ddyled
- y gwaith yn rhy anodd
- dim sicrwydd gwaith ar ôl gorffen
- methu gwneud ffrindiau newydd

Gweithio

Anfanteision

- gorfod derbyn gwaith diflas
- y cyflog ddim yn ddigon i fyw arno
- colli gwaith heb lawer o gymhwyster am waith arall

Teithio o Gwmpas y Byd

Anfanteision

- afiechydon
- dy gael dy hun mewn sefyllfa beryglus
- colli allan ar flwyddyn o addysg neu waith a theimlo dy fod yn llusgo tu ôl i dy ffrindiau

Mae symud allan o'r hen rigol a mentro i sefyllfa newydd yn gallu bod yn dda ac yn agor y drws i gyfleoedd bywyd. Ond mae mentro i rai sefyllfaoedd newydd yn gallu bod yn broblem hefyd gan eu bod yn dy arwain i sefyllfaoedd cymdeithasol peryglus ac o bosib yn dy ddwyn wyneb yn wyneb â chyfraith gwlad.

Dewis doeth?

Ond yn yr un modd ag y mae hi'n bwysig dy fod yn meddwl am dy ddiogelwch pan fyddi di'n ystyried dringo mynydd, canŵio mewn dŵr gwyllt, neu neidio allan o awyren, mae hi hefyd yn bwysig dy fod yn ystyried y peryglon pan fyddi di'n cymryd rhan mewn rhai **gweithgareddau** cymdeithasol.

Mae'n bwysig dy fod yn cymryd dy ddiogelwch o ddifri. Mae yna adegau pan wyt yn dy ystafell ac yn meddwl dy fod yn ddiogel pan wyt ti mewn perygl.

Faint o'r rhain sy'n beryglus?

★ Rhoi manylion personol dros y we neu'r ffôn.
★ Sgwrsio mewn ystafelloedd sgwrsio ar y we.
★ Ymateb i e-bost oddi wrth rywun nad wyt ti'n ei adnabod.
★ Prynu rhywbeth heb ei weld.

Mae angen bod yn ofalus!

- Mae rhoi manylion personol dros y we neu'r ffôn yn gallu bod yn beryglus.
- Mae bod yn rhy gyfeillgar gyda phobl nad wyt yn eu hadnabod yn gallu bod yn beryglus. Mae cael ffrind o'r un oedran â ti sy'n byw mewn gwlad dramor yn gallu bod yn brofiad gwerthfawr, ond a wyt ti'n siŵr ei fod e'n dweud y gwir amdano'i hun?
- Mae sgwrsio mewn ystafelloedd sgwrsio ar y we yn gallu bod yn hwyl, ond gall pethau droi'n beryglus os oes rhywun yn gofyn cwestiynau personol, neu am drefnu cyfarfod. Alli di byth fod yn hollol sicr pwy ydy'r person arall, neu a ydyn nhw'n dweud y gwir.
- Mae rhaglenni dieithr yn gallu lledu firws drwy dy gyfrifiadur.
- Mae bargeinion di-rif i'w cael ar y we ond a ydyn nhw'n fargeinion? Ydyn nhw ar gael mewn gwirionedd? Neu a fydd y gwerthwr yn diflannu unwaith rwyt ti wedi anfon dy arian?

- Mae'n rhaid i ti amddiffyn dy gyfrifiadur os wyt ti am dy amddiffyn dy hun.
- Paid â rhoi manylion amdanat ti dy hun i rywun nad wyt ti'n ei adnabod.
- Paid â llwytho rhaglenni nad wyt ti'n gwybod o ble maen nhw'n dod.
- Paid ag agor e-bost os nad wyt ti'n gwybod pwy sy wedi ei anfon.
- Cofia osod **rhaglen gwrth firws** er mwyn atal pob math o sbwriel.

Cario cyllell

Mae rhai'n teimlo'n fwy diogel os ydyn nhw'n cario cyllell, rhag ofn bydd rhywun yn ymosod arnyn nhw. Ond mae **ystadegau** yn dangos bod rhywun sy'n cario cyllell yn fwy tebygol o gael ei drywanu.

Mae rhai pethau eraill mewn bywyd bob dydd yn gallu bod yn fentrus neu'n beryglus.

Bodio lifft ar dy ben dy hun

Efallai fod bodio lifft yn ffordd rhad o deithio, ond pwy sy'n gyrru'r car sy'n cynnig lifft? Mae'r person yma'n gallu bod yn fygythiad i dy eiddo, neu yn waeth fyth, i ti dy hun.

Dechrau dadl gyda rhywun

Mae perygl i sgwrs ddiniwed am bêl-droed droi'n ddadl ac yna'n ymladd mewn dim amser pan fo un ochr yn rhy ddifrifol neu dan ddylanwad alcohol.

Arbrofi â chyffuriau

Mae rhai'n meddwl bod cyffuriau'n ffasiynol. Maen nhw'n chwilio am wefr – y *buzz* mae rhai yn ei gael drwy gymryd **cyffuriau**. Ond, mae nifer mawr yn dod yn *junkies*, er nad ydyn nhw'n credu y byddan nhw byth yn cael eu caethiwo.

Peryglon goryfed

Mae dathlu yn beth naturiol i'w wneud. Ond, yn aml mae 'dathlu' yn golygu yfed, ac yn aml iawn mae yfed yn arwain at oryfed.

Derbyn diod oddi wrth ddieithryn

Mae yna elfen o berygl mewn derbyn diod oddi wrth ddieithriaid. Alli di fod yn siŵr nad yw'r ddiod mae rhywun wedi ei phrynu i ti yn ddiogel, neu a yw'n cynnwys cyffur? Mae cael dy ddiod wedi ei sbeicio â chyffur neu alcohol yn berygl real iawn.

Iechyd ... a diogelwch

Mae'n bosib mynd yn rhy bell!

Mae chwaraeon eithafol, a chwaraeon 'peryglus' traddodiadol yn cynyddu mewn poblogrwydd, ac os ydy pobl yn ymddwyn yn anghyfrifol yna mae'n naturiol bod y llywodraeth ac asiantaethau yn poeni am bopeth mae pobl yn ei wneud.

Efallai dy fod yn meddwl bod dy iechyd a dy ddiogelwch yn dy ddwylo di, ond os wyt ti'n ddi-hid o dy ddiogelwch, pam ddylai pobl eraill boeni amdanat?

Ond nid dyna mae pawb yn ei feddwl. Mae rhai pobl yn meddwl y gallan nhw fwyta cymaint o fwyd, neu yfed cymaint o alcohol, neu gymryd cymaint o gyffuriau ag y maen nhw'n ei ddymuno ac mai cyfrifoldeb y **Gwasanaeth Iechyd Cenedlaethol** ydy gofalu amdanyn nhw.

Binge drinking over New Year's Eve could cost NHS £23m
The Guardian

Obesity to cost NHS £6.3 billion
http://www.inthenews.co.uk

£22million bill for heroin substitute prescribed to addicts on the NHS
The Daily Mail

Oherwydd y gost y mae rhai yn dadlau na ddylai'r Gwasanaeth Iechyd wario'r holl arian ar bobl sy'n mentro'u bywydau, ond yn hytrach dylid ei wario ar bobl sy'n dioddef o afiechydon fel canser ac Alzheimer.

Mae ffordd o fyw heriol rhai pobl yn gallu peryglu bywydau pobl eraill … yn ogystal â'u bywydau eu hunain. Oherwydd hyn mae cyfreithiau a rheolau iechyd a diogelwch wedi cael eu cyflwyno.

Gwisgo sbectol ddiogelwch wrth chwarae concyrs

Ydy cadw at y rheolau iechyd a diogelwch yn bwysig? Pwrpas y rheolau hyn ydy gwneud yn siŵr nad ydych chi'n mentro gormod. Ond mae rhai yn meddwl fod pethau wedi mynd yn rhy bell a bod angen i ni edrych ar ôl ein hunain. Mae rhai'n dweud bod rhai deddfau iechyd a diogelwch wedi mynd dros ben llestri.

Mae rhai yn dweud bod gwisgo sbectol ddiogelwch wrth chwarae concyrs yn un o'r rhain. Mae rhai cynghorau yn gwahardd gosod basgedi blodau uwchlaw'r stryd rhag ofn i'r fasged ddisgyn ar ben rhywun sy'n cerdded o dan y fasged. Beth ydych chi'n feddwl? Ydych chi am fentro chwarae concyrs heb sbectol neu gerdded dan y fasged flodau? Beth fyddai'n digwydd os fyddech chi'n brifo?

Mae rhai yn gwrthod cael coeden Nadolig mewn ysgol neu swyddfa rhag ofn iddi ddisgyn ar ben rhywun neu i rywun faglu drosti. Ydych chi am fentro i nôl yr anrheg o dan y goeden Nadolig?

Mae rhai Cynghorau Sir yn gwahardd rasys **crempogau** rhag ofn i rywun ddisgyn a brifo. Mae rhai ysgolion yn gwahardd rasys ble mae rhieni yn cymryd rhan mewn ras … rhag ofn iddyn nhw gael eu hanafu. Ond, beth fyddai'n digwydd os byddai rhywun yn mentro gormod ac yn cael ei anafu? Fyddai'r ysgol yn gorfod talu iawndal?

Yr hyn sy'n rhaid ei wneud fel arfer ydy gwneud asesiad risg. Hynny ydy, gweld beth ydy'r risg. Os oes yna risg, yna sut mae lleihau'r risg hwnnw fel bod pawb yn ddiogel.

Ydych chi am fentro dan y goeden?

Ras Grempogau yn Rhuthun

Pwy sydd ar fai?

Yn sgil yr holl boeni am ddiogelwch a'r holl ddeddfau a rheolau, mae diwydiant cyfreithiol sy'n edrych ar hawlio iawndal wedi tyfu.

Mae hysbysebion fel hyn yn gyffredin iawn ar y teledu, y radio ac ar y we. Maen nhw'n dangos ar y naill law fod rhywun yn poeni amdanat, ond ar y llaw arall ein bod ni bellach yn credu fod pob damwain yn ganlyniad i esgeulustod rhywun.

> **'Wedi cael damwain yn y gwaith?**
> Nid arnat ti oedd y bai?
> Yna cysyllta â'n cwmni ni,
> Mae Rhywun ar Fai Cyf.,
> **ac fe awn â nhw i'r llys a chael arian mawr yn iawndal i ti.'**

Ar un adeg roedd pobl yn arfer dweud 'mae damweiniau'n digwydd', ond bellach mae mwy a mwy o bobl yn credu bod rhywun wedi achosi'r ddamwain honno. I bob pwrpas does dim y fath beth â damwain yn bod bellach.

Pwy sydd ar fai?

Pa fath o ddamwain?

- Damweiniau yn y gwaith
- Baglu ar y stryd
- Damwain car
- Cael y moddion anghywir
- Llithro mewn siop
- Cael damwain neu salwch ar wyliau

Mae'n iawn fod pobl yn cael iawndal am ddamweiniau sy'n cael eu hachosi gan ddifaterwch eraill – hawl nad oedd i'w chael mewn pyllau glo a diwydiannau trwm yng Nghymru adeg y **Chwyldro Diwydiannol**. Ond mae rhai'n poeni ein bod wedi mynd yn rhy bell, ac mai cael swm sylweddol o arian ac nid cyfiawnder sydd wrth wraidd rhai o'r achosion am iawndal.

Mentro gormod?

Er gwaethaf pawb a phopeth ... Mentra!

Yn wyneb yr holl ddeddfau a rheolau hyn mae'n naturiol bod rhai yn adweithio yn eu herbyn. Erbyn hyn mae gwefannau a llyfrau ar gael sy'n annog pobl a phlant i fentro ychydig yn fwy. Er enghraifft, mae'r llyfr *Fifty Dangerous Things (You Should Let Your Child Do)* yn annog darllenwyr i fynd y cam nesaf: "Mae cerdded yn weithred beryglus pan ydyn ni'n fabis, ond rydyn ni'n dyfalbarhau ac mae'n dod yn ddiogel. Y peth nesaf rydyn ni'n ei ddysgu ydy dringo a mynd lawr grisiau. Ond pam aros fan'na? Pam nad ymarfer a dod yn fedrus ar gerdded ar do'r tŷ neu ar raff dynn?"

Mae'r llyfr hefyd yn cynnig cynnau tân, taflu cerrig, a hyd yn oed llyfu batri 9v er mwyn deall beth yw cael sioc drydanol!

Mae'r Gymdeithas er Atal Damweiniau am leihau'r perygl o ddamweiniau. Ond, maen nhw hyd yn oed yn meddwl bod rhieni'n goramddiffyn eu plant … a bod y plant yn colli pob synnwyr o beth ydy gwir berygl.

Ond heb fynd yn rhy eithafol, faint o blant sy'n gwybod sut i reidio beic, neu sy erioed wedi dringo coeden, neu swingio ar draws afon? Pethau roedd bechgyn, a merched, yn arfer treulio'u hamser hamdden yn eu gwneud.

Un o fanteision amser hamdden yw ein bod yn gwneud rhywbeth sy'n wahanol i'n bywyd bob dydd. Mae hynny'n ein helpu i ymlacio ac i adnewyddu ein brwdfrydedd dros bethau bob dydd. Felly beth am ddechrau cymryd rhan mewn camp wahanol?

Mae'r rhan fwyaf o blant yn cymryd rhan mewn chwaraeon yn yr ysgol gynradd, ond mae'r nifer yn mynd yn llai ar ôl mynd i'r ysgol uwchradd. Mae'r nifer yn llai fyth ar ôl mynd i'r coleg neu ar ôl dechrau gweithio.

Ond yn lle torri'r arfer, beth am ddechrau'r arfer? Beth am wneud rhywbeth sy'n dy herio, yn dy ymestyn ac yn gwneud i ti chwysu ychydig?

Ond does dim rhaid iddyn nhw fod yn bethau mawr, nac yn gampau. Mae yna ddigon o weithgareddau ysgafn, sy hefyd yn ymarferion i ddechrau cael rhywun yn ffit cyn iddyn nhw ystyried rhedeg **marathon**:

- mynd â'r ci am dro
- helpu o gwmpas y tŷ
- tacluso'r ardd
- golchi'r car
- helpu gyda'r siopa

A does dim rhaid iddyn nhw fod yn bethau corfforol hyd yn oed. Beth am roi cynnig ar ddysgu chwarae offeryn cerdd, arlunio, ysgrifennu creadigol? Rhywbeth, unrhyw beth, sy'n dy herio.

Mae llawer mwy o fendithion na melltithion i'w cael o fentro ar weithgareddau sy'n dy herio i gyflawni pethau sy'n ymestyn dy allu ac yn ychwanegu sgìl arall i dy CV.

Mae mentro yn gallu:

- ✓ dy helpu i ddatblygu sgiliau newydd
- ✓ dy herio i wneud rhywbeth gwahanol ac annisgwyl
- ✓ cynyddu dy hunanhyder
- ✓ gwneud i ti deimlo'n well am dy hunan
- ✓ dangos i eraill ochr wahanol i dy bersonoliaeth

Mae bywyd mor brysur, a dim llawer o amser i'w dreulio ar weithgareddau hamdden, ond beth am dreulio hanner awr yn llai o flaen y teledu, ar y cyfrifiadur, yn gorwedd yn dy wely, a'i dreulio'n gwneud rhywbeth gwahanol?

A phwy a ŵyr, efallai y byddi di'n ei fwynhau.
Dere 'mlaen.
Mentra!

Geirfa

adrenalin – cemegyn naturiol yn y corff sy'n cynyddu curiad y galon ac yn tanio'r corff. I'w weld pan mae'r corff dan bwysau neu pan mae person yn cael braw

ceubyllu – y gamp o archwilio ogofâu tanddaearol

crempog – math o bwdin neu gacen *(pancake)*

cyffuriau – sylweddau sy'n gallu gwneud i bobl deimlo'n dda ond mae nifer yn mynd yn gaeth iddyn nhw

chwaraeon eithafol – chwaraeon sy'n wahanol ac yn anturus iawn

Chwyldro Diwydiannol – cyfnod rhwng 1760 ac 1850 pan fu cynnydd mawr mewn diwydiant, gyda nifer o beiriannau newydd yn cael eu dyfeisio

egni (*stamina*) – nerth i gario ymlaen i wneud rhywbeth dros gyfnod hir o amser

endorffin – cemegyn yn dy gorff sy'n gwneud i ti deimlo'n dda, yn enwedig wrth i ti wneud rhywbeth corfforol

gornest – cystadleuaeth rhwng dau neu fwy i weld pwy ydy'r gorau neu'r cryfaf

Gwasanaeth Iechyd Cenedlaethol – sefydliad sy'n darparu gwasanaethau i wella pobl sâl, fel ysbytai, meddygon, nyrsys, ayyb

gweithgareddau – pethau sy'n cael eu gwneud

gwrthwynebydd – rhywun sy'n dy erbyn

iechyd corfforol – pa mor iach neu ffit yw dy gorff

marathon – ras hir i redwyr o tua 26 milltir

neidio BASE – neidio oddi ar adeiladau uchel, pontydd, ayyb, gyda pharasiwt

paragleidio – camp sy'n gofyn i ti eistedd mewn harnais dan adenydd. Wrth redeg oddi ar fynydd bydd y gwynt yn dy gynnal

parcour – camp sy'n meithrin sgiliau neidio a dringo wrth i ti osgoi rhwystrau

rhaglen gwrth firws – cynllun i geisio atal firws

rhydwelïau – tiwbiau sy'n cludo gwaed o'r galon i weddill y corff

ystadegau – casgliad o ffeithiau neu fesuriadau